MOST DANGEROUS GAME

by

Daryl E.J. Simmons

MOST DANGEROUS GAME

Copyright © 2019 by Daryl E.J. Simmons

All rights reserved. This book or any portion thereof may not be reproduced, distributed, or transmitted by any means, including photocopying, recording, or other electronic or mechanical methods, without the prior written permission of the publisher except for the case brief quotations embodied in critical reviews and certain other noncommercial uses permitted by copyright law. For permission requests, write to the author at the address below.

Thinkery Group, LLC
P.O. Box 1138
Skiatook, OK 74070

Printed in the United States of America

First Edition, 2019; Second Edition 2022

ISBN: 9781099500817

Cover images taken from the public domain. Layout and design Copyright 2019 by Daryl E.J. Simmons

Edited by Heather Nuttall Westover

Author photograph by Cindy Kay Photography

The story and all names, characters, and incidents portrayed therein are fictitious. No identification with actual or historic persons, places, buildings, programs, or products is intended or should be inferred. Any similarity or resemblance between the contents of this story and any locations, events, objects, or persons - living or dead - is purely coincidental.

This story is a work of fiction created purely for the purpose of entertainment. It is entirely contrived by the author's imagination, with absolutely no involvement of the United States Government, its officers, offices, or subsidiaries. In accordance with the Information Security Oversight Office, Executive Order 13292, 13526, 13556, 13587, *ad nauseam*, as well as any and all applicable Department of Defense directives and instructions, no privileged or classified material is contained herein, nor was used in the creation of this story. This story is not authorized or endorsed by the United States Government, any of its branches, divisions, or subsidiaries. Any similarity between any portion of this story and any real government activities, offices, or programs is purely coincidental, and not based on any forethought, foresight, or foreknowledge the author may or may not possess.

DEDICATION

First, foremost, and always: I thank Jesus Christ my Savior, who carried me through the valley of the shadow of death. Several times.

This book - every word and letter - is dedicated to the brave men and women past and present who serve our country in uniform: my brothers and sisters in the military and law enforcement. We are the one-half of one percent. Nobody who hasn't been where we have been can truly understand what it feels like to sacrifice your time, your livelihood, your family, or the promise of a future in order to secure the Blessings of Liberty for millions of strangers. Remember that the promise we made had a purpose. Stay strong for each other. We are the real Americans.

My continued thanks and love to my wife. No man has ever known a better friend, more faithful companion, or loving mother.

To Major Chris Morse, my friend of many years and brother in Christ; "he who was my companion through adventure and hardship, is gone forever." And to Coyt "Thumper" Hargus, the absolute greatest of mentors, who showed me every day we worked together the difference between a boss and a leader.

Last but not least: to you, my readers. Whether you've been a fan from the beginning or you've just started reading the Wakefield books, thank you for joining the rest of us on this journey. I hope you get something out of this story. And that I continue to write things that you read on purpose.

Be sure to catch the rest of the Oath Keeper series by Daryl E.J. Simmons:

Oath Keeper
Land of the Free
Blood of Patriots

And the sequel to this book:

Justice for All

As well as the original hit sci-fi western:

After the West

And, coming soon:

Intent to Kill – Book six in the addictive and thrilling Oath Keeper series
The Man from Earth – an all-new sci-fi adventure

PROLOGUE

THE DIFFERENCES between a killer and a warrior are numerous. Nonetheless, the simple fact remains that those distinctions are often lost on lay people. And the world is worse for that confusion.

A killer is simply that - one who takes another's life. Killing is a part of nature. Predators hunt prey. And in times of desperation, though it might not be their preferred choice, sometimes the would-be victim must kill to defend themselves from their assailant.

Criminologists, legal analysts, and law enforcement professionals state that on average, three out of every four violent crimes committed in modern America are of such severity and circumstances that the target is fully justified - legally and morally - to use deadly force to defend themselves. And yet every year, millions of Americans choose to be a victim rather than a victor.

Those people are so averse to causing another person harm that they choose - consciously or not - a point of interaction at which they would rather concede to their assailants than risk hurting the other by standing up for their rights - even the right to live.

There comes a time when the results of such ultra-pacifism can no longer honestly be called "tragic," *per se*. A tragedy is when something unforeseen and unpredictable occurs. When something unfortunate happens to you and yours after you have willfully adopted a lifestyle that inevitably leaves you vulnerable to a clear and present threat, it is not tragedy; it is voluntary victimization.

There is also no small irony that stares every American in the face. Yet, like the proverbial elephant in the room or the emperor's nudity, is not openly discussed. The fact is that many of these pacifists who find virtue in victimhood, who are unwilling to draw a gun to protect themselves - and who vocally argue that others should not be allowed to do so, either - hold a casual attitude about killing unarmed, nonviolent, unborn children. Indeed, a plurality of these people who claim to value non-violence feel they hold the unassailable right to kill a baby if they find its arrival to be personally inconvenient. One wonders if the abortion doctor used an AR-15 instead of a surgical vacuum, which of these self-appointed moral guardians' principles would crumble first.

In many ways, the warrior stands as the antithesis of the killer - even though their results and methods may be similar. Where the killer's objective is the end of a life, the warrior's goal is to preserve and protect that life. Either may fight as fiercely as their opposite, and one or the other may just as likely bring about their adversary's demise, but the conflict between these foes is at least as old as humanity, as they are each in their nature driven by a primal force - for the killer, *thanos,* the urge to destroy; and the warrior, *eros,* a passion for life.

The sheep, it is said, often have problems telling the difference between the wolves and the sheepdog. Though the either would gladly slay the other, it is the latter who willingly sacrifices its own safety for its charges. Occasionally, the more vocal members of the flock cry out and complain. They try to convince the sheepdog to grow his coat out, learn to eat grass, and *bleat* like the sheep do. Generally, though, they tolerate the sheepdog with quiet indifference. But when the wolf comes - and sooner or later he always comes - the sheep will trade anything for a big, strong protector to keep them safe from harm.

Most people are sheep. They spend their days mindlessly consuming things which are produced and producing things which are consumed. They are mostly harmless, though sometimes unpleasant. And they generally ignore their protectors - except when they take the time to complain about the police or condescend to soldiers and veterans - until some predator comes their way. In the fearful moment when they stand face-to-face with a genuine threat, even the most peace-loving hipster will trade a lifetime supply of skinny jeans and low-fat mocha frappuccinos for a big, strong man with a gun to stand on their behalf. Tears will run from behind their designer glasses down into their styled beards as they beg for some neanderthal with a heart of gold to deliver them from evil.

But when the scrape is over and the warrior nurses his wounds, the very sheeple he saved from the wolf have an obligation not to forget that their safety is bought with the blood, sweat, and tears of rough men who are willing to hunt things that go bump in the night.

CHAPTER 1

INTERSTATE 25 RAN uninterrupted from Del Rio, Texas all the way to the other side of the American/Canadian border. If a fellow was so inclined, he could drive all the way from the Rio Grande to Calgary without ever changing roads or so much as looking at a map. And Justin Gage was just so inclined. While Jimmy, the younger of the two adult brothers, stretched out in the back of their big cab, Justin steered the 18-wheeler up the last stretch of US highway. He liked to handle the first and last legs of their run, even though he usually swapped out with Jimmy every third hour or so on the long haul up the country's spine. Justin knew he was the better driver between his brother and himself, but it paid to keep a fresh set of eyes and an alert driver behind the big wheel.

Commercial trucking companies had rules, limits as to how many hours or miles an operator could drive on a given day. Those regulations were a bit more flexible if you had a partner to split the trip with you. But the Gage brothers learned years ago that the real money was to be made not in hauling frozen food, or chemicals, or even oil equipment. No, the lifelong troublemakers finally started to make some real cash after they bought their own truck, left Overland Freight Family, and started hauling Ecstasy for an upstart Mexican crew that called itself the Jalisco cartel.

Gringos love X, Gage smiled. Justin knew the drug well. Ecstasy was one narcotic that was properly named. It was popular at clubs, bars, and schools, and up until a few years ago almost all of it came into the States from somewhere in Europe that he could not remember. *That's Capitalism for you*, he hummed to himself. *People will pay for what they want.*

And so it came to be that some time around dawn, Justin was northbound passing Odessa as he hauled a pair of tandem trailers loaded full of Mexican Ecstasy - MeX, as it was called on the street. Jimmy's leg of the drive included their usual stop in Denver yesterday. If the distributors and sellers moved quickly, they could get the MeX into consumers' hands during Thursday night's raves; if not, there was always the weekend crowd. And here, on a Friday night, Justin Gage was about two hours out from delivering a load of candy to the Jaliscos' Canadian arm - a crew that called itself the NewGen gang - for next week.

It was easy money, simple hours, and in two weeks he and his brother would do it all over again.

Justin called back into the darkened cab. "You know, Jimmy, next month we'll've been doing this for right on five years."

"So?"

Justin was surprised to even hear that much of a reply. Jimmy never was much for conversation, and he was even less sentimental than his older brother. "So," he continued, "before we left, Hector told me that after this load we could maybe switch to the Chicago Run."

"That's the money line," Jimmy perked up. "Ain't like we're retiring."

"It's like I told you all along, Jimmy. Prove to these wetbacks that they can trust us and we'll be rolling in dough."

"The Brothers' cash spends just like anyone else's." Jimmy rose in his bunk. "What'd'ya tell Hector?"

"Whaddaya think I told him?" Justin saw the bright lights over an all-too-familiar customs station on Montana's northern state line. The career driver downshifted and let the rig's engine do most of the braking for him. He saw a uniformed figure don a thick coat and step out of the guardhouse. Justin dimmed his headlights and downshifted again. When he came to a stop short of the lowered swing arm, a familiar face blew a smokey cloud into the frozen December night.

The oldest Gage brother rolled his window down with one hand and reached between the seats with the other. The fingers of his right hand wrapped around cold metal. "Evenin', off'cer," he smiled.

"Good Evening," the familiar Border Patrol agent nodded. The Gage brothers passed through this particular checkpoint periodically, so Justin easily recognized the same three or four guys who rotated through the booth. Most times, they let the truck pass through with barely a pause. Sometimes the agents checked their identification, just to make sure. This shift's agent took Justin's driver's license, painted the driver's face with a flashlight, then waved for another man in the booth. "Would you mind stepping out of the cab, please?" It was not a request.

"Sure thing, off'cer." Justin grabbed his denim jacket, hopped out of the cab and landed heavily on the cold ground. He slipped the faded blue garment on over his knit thermal shirt and coveralls that carried a swollen stomach like a kangaroo's pouch. Then he reached back to the door and thrust his right hand forward. An aluminum clipboard loaded with half-forged mileage logs and innocuous weigh-ins hung in midair between himself and the agent.

"What'cha hauling tonight?" the officer asked as they walked to the back of the trailer. He looked to be in his mid-to-late-twenties, about Justin's age, though softer for it. The agent's oversized flashlight washed the undercarriage in an obvious search for stowaways or poorly concealed contraband.

"Look for yourself," Gage invited, as if he had some sort of say in the matter. This was the same border patrol agent Justin saw at least once a month. They were not exactly friendly, but there was a level of familiarity between the two, like his usual cashier at his favorite drive thru burger joint. The officer signaled him to unlock the trailer doors, then bathed the chamber's interior with his light. The trailer was filled - wall to wall, floor to ceiling, stem to stern - with cardboard boxes. Each of the cases was sealed and stamped boldly to read "Vitamin E Supplement." They even sported a convincing forgery of a popular nutritional label's logo.

"You know," the savvy agent commented, "transporting pharmaceuticals across the border requires a special license."

Gage presented the clipboard again. "I'm pretty sure I've got all the right paperwork, off'cer." The agent, skeptical, took the metal apparatus, flipped through the loose pages clipped to the top, then opened up the hinged compartment to reveal a stack of green paper. Only, instead of an endorsement from the United States Food and Drug Administration, these pages sported pocket-sized portraits of the late Benjamin Franklin. The agent looked at Justin. Then he glanced over each of his shoulders. He pocketed the greenbacks, snapped the clipboard closed and handed it back to the driver.

"Right. Everything looks to be in order here," the agent blew out another smoke cloud. "Go ahead and button it up. And watch for ice up the road."

"Will do." Gage secured his cargo and made his way back to the cab. The border patrol agent, back inside the warm sally port, had just reached for the button to raise the red and white armature when his window shattered with a *crack-chink!* Justin saw the spiderweb explode across the glass and dove to the frosty ground. "Jimmy?" he shouted through the cab's open door. "Jimmy!"

Shadows wavered. Shimmering forms walked out of the nearby trees. First a few, then several bodies approached the truck from all around. Over a dozen assailants dressed in winter camouflage and tactical gear whispered to each other and pointed as they moved. Justin could not quite make out what they said, but it did not sound like English. One of the gray and white forms padded through the snowdrift, until it stood over him and aimed a small, suppressed pistol right between his eyes.

"*Buenos noches,*" a muffled voice announced, "*de los Sinaloas.*"

A scream sounded from the far side of the cab. A second later, Jimmy's body slid on its side from behind the tractor's rear wheels. Jimmy reached up, and a pistol *popped* twice in rapid succession. Heavy fabric puffed and tore as holes erupted in Justin's would-be executioner's chest. The camouflage-clad assassin fell to the snowy white ground.

"Drive!" Jimmy shouted as he rolled to his feet. Justin leapt into the cab. Another figure in winter fatigues appeared out of nowhere. The hitman clamped down on Jimmy's hands in an attempt to wrestle the pistol from him. An armored kneepad drove itself into Jimmy's left leg, which buckled. Jimmy turned his fall into a clockwise spin and swept his right leg behind the grappler, taking the fighter down backwards. Jimmy shot him once in the temple. The pistol's slide locked back, so the smuggler tucked it into his belt and produced a wickedly curved knife in its stead.

Justin Gage punched the truck's throttle and drove through the check station gate. Jimmy twirled his karambit so that its beaklike blade was held downward while he ran alongside the lumbering semi. The engine lulled for just a second as Justin pushed the vehicle into second gear. Jimmy leaped into the space between the cab and the trailer, sprung off the exposed frame rails, and flew out through the gap on the passenger side. His blade caught another figure with a flash while he was still mid-air. Jimmy landed on the run, ready to cut down anyone else in his way. He sprinted back to the passenger door and launched himself into the cab as his older brother shifted into third gear and picked up some real speed.

"You okay, Jimmy?"

"I'm fine," the younger brother fought to catch his breath. "You hit?"

Justin shook his head in the darkened tractor cab. "Not for lack of tryin'. Thanks. I mean, for savin' my bacon back there."

"We're brothers, Jay. You'd'a done the same for me."

"I wouldn't need to," Justin scoffed. "Ain't never seen you caught flat-footed. Not yet."

"Yeah, well, remember that next time you give me lip about not pulling my weight." It was true. The older Gage brother logged most of the driving miles and did most of the talking on these runs, but on those rare occasions when things got more intense, Jimmy was worth his weight in gold - brother or not.

Justin drove the truck into the cold Alberta night. Calgary was a short hitch up the road. And he had quite the story for his NewGen contact at the delivery point. Running loads of MeX was one thing, but doing it under fire from a rival drug cartel? As far as he was concerned, the price for the Gage brothers' services just went up.

Daryl E.J. Simmons

CHAPTER 2

DANNY LAID ON his belly, stretched out in the tall, frost-encrusted grass. A breeze blew over the Montana plain spread out before him. It transformed the overgrown plant life into green waves whose snow-white caps seemed to roll and crash into the distant mountain line. He breathed out slowly, forced himself to stay relaxed as he huddled inside his thick jacket. Tense muscles actually make a body colder faster, he remembered from survival school. The sun was about halfway over the ridge behind him, its rays had not even warmed the morning air past freezing yet. And Danny knew that the broken tree line under which he had camped last night would still cast long shadows all around him well into the day and keep him from ever really heating up.

Light patches of snow clung to the ground. Winter had been mild up to this point. Instead of a solid blanket of thick powder, a broken pattern of white laid atop Montana's dormant grasslands. Danny's vision blurred a bit as his mind wandered back into a still-fresh memory: a green field marked with white grave markers, a few weeks ago and a thousand miles behind him. A single thorny rose left against a smooth marble cross with his partner's name freshly carved into its face.

The great plain never produced frost like the ice that trapped Danny's soul on the day he watched them lower Sandra into the ground at Arlington. The whole world grew cold and gray around him. Out there among the people he had to keep it together. He had to stay strong. That was what people expected from him.

If the former Marine broke, then the bad guys won. Sandra's killer would get one last posthumous victim. Nick, the supervisor who hated him, would finally have the ammunition he needed to end Danny's career once and for all. Anyone who bothered to notice his plight would have simply chalked it up to just another case of Post Traumatic Stress Disorder: another shattered vet; a sad statistic and testament to all that was wrong with whatever laws or policies they had chosen to rail against on that particular day.

Danny could not stomach the thought of being a talking point for a bunch of progressive idiots, nor would he ever give "Nick the Dick" such sweet satisfaction as firing him. And a pair of 600-grain hollow points from his .458SOCOM carbine back in D.C. made sure that the Constitutional Killer's body count had officially stopped. *No*, Danny braced himself against the cold, dark world, *you will not break me,* he resolved.

His mind snapped back to the present. A frozen brook slipped and slid through the open country about forty yards to Danny's left. Just under a hundred and fifty yards downstream, the creek hooked to the right and cut a long, jagged path across his view.

Beyond that creek was another couple hundred yards or so of brush and grass, then another wooded area. Without really moving, Danny shifted his weight just the slightest bit. He felt the disposable hand warmers stuffed into his pants and shirt find new areas of his legs and torso to heat through his thermal base layer. His mind travelled back to his small, low tent a few yards away, just behind his outstretched feet. The minimalist shelter was barely larger than his down-filled sleeping bag and heated via the business end of an Apache fire hole he dug out yesterday. An old trick used by Native Americans and survivalists alike, the Apache stove was a vertical, j-shaped trough dug into the ground. At the base of the longer neck, a small fire burned to produce very little flame but a significant amount of heat - most of which went out the upright chimney, but some of which funneled up the curved vent that angled into Danny's tiny shelter. As long as his little fire did not burn out, his little nylon cocoon would stay nice and toasty on the inside with only the slightest wisp of smoke - which easily disappeared with even the hint of a breeze - discharged from the chimney. *Twenty more minutes,* he thought, *and I'll climb back inside. Warm up a bit. Then come back out here. Maybe reposition for tomorrow night.*

All of the land he could see from the ridge behind him to the mountain on the far side of the plain belonged to the Johnson family. They were cattlemen by trade and his father's friends. But the animal that emerged from the woods almost three hundred yards to the west was no cow. A big buck elk scanned the fields with the same caution that had helped him to survive yet another hunting season with his massive rack and life intact, then picked his way carefully to the stream almost straight ahead of Danny and below him. *Too easy,* the former Marine smiled as he peeked through his rifle's scope. *Might as well be a shooting range.*

The bipod upon which Wakefield's Remington 700 was perched kept his rifle and his view steady. Dull colored yarn hung from trips of burlap wrapped around the gun from the suppressed muzzle to the bolt action and made the weapon look like grass on a knoll. The stealthy effect continued with a ghillie hat worn over his warmer knit cap, and an old pair of desert camo pants and a greener jacket blended Danny's body into the rest of the hillside's vegetation.

The human shrubbery steered his long gun from its aftermarket stock with his left hand while his right hand rested on the grip - perched, but relaxed. The former sniper ran through a mental checklist as he prepared for his opportunity. *Breathe out. Arm relaxed. Hand limp. Breathe in. Breathe out. Body loose. No tension. Breathe in.*

Another wave rippled through the grass as the buck dipped his crowned head for a drink. Danny used the elk's distraction and the terrain's natural motion to mask his own subtle movements as he repositioned himself just a few millimeters into an even more optimal angle. The elk gave no indication that he noticed the former Marine. Danny breathed slowly as he found the buck in his glass, rested his crosshairs, and waited for the right moment. He was a big one, probably eight hundred pounds on the hoof. That was a lot of naturally wonderful, tasty meat, all bundled up in soft, brown, velveteen gift wrapping. The mature male dropped his crowned head and munched on the lush greenery that grew next to the trickling water.

Properly dressed and quartered, Danny knew that the buck could provide a small family with their primary meat for a good long while. Memories of morsels derived from the animal made Danny's teeth sweat: elk steaks, roasted haunches swimming with vegetables in a stew pot, elk jerky, ground rib meat, and spicy elk sausage... The marksman moved his scope up to the animal's head, counted fourteen points on the buck's rack, then shifted his aim back to the money shot. At this range, a 77-grain boat tailed hollow point projectile would drop even larger game if it was placed properly. The buck's ear twitched, then its head come up as the elk looked to and fro.

Another burst of wind blew. The elk's neck turned fully away from Danny, who used the opportunity to silently thumb his rifle's safety switch into the *Fire* position. He kept his scope trained on the elk and waited for his shot.

Breathe out. Cheek weld. Touch the chassis for luck. Breathe in. Danny had struck out yesterday afternoon. Last night was equally unproductive. He fought to keep his pulse and respiration steady, but the thought that all of his stalking, sneaking and shivering might be about to pay off brought a surge of adrenaline into his system. *Buck fever*, hunters called it. Sometimes it seemed like a hunter's excitement was all it took to scare game away, as if these creatures could hear a buzz of adrenaline from an unseen predator.

Danny let his imaginary armor down and allowed the weight of his life in, just for a moment. His mind quickened and his body operated on well-trained reflex rather than conscious control. If ever there was a time when being emotionally numb was an advantage, this was it.

The big elk startled and bolted to Danny's right. A massive tawny puma sprung from the grass several yards behind the buck and gave chase. Danny panned his rifle as his target streaked along. He tracked the animal, led it a bit, and exhaled again as he pressed the gun's glassy trigger.

*   *   *

At just after two o'clock in the afternoon on a chilled Saturday in mid-December, Daniel Wakefield pulled up his father's driveway astride his big four-wheeled all-terrain vehicle. His coyote tan backpack was slung on his back. His rifle was nestled inside a tan range bag which was, in turn, strapped to a rack in front of the ATV's handlebars. The tubular cargo carrier on the back of his ATV was loaded down with a 190lb. mountain lion neatly wrapped inside a patchwork of black 50-gallon garbage bags and sealed with duct tape. Danny rode around to the back yard and parked near the door to his father's walk-out basement. He dismounted, unwrapped the big cat and hung its corpse from a set of pulleys bolted into the deck above him which serviced the dining room on the house's main level. The split-level home was not fancy, but it was plenty big for a retired cop with an empty nest and plenty of life left to his years.

Claire Wakefield died when Danny was seventeen. She was survived by a husband who had adored her every day of their shared life. Danny's widower father, David Wakefield, served out the rest of his time with the Bozeman Police Department, then retired and tended to the modest cattle farm that had been in their family for generations. Big sky country was all around the house. Open air. Quiet days. Lingering memories.

Danny looked down to the south range and saw his father trot up in his direction. David rode Powder, a dusty gray mare speckled with dirty white spots. The older man spent more money on his saddle than he did on the horse under it. Powder was a mustang from an adoption center that was about to be put it down, but David saw something in the horse - something more valuable than a bag of dog food. Powder was past her prime when David brought her home. In the years since, she never gave him reason to question the decision.

Danny checked the anchor line that held the mountain lion aloft, then grabbed his gear and hauled his bags into the basement. A high-pitched whistle beckoned him back outside before he could loosen his boot laces - not that Danny seriously thought for a moment that he was actually going to take his boots off. That would have implied that he was going to get to stay inside for a while and actually warm up after two days in the frigid wild.

Powder stepped from side to side and dug her hooves uneasily into the dirt as David fought to keep her close to the cat's corpse. "Hey, Dad," Danny waved.

"You know, son," the gray haired man nodded toward the dead cat, "when you told me you were going out to hunt some pussy the other night, that isn't exactly what I thought you meant."

"Didn't you hear when old man Johnson was complaining that he lost some of his heifers?"

"I did," David replied from the saddle, "but I also heard him say that his niece was up visiting over Christmas break. Kinda figured your priorities were somewhere else."

"You think Mom would approve of you letting your son live like that?"

David looked his son square in the eye. "We're Catholic, Danny, not stupid. And if your mother was still here, she'd be even less deluded than I am about the realities of your life - or the lifestyle that comes with it."

Danny sniffed the cold mountain air. "Nice to know that if I decide to cat around," he flashed his eyes to accentuate the pun, "that I can always count on parental support."

"I didn't say that," David furrowed his brow. "Knowledge isn't the same as acceptance. All the same, I guess it's best that you're not stirring up friction with the neighbors. But a fella could do worse than Gus Johnson's little girl. Biology professor up at the college and all."

"You can relax, Dad. I came back to clear my head. Maybe pull a few critters out of circulation that need it. I ain't hunting any trim. Not this trip."

"I wasn't looking when I found your mother, either, son." David held up a hand wrapped within a rough leather glove to stave off his son's inevitable protest. "I know, I know... Just saying. It ain't like D.C. out here. Pickin's are slim. A good woman can be hard to come by. Deke Connors - you remember Deke, don'cha? - well, his boy Caleb had to order his bride online."

"I thought Connors said they met in a chatroom," Danny countered.

"Catalogue... interweb," his dad shrugged, "mail order's mail order. Either way, most o' the dudes 'round here are goin' dry while you're passing up easy water."

"Now's really not the time, Dad." Danny was still raw from losing Sandra the way he did. He had just started to reach a point where if he worked really hard and kept his mind off of anything that reminded him of her, he was almost numb - as if the great northern cold could somehow seep into his psyche and freeze his heart as solid as the glacial tundra. Almost. It was as close to good as he dared himself to feel. It was, in his estimate, better than he deserved to feel.

"I know, I know. But son, sooner or later, you'll get back into the saddle. You may not feel like it now, but you will." The older Wakefield looked the big cat's corpse up and down. "You gutted that beast up at Johnson's? Well, the cold'll keep the rest of your cat from getting funky. Now we've gotta see to mine."

"You see puma tracks out on the range this morning?"

"Not today. But you need to go get yourself cleaned up. I told Kitty that we'd be there by four."

Speaking of cats on the prowl, Danny inwardly mused. *And getting back in the saddle.* For the longest time after his mother's death, Danny's dad had lived a solitary life. But about a year ago, the younger Wakefield noticed that his father had taken to spending a considerable number of hours with Katherine 'Kitty' Malone, the gracefully aged lass whose now-ex-husband had gotten wealthy enough that he decided he needed a new trophy wife.

"We're supposed to play at Kitty's tonight with that daughter o' hers. Remember?" David gave his son the sort of look that put the *b* back in subtle. "You know, a fella could do worse than Stacy, too. Real looker, that girl. That dude who walked out on her and her little dumplin' is about as dumb as they come. She's about your age, too, you know."

Danny ignored his father's heavy-handed attempts at playing matchmaker. "I know, Dad. But I thought setup was at eight."

"Our stuff's already there. It'll only take a few minutes to plug in and tune. Besides, I told Kitty we'd help her open."

Kitty Malone had funneled a hefty chunk of her ex-husband's considerable alimony payments into starting her own restaurant and bar - Miss Kitty's Saloon - on the outskirts of Bozeman proper.

"You know, Dad, I couldn't be happier that you're seeing someone up here. Really. I like her. I do. And it's cute that you help her around the saloon, but you can't just pimp me out for free labor."

"Well," David looked at his son judgmentally, "I'm sorry if turning a few chairs over for your old man puts you out. Maybe too much time in Washington's made you forget the value of real, honest work."

Danny tossed a thumb over his shoulder toward the feline carcass. "I've got a kitty of my own that needs some attention. I need to skin this cat and get a tooth up to the ranger station."

"The law says you've just gotta notify him in a timely manner. Just about everyone'll be at Miss Kitty's tonight. You're bound to run into Ranger Young there. Tell him then. You can take care of the taxidermy tomorrow. Cat won't spoil in this weather."

"But what if I needed to pick someone up, Dad?"

"You just said a minute ago that you weren't seeing anyone," David reminded him.

"Well, yeah, but you didn't know that when you made plans for me."

David's hat tilted with just the slightest change of angle. "Not everything needs a written notice, son. Now, I'll saddle Cinnamon for you while you get yourself cleaned up."

Most cops and prosecutors had a virtually nonexistent tolerance for folks who drove while under the influence. The sober truth of the matter was that drunk driving was equally dangerous and stupid. DUI was the single most preventable crime in modernity - it was the result of no less than five conscious decisions to override plain common sense. And those most familiar with the outcomes of such felonious stupidity tended to hold those who engaged in such behavior in very low regard and cut them absolutely no slack whatsoever.

This conflict of interests created a certain dilemma for people who drove themselves to bars. On the one hand, they wanted to drink. On the other, they did not want to go to jail. And the dilemma only became more contentious when the people who went to those bars were, themselves, involved in law enforcement.

Kitty Malone's profits depended greatly on the sale and consumption of alcoholic beverages, and a relationship with David Wakefield would have been strained well beyond the breaking point if the former cop interfered with the goings on at Miss Kitty's. And the former-cop-turned-hobby-rancher could neither face himself in the mirror nor look his son the federal agent in the eye if he ever drove home from a night helping Kitty at her saloon - her *restaurant and bar*, as David preferred to call it - under the influence. So the elder Wakefield solved the problem in true Montana cowboy fashion.

He rode his horse to Miss Kitty's.

This solution allowed David to go see Kitty at work - and even enjoy a few rounds - without the presumption of staying with her until morning, though Danny and the rest of Montana knew that Kitty would welcome David to do exactly that. It also afforded the former cop a self-driving mode of transportation that could easily find its own way back to the Wakefield ranch with an inebriated rancher on its back. And it also meant that Danny had to ride along with him when they went to Miss Kitty's together.

The first few minutes of their ride passed in silence - David astride Powder and Danny right beside him atop Cinnamon. Like her older gray counterpart, Cinnamon was a mustang mare that David had acquired somewhere along the way. But she was younger, spryer, and sported a sweet brown coat mottled with white and drizzled with a bleached mane. Saddle oil, perfumed blankets, and days spent in the open air rather than cooped up in a stable helped keep both horses' smell at bay.

In the time it took Danny to shower off and make himself presentable, his father had not only saddled the other horse, but had washed himself and changed into a fresh shirt, clean jeans, his nice leathers and most crisp hat. As the Wakefield house shrank behind them, David cleared his throat. "You know, son, we've never really talked about it, but I was in a few scrapes while I was on the force. But in all that time I only had to shoot one guy."

The older Wakefield kept his eyes forward as he told the tale. Danny listened intently. He had never heard his father share this story.

"Call was for a domestic disturbance. Back in the old days, we'd've told them to sort it out themselves. But, then the '90s came and the higher ups expected everyone in the department to be a marriage counselor with a badge. Sensitivity training and all of that nonsense… Anyway, it's night. I arrive on the scene and there's this half-dressed woman with blood coming from her nose and an eye that's swelling shut and turning black as I watch. Her live-in boyfriend is in his pajamas. Drunk. Or high. Or both. But he's obviously out of it. Anyway, they'd evidently been getting into it. One thing led to another, and she jumped him with a kitchen knife. Somehow, he managed to keep her from cutting him while he disarmed her, but during the struggle he cold-cocked her. That was their story of what all happened before I arrived."

"That was both of their stories?"

"Yep. Both in accord. I'm skipping the details of who called who what name and who accused who of cheating with whom. But, yeah. They both basically told the same tale." David sniffed, then continued. "So, just telling me their sob story gets these two mopes to arguing again. I separate them, but the yelling just keeps up. So I tell the dude to stay in the living room while I walk into the kitchen with the wife. It's one of those cheap apartments where the living room, dining room and kitchen are all one open area, so I can keep an eye on him while she just goes on and on about all of this crap in their lives together when she pulls this big freaking butcher knife from the counter and lunges. Now, in hindsight, I think she thought she was trying to stab him. But I was between the two, so the knife's coming right at me. Now, I step out of the way, parry, get control of the knife, and put her down. But as I'm cuffing her, he comes swinging an aluminum baseball bat that was evidently resting next to the couch and yelling 'Get off her you dirty pig!'

"I roll backwards outta the way. His swing passes just over me and catches the kitchen cabinet. I immediately pop him with my Taser, still on my ass. That was back when Tasers were still pretty new, you know? Anyway, while the dude's flopping on the floor like a fish, that harpy of his grabs the knife again, screams 'Don't hurt my husband!' and tries to stake me like a vampire."

"Geez, Dad..." Danny had known all of his life that his dad was a cop, but he had never heard anything remotely like this story. And he was beginning to understand why. Most parents would think long and hard before they ever told their kid about such a harrowing experience.

"I know, right? Well, I did the only thing I could do. I pulled my Glock and drilled her. Double tap. Center mass. Almost point-blank range. She falls across me. The knife misses me by a few inches. I slip out from under her, backpedaling across the floor on my back like a crayfish. She's screaming and hollering, rolling around on the floor. I secure the scene, call for backup and EMS. All by the book."

A heavy breath passed through David's nose. "By the time help arrives she's dead in a pool of her own blood. The husband's a mess, you know? On top of all that, one of those nine-mil rounds passed through the wall behind the woman and sailed through the apartment next door. The other one exited her and punched into the apartment upstairs right through the kitchen sink. Under the circumstances, we were all just lucky none of the neighbors got hit, too."

"I'm sorry, Dad," Danny hissed as his horse trotted along. "That's a messed up situation."

"Trust me, son. I know." When David looked at his son, his icy blue eyes cut into Danny soul. "I still see her face. You know? Of course you do. You never really shake something like that outta your head. Not unless your mind ain't wired right. But it was her or me. You know? It ain't fair. It ain't right. And it ain't the way we want it to be. But it is the way it is. It's just part of the job. That's why they give us guns and teach us how to use them. And when.

"And that's my point, Danny. I saw the footage of what happened with you in D.C., son, and there's no way anyone could tell me that wasn't a righteous shoot. These things happen. You do what you have to do. What you're trained to do. And that's to stay alive. And then you deal with it." Eight hooves clomped through the frozen grass.

"Oh, we're dealing with it, Dad. Why do you think my boss let me drop a leave bomb on his desk? Wiley wants me out of D.C. until this blows over. The last thing anyone needs is a media circus back at HQ right now. Hell, things barely died down since the Daggenhart assassination. And that was my fault, too. At least, according to the press."

"A lot of folks will talk, Danny. But it's just talk. They don't know what they're talking about. They're just feeling out loud. You know that, son. And you should also know that you're not the only guy who's had to walk this road. If you need anything - to talk, whatever - I'm here for you. I understand what happened, son. I know what you're going through."

In all of his years, Danny had never heard this story. It revealed a side of his father that he never knew existed. Hidden tears threatened to flow out from behind Danny's sunglasses, but he kept his voice steady. "Thanks, Dad."

"I love you, Son. And I'm damn proud of you. And your mother would be, too."

Danny stared out into Montana's afternoon sky. Sunset was still a while out, but the sun started to paint the underside of some of the higher clouds. "That's nice, Dad, but I'm not sure you should be."

"What're you talking about? You stopped a serial killer, son."

"Not before he -" Danny stopped as a lump caught in his throat. He swallowed hard and forced himself to continue, though his voice lost much of its strength. "Not before he got Elbee."

"And I'm sorry about that, son. I truly am. I know she was your partner. And I know that she meant a lot to you. But that was beyond your control, Danny. That was all him. And you took the bastard down for it."

The memory of Thanksgiving night played itself out in Danny's mind for the millionth time. The explosion, meant for the president, that vaporized his lover. The chaos as Danny chased the assassin through Washington's streets. And the moment when he gunned down the murderer. That memory visited him every night when he tried to sleep and every waking moment when he let his thoughts idle. Danny did not need to be reminded of it. He would never forget.

"I shot him in the back," he confessed. "You saw the video. Hell, Dad, the whole world saw the video."

"That guy was a serial killer and a highly trained combat veteran," David protested. "So long as he was alive, he was a threat to everyone around. You did what you had to do."

"Yeah, but I shot him *in the back*."

"That dude was a demonstrated threat to everyone on that scene and the public at large." David recited a sermon that was preached to every member of the military and law enforcement communities. "He killed before. He'd've killed again. Your first mandate is the preservation of innocent lives. If you hadn't done it then somebody else would've."

"Dad." Danny gritted his teeth. "I shot him. In the back. Like a coward."

"Deadly force is either justified, or it isn't." Even in the failing light, Danny saw that his father rode tall in the saddle. "Doesn't matter if you shoot 'em in the face, blast 'em in the guts, or use a hand grenade. They're just as dead, either way."

"I think you're kinda missing my point, Dad."

"No, son. I'm not. Back when I first put on the badge, we stopped criminals. That's what cops did. We deterred them when possible, caught 'em when we could, and shot 'em when we had to. Now, I've seen what's become of the world, son. These days, seems like folks're more concerned about making sure the crooks' feelings don't get hurt than in protecting innocent citizens from the predators all around us. You've always been a sheepdog, Danny. Ever since you were a boy. And I've watched you grow into a good man. You can't just sit there and watch bad people do bad things. You feel the need to stand between folks who can't protect themselves and those who would do them harm. There's nobility in that mindset, son. And don't ever let anyone tell you different."

"Some folks'd say that it was cowardly, Dad."

"It's a war out there on the streets, son. Certainly was with this guy. Special Forces Ranger and all that. And in war, it's just killing. Cowardly or not just doesn't play into it. Either it needs to be done, or it doesn't. If it does then you're a hero. If not, a criminal."

"Sure doesn't feel heroic," Danny sighed.

David's big, gloved hand found its way onto Danny's shoulder. "I know it doesn't, son." He squeezed hard enough that Danny felt it through his warm leather jacket. "That's how you know you're not the bad guy."

CHAPTER 3

THE FINGERS ON Danny's right hand walked across his guitar's upper E, B, and G strings, punctuated occasionally when his thumb plucked a deeper note out of the A or lower E string. The heavy gauge bronze strings on his black Fender acoustic-electric guitar and a little distortion from his amplifier produced a fuller, subtly edgier sound that complemented the brighter, crisper chords Stacy strummed out her own steel-strung, six stringed Yamaha. As the two guitars played in harmony, Stacy closed her big eyes, smiled at an image painted beneath her coppery hair, and drew in a deep breath.

"She's got a smile that it seems to me," Stacy sang in a gentle yet confident voice, "reminds me of childhood memories, where everything was as fresh as a bright blue sky…"

Most of the cowboys in Miss Kitty's Saloon were either too drunk or too uncultured to appreciate

Stacy's talent. But that did nothing to stop the boys from staring whenever Miss Kitty's daughter graced them with a performance. Stacy Malone grew up as a teenager with visions of a singing career that would someday take her out of Bozeman and into the big lights and concert halls that accompanied fame. She had poured all of her energy into making that dream a reality - right up to the moment a few weeks after her sixteenth birthday when she discovered that she was pregnant. Things changed so quickly after that. Her boyfriend deserted Stacy and the baby. Her little girl demanded her time. And the jobs she could land with only a GED did not pay nearly enough for her to be able to afford a voice coach.

Someday never came. By nineteen, Stacy faced the music and transitioned from being the starry-eyed wannabe Nashville starlet into a career as a dental hygienist in Helena. But ten years after she traded her dream for reality, she still loved to perform. And though her usual venue was nothing more than the occasional session at her mom's watering hole, she relished every moment of it.

Miss Kitty watched the modest stage from her normal station behind the bar with a wistful eye. David hammered a light rhythm on a big deerskin drum behind their respective children with his hands as Danny and Stacy crescendoed into a more energetic second verse. "She's got eyes of the bluest skies, as they thought of rain," Stacy's bright voice continued. She played a steady rhythm of chords as light and gentle as her voice while Danny picked out the more complicated part on his Fender. "I hate to look into those eyes and see an ounce of pain…"

Danny knew that Stacy's heart was focused on her daughter - the 'sweet child' of whom she sang so sweetly - just as surely as he could see that Miss Kitty's adoration was split between the daughter she was so proud of and Danny's own dad. Kitty Malone's steady boyfriend volunteered at the saloon on the weekends. He claimed it was to pay off his tab, but Danny knew it was because the silver-haired cowboy was too smitten with the proprietor not to hang out with her whenever he could. With platinum blonde hair, eyes as big and blue as the Montana sky, and an almost permanent smile on her gentle face, Kitty Malone was still a looker well past fifty. The saloon and her little hobby farm kept her fit and trim without the artificially thin appearance of some midlifer who spent half her day rotating between tanning beds, yoga classes, and treadmills. After a few rounds it was not uncommon for one of the less-than-gentlemanly patrons to make a clumsy pass at the silver fox. Danny figured that preventing any outside amorous advances was just another reason for his father to hang out at the saloon.

Out of the corner of his eye, Danny caught an exchange between Kitty and a lithe brunette about his own age. Kitty gestured toward the stage just as Stacy was about to finish the second run through the chorus. "Oh, oh, oh, oh sweet love of mi-ine." With three heavy strums and a rap, the younger Wakefield segued into his solo.

Danny plucked a melody with his right hand - a series of quick notes sporadically interrupted by one held long enough for his left hand to pull the string out of tune and bend the tone into something more raw, followed by another quick run or arpeggio. The fingers on his left hand worked their way across the frets and walked up and down the guitar's neck. Finally, he wrung a few high notes out of the last inch offered by his E string before the guitar's gaping mouth left him with nothing to press against the string. He spent the last measure of the solo on a series of triplets that descended back into the song's original registry.

The whole time Danny played, every set of eyes in that cowboy bar was fixated on the pretty lady who strummed simple background chords out of the vanilla guitar next to him. Every set, that was, except the dark eyes of the mysterious brunette who worked her way from the bar at the far side of the room to the space directly in front of him. She wore a plain white t-shirt under her open, black leather jacket and snug, dark jeans that were definitely not used for riding horses. As she maneuvered through the crowd, she left a wake of downturned eyes as the cowboys caught sight of a new mare in the field. Finally, she stopped a handbreadth from the barely raised dais. Her eyes were fixated squarely upon Danny.

"Oh, oh, oh, sweet child o' mine," Stacy crooned. "Oh, oh-oh, oh, sweet love of mine." She repeated the stanza again, louder and higher at first, but her shaking head cued the Wakefield men through the last couple of measures and a *decelerando* that ended the song on a sustained G chord from both guitarists and a quick drumroll from David behind them. Stacy thanked the applauding cowboys and signaled the band's break, but assured everyone that there would be another set of songs in a few minutes.

Wakefield noticed the brunette made sure that when he walked off the stage, Danny stepped up to her - not that he minded the chance to meet her. More than a few guys had started to notice that there was someone in Miss Kitty's who was in a league all her own.

"You Wakefield?" the beauty knowingly asked.

"I am tonight," he smiled. "And who might you be?"

"Wilson. Anita Wilson."

Danny ushered Anita toward a booth in the back corner with a handwritten sign that read *'Reserved for Band'* and waived at the bar to signal a round of drinks. One or two of the dozen cowpokes they passed gave Danny an encouraging word about his performance. Every one of them cast an appraising, hungry look at his new companion.

"Please join us," Danny invited as the crew all fell into the booth. Out of habit, the Wakefield men sat on the outside, with the women nestled comfortably in the uncrowded and protected space between the men and the saloon's wall. Complimentary beers were delivered promptly and still cold. Danny managed a quick round of introductions before the waitress left with their order for the next round of drinks.

"I thought I knew just about everyone around here," the elder Wakefield's voice remained casual, but there was no hiding all of the suspicion from his face. "What brings you to our little corner of paradise, Miss Wilson? Or is it *Officer* Wilson?"

"*Constable* Wilson, actually," she pointed. "But, yes, I'm a detective. With the Royal Canadian

Mounted Police." Anita's pale complexion and slight build told Danny that she primarily worked indoors.

"Did you fly south for the winter," Danny tried to smile despite the sinking feeling that grew in the pit of his stomach, "or are you here for business?"

"I'm working a case. My suspects bolted down to this side of the border. My people talked to their people, who talked to your people, who pointed me to you."

"I'm on vacation," Danny countered. "But good luck with that. I'm sure some marshals or somebody would happily help you sort it out."

Constable Wilson pulled a thrice-folded piece of paper out of her inner jacket pocket. "Orders," she handed the page to him. Danny quickly examined the message. It looked authentic, and according to the addresses in the message header it had at minimum come through his boss, if not from him. Danny knew that Dr. Wiley, the head of the Analysis Division at Secret Service headquarters in D.C., was well aware of Wakefield's emotional and mental state after the incident at the White House and the shooting on the Arlington Bridge. The fact that the guy Danny shot was a highly trained and accomplished serial killer who had just murdered Wakefield's lover did little to put the former Marine at ease over gunning down a fellow veteran.

In the aftermath of the shooting, it seemed as though a billion people had inserted their own opinions and insights into Danny's private Hell, and thanks to social media and broadcast sensationalism there were plenty of outlets for them all to share those unearned opinions. Danny's office had been bombarded by requests for interviews from various media outlets. His face was all over the news. His neighbors had started voyeuristically tracking his movements and activities and his ex-wife, Yvette, had taken all-too-keen an interest in his life again. His privacy was gone.

In doing his duty Daniel Wakefield had become a celebrity, and that was no way for a Special Agent with the United States Secret Service to live. That was why Danny cashed in the copious amount of leave he had accrued and disappeared into the Montana wild lands for the last few weeks. He needed to disappear for a while. He knew that the world would forget about him as soon as the next big, shiny thing came across their screens. And he also knew, given all of the factors and feelings in play, that Jonas Wiley knew all of those things, too. His mentor - the man he jokingly nicknamed Father when he was back in D.C. - would not cancel Danny's leave lightly. Whatever this Mounty's case was about, Danny's boss obviously felt it required his particular skills.

"You know, Wakefied," Wilson shook her head, "I've gotta say that after everything that happened, I'm a little surprised that you still have a job." She looked at the scraggly beard that had sprung up on Danny's jaw since his last day at the office. "Okay, very surprised."

"Well, like they explained on the news, Constable Wilson, it was all really part of an undercover operation designed to lull Phillips out of hiding."

Anita choked on her beer. "You don't actually expect me to believe that, do you?"

Without meaning to, Danny called to mind the high price that had been paid for the official story, real or not, to become the narrative. Dr. Wiley spent no small amount of political capital and cashed in more than a few favors to save Wakefield from facing the worst consequences of his actions. But no friendly phone call, blackmailed acquaintance, or bribed reporter could salve Danny's conscience over what he did - and what he failed to do. "I really don't care what you believe, Constable. And if you've got a problem with it then you can walk your happy ass right back to Canada and deal with it yourself." He tossed the orders back across the table. "I'm perfectly happy right here."

"I'm truly sorry, Agent Wakefield. I wish I could do this on my own, but that really isn't an option here. I do need your help."

"You'd best get going, son," David announced while he looked into the bottom of his mug. "Duty calls."

"He said 'dootie'," a new voice giggled. Two fellows in dirty flannel shirts and battered ball caps appeared next to the table. The latest in what had obviously been a long line of beer bottles were held in each of their right hands.

"Evening Gus," Danny nodded. Gus Hatfield was in the same class as Danny back in high school. Gus was a pudgy idiot back then, and the only thing that had changed over the years was that now he could buy his own booze without a fake identification.

"Miss Wilson," David sighed, "this is Gus and Cody Hatfield. You know how they say every village has an idiot? The Hatfield boys take turns."

"We were just leaving," Danny announced as he stood. Gus and Cody each yielded a step to the bigger man.

"Go?" a bewildered Gus managed, "but she just got here."

"You work fast, Dan." Cody - a few inches taller and several pounds lighter than his brother, but still barely average sized - snickered.

"And don't you have more songs to play?" Gus smirked. "How's about you go up and play on yer gi-tar whiles I keep your lady friend here company?" He flashed a wry smile. "Now don't you worry, miss. I'll make sure nobody bothers you." Gus still wore that idiot grin of his as he took an overly confident pull off of his beer.

Anita casually reached up and gave the bottom of Gus' bottle a deft, outward pull away from his bemused face. The seal between his lips and the bottle's top broke. Cold, pale liquid poured down Gus' frontside and did not stop until it was well into his gusseted nether region. Gus half-choked on what was left in his mouth. "Summ-bitch!" he stammered over a chorus of laughter.

The short drunk started forward, but Anita reached across him, pulled hard on his far shoulder, and dropped him onto the vinyl bench Danny just vacated. "Sit, doggy," she ordered, then quickly regained her casual air. "Now, if you'll excuse us, I believe we have places to be."

Gus managed a snort, but his soaked britches kept him in an ill mood. "Ain't nobody leavin' till she gets me another beer," he declared.

Danny pointed to the half-full bottle on the table in front of the drunk. "You can finish that one. Looks like I'm done for the night."

Gus took the bottle in hand, then quickly jerked it up and away from himself. A fountain of beer leapt up and slapped across Anita's chest. Her mouth gaped open in shock as she tried to wipe the liquid off of her leather jacket and keep the dripping draft off of her jeans. Her white shirt, however, seemed to dissolve right before everyone's eyes. Still standing beside her, Cody's laughter reached a boil.

"Now we're even," Gus giggled.

Stacy reached up and slapped Gus repeatedly about the head and shoulders. From the opposite end of her arm, her previously melodic voice grumbled obscenities and insults at the older of the two Hatfield brothers. Cody's anger flared. He leaned in behind David to say something, but the elder Wakefield just grabbed Cody' wrist, slammed it down onto the table in front of himself, and shook his head in warning.

The sudden ruckus must have ignited somebody else's temper, too, because somewhere a few tables away a barstool crashed to the ground. Rough men all around Miss Kitty's Saloon took this as the signal to vent their grievances against one another. Some guy was instantly laid across the distant pool table. Two burly brutes began to wrestle in one of the other booths.

Gus was on his feet in a flash. Danny barely saw Anita's right hook fly through the air. Gus missed it entirely - until it connected with his nose and spun his face hard to his own right. Danny took a giant step back - more out of experience and instinct than some consciously perceived danger - just in time to see a bottle sail past the space that had just been occupied by his head a second ago. The bottle seemed to tumble in slow motion until it hit Cody Hatfield in the head. The blow was not hard enough to knock the man out, but it was certainly enough to make him pop his top.

Cody slipped his wiry hand out of David's wrist lock, pushed off the table and rushed at Danny. He charged like a bull with his head down in a classic tackle, but the former Marine caught the smaller man by the back of his jacket and deflected him away with a hard shove. Cody tackled a table at Danny's seven o'clock - a table whose occupants must have thought that Wakefield was their assailant's cohort, as they threw Cody right back toward him.

David Wakefield, still in his seat, sipped his brew with an amused grin and watched for flying debris or bodies that might pose a threat to his girlfriend's daughter.

Gus grabbed a fistful of Anita's jacket and pulled himself up into a body blow designed to double her over, but the lithe woman slipped out from her place deep within the booth, pirouetted under his offending arm, and twisted it hard into an awkward angle. Pain shot up his arm and shoulder, stopping his punch before it was ever thrown. Anita bent the appendage into a configuration God never intended, then snapped downward. Gus' head hit the table hard. Gravity pulled him the rest of the way to the floor in a disheveled heap.

Meanwhile, Danny slipped and parried a series of wild punches from Cody. A particularly sloppy right cross was answered when Danny grabbed Cody by the scruff of his neck and drove his own right knee into his opponent's midsection. The drunken Hatfield brother dropped to the ground, puked, and fought to breathe again.

A flash in David's eyes was all the warning Anita got before a heavy pair of arms wrapped around her from behind like a bear and picked her up off the ground. Her arms were pinned against her sides and her legs kicked uselessly in the air, so she snaked a hand between her taught backside and the man-bear who unwantedly hugged her until, groping, she found his elderberries and squished them into jam. Her assailant - some random local who evidently took exception to the way she treated Gus - groaned in agony. His grip immediately slacked enough for Anita to drop out of his arms, duck down low to cup his ankle with her left hand and ram her right elbow through his right knee. She rolled her shoulder into the blow and drove hard with her legs until the joint buckled at an unnatural angle with a wet *pop*. The big brute fell to the floor and cried in pain.

The elder Wakefield assured Stacy with a calming gesture that said, *You're okay. Just sit still and enjoy the show.* David hoisted his mostly-empty bottle toward Anita in salute.

Several different fights broke out in little pockets around Miss Kitty's. Then, just as quickly, they all started to die down. Danny sauntered up to Anita as the whip of a woman regained her composure.

"Let's get outta here," he invited.

Anita nodded her assent. On the way out the front door she half-turned to him. "Don't we need to stick around and sign a report or something?"

Danny smiled sheepishly at Kitty, who stood behind the bar with her arms crossed and a displeased look painted across her face. "I wouldn't worry too much about that. Just an honest brawl among simple folk. I bet it'll all get sorted out here in a minute."

Fights were not exactly common as Miss Kitty's. Nor were they exactly unheard of. So long as nobody needed an ambulance and the joint remained mostly intact after the commotion, things usually ended with the matron giving all of the parties involved a good tongue lashing and a slightly padded bill for her estimate of their part of the damages. Even so, Danny knew that his father's girlfriend would give her beau an earful later over what he also knew would end up somehow being his fault. He tried not to think about the tub of hot water he just dumped his own father into - partly out of sympathy, but also because he knew that water flowed downhill, which meant that Danny was assured a good talking-to of his own in the very near future.

Anita and Danny heard the yelling inside of Miss Kitty's from the parking lot. It made the sub-zero air outside the bar much more tolerable. "So what's this case of yours about?" Danny's breath condensed into small clouds that floated away as he asked. "Must be important if it couldn't wait until morning."

The female Mounty fought off a shiver from within her jacket. Even with her coat fully zipped, her beer soaked shirt worked to steal away all of her body heat. "I'm after a pair of Americans, actually," she explained through her clenched jaw. "The Gage brothers. They're mid-level dirtbags. Runners for a drug network out of Calgary. My partner and I just about had them a few weeks ago when they bolted." Danny smiled a little as her accent transformed the word *about* into *a-boot*, but he remained quiet and listened. "The other night, they got into a firefight with a rival cartel while crossing back from delivering their latest load. One of our officers got caught in the middle. He didn't make it."

Danny shook his head. "Sorry to hear that."

"Thanks. Anyway, The Gages did a touch-and-go on our side, then bolted back down south of the line. My people have lost our sense of humor with these mopes. So my section chief worked a deal for me to come down and hunt them a little more aggressively, rather than just wait for them to appear on our side again in their own due time."

"That's a lot of cop work for some pretty small fish," Danny sniffed. "What aren't you telling me?"

"They've been smuggling drugs and money across the border for years," she continued. "That's a lot of unaccounted cash which could be funding all sorts of illicit activity beyond narcotics. Hence our assumption of the Secret Service's interest, as the action arm of your Treasury Department."

"Not what I meant." The cool night air helped to sober Wakefield - not that he had had much to drink before the festivities began. His eyes became as cold as the mountain snow and bored into hers for answers.

Wilson waited. She kicked at the gravel under her boot. Her plentiful lower lip curled into her mouth as she chewed on it, obviously considering whether to disclose some sensitive detail. "The younger Gage brother, James," she relented. "He knifed my partner. Back in Calgary. A few weeks ago, when we tried to arrest them."

"I'm sorry." Danny nodded in sympathy. "That explains a lot."

"Both of the Gage brothers are bad apples," she glared, "but James is a total psychopath. My partner wasn't the first person he's -" Anita blinked, sniffed, and planted her hands on her hips. "Look, Wakefield. I just wanna get these guys. I've memorized their file. I know their faces. Their routes. Their contacts. I know where they bed down."

"Sounds like you've got this. Why do you need me?"

"First off, my jurisdiction ended at the 49th parallel," she pointed. "I can't arrest or detain one of your citizens on American soil all by myself. Secondly, in addition to your cooperation and credentials on site, I may need you to access your own law enforcement and government agencies for information. Updates. As the case may need."

"You need a liaison for a bilateral operation," Danny nodded. "Keeps everything official and on the up and up."

"There's one other thing," Wilson confided. "I feel like I should tell you this up front. The best information that we have right now indicates that they're holding up on the reservation."

Wakefield shook his head. "Oh, this just keeps getting better and better."

"According to our records, the Gages' biological father was Native American - Shoshone, to be exact. Their parents weren't married, but our informants have indicated to us that they grew up with some semblance of a relationship with their father. Which is why I don't just need a federal agent," Anita pointed. "I need a local native who knows the lay of the land…"

"And who might be able to provide you with an 'in' on the rez?"

"Exactly."

His father's remark from earlier in the evening echoed in Danny's head. An agent needed his help. Not that he had any choice in the matter, what with Anita having come down fully equipped with an official request for support and orders from on high. But even if the Mounty had shown up empty handed, how could he look at himself in the mirror - or at his own father, a retired cop - in the eye if he ignored a fellow officer chasing after her partner's killer?

Like it or not, Danny was the one person who seemed uniquely suited to render her the exact type of aid she seemed to need. And the challenge of tracking down a cop killer on the run in big sky country had already set his mind into motion. *You're getting to be closer to forty than twenty…* Danny slapped the iconic scene of one of his favorite cop movies out of his imagination. *No*, he told himself, *I'm not getting too old for this.* "Where're you staying tonight?"

"There's a little motel on the outskirts of town. Thought I'd get a room there."

"Don't bother," Danny shook his head. "We've got a spare room back at my Dad's place. You can crash there. It'll let us get an earlier start in the morning. Where're you parked?"

Constable Wilson thrust a thumb toward a miniaturized automobile parked a few spaces away from them. "That's me."

"What, the little half-a-car?"

"The Smart Car is very economical."

"It's also about the dumbest thing you could possibly try to drive out here," he frowned. "One little patch of slush and that thing becomes an ice skate."

"Oh, really?" she waved her hand at the collection of lifted pickups and dual axle behemoths crammed into the lot. "And which one of these penis mobiles is yours?"

"I rode in with dad tonight," he sniffed as he casually avoided any mention of what, exactly, he rode. "But if I did own a dually, I'd probably keep a Smart Car in the back, just in case I got a flat or something. Probably lighter and cheaper than a full spare."

"You Yanks and your cars," she huffed. "Maybe I should just try the hotel."

"Oh, I'm just teasing, Wilson. C'mon. It's getting cold out here."

CHAPTER 4

JAMES GAGE WALKED out of the back bedroom with a self-satisfied smile on his face. That smile had gotten him out of almost as much trouble as it had gotten him into over the years - especially with the ladies. Early into adolescence James learned that a smirk and a flash of his bright blue eyes could get him a lot further than what little effort he could be bothered to invest into most endeavors - especially with the ladies. A lot of gals were addicted to the rush of excitement promised from playing with a bad boy like James. By the time most of them learned what kind of a wolf he was underneath the fleece, *his* clothing usually was not the only thing on the floor.

The youngest Gage carried his worn-out boots in his left hand. His beat-up denim jacket was draped in the crook of that same elbow. His cracked leather belt rattled as he sauntered around with his faded jeans still unfastened.

"You 'bout done, Jimmy?" his older brother asked impatiently from the trailer home's front - and only - door as he rubbed his bloated belly.

James dropped his boots unceremoniously onto the floor and snickered at his more rotund sibling. "Yeah," he finished dressing his lean frame, "she ain't gonna be no good to anyone." His smirk lightened. "At least, not for a while."

"Did you get what we need?" Justin pressed.

"I got what *I* need," James pulled on his boots and stomped his feet into the toes. Then he pulled a scrap of paper out of his pocket and dangled it in the air. "And I got what *we* need. Address where the wetback keeps his stash."

Justin humorlessly swiped the note from his little brother's fingers. "Took you long enough," he scowled. "What happened?"

"Well, you know me," James tugged his beat-up jacket tight and tussled his dirty blonde hair. He was the looker between the two, and there were plenty of gals out there who dropped their guard with little more than some tussled locks and a blue-eyed smile. "I like to stop mid-rape, lean in and whisper, 'I'm just not that into you' into their ear." His own idiot giggle was matched with his brother's chortle. "Puts a little more fire into them." Dressed and satisfied, he nodded. "So, yeah, now we can go get us some payback."

"Yep," Justin grinned. "C'mon, Jimmy. Let's park our load over at Salvadore's and pick up some free goodies."

*   *   *

Danny nursed wakefulness from a thick ceramic mug at the kitchen table. He dressed for a day out in the cold world with a pair of brown pants made from the same heavy canvas as firehoses and lined with a soft fleece interior. A simple black turtleneck helped his core retain some of the equally black coffee's heat. Thick wool socks kept his feet cozy and relaxed. It was the little things, he told himself many times, that helped him ease his way into the day.

The rustic seat at the head of the country table remained empty. Either Danny's father stayed with Kitty the night before or he had long ago risen, ate his breakfast, and headed out on the range to check his livestock. But the table's heavy wooden planks practically echoed with the older man's cautious voice as Danny imagined the words his father would probably serve up with breakfast:

Make good choices, son.

Constable Wilson padded up the hallway from the guest room where she slept away the previous night. A full night's sleep and a full shower made her look refreshed. Her black leggings, white knit shirt and a puffy, cream-colored ski vest were as suited to the cold Montana day as her designer jeans and leather jacket were to the bar the previous night. "Thanks for letting me crash here last night, Wakefield. Sorry if I slept in a little late."

"No problem," he pushed himself up and set to work in the kitchen. "I was just gonna whip up some breakfast. How do you like your eggs?"

"Oh, you don't have to -"

"It's no bother," Danny pulled a handful of free-range eggs from the fridge, "I haven't eaten yet."

"I'm a vegan," Anita explained. "But do you have some grapefruit or something? Whatever's easiest."

"Grapefruit? In cattle country during the middle of winter?" He shrugged. "I doubt Dad's got much rabbit food laying around. Toast? Waffles?"

"Toast is fine."

Danny snatched a loaf of bread from the pantry, then thought for a moment. *What are rules for vegans, again?* "You can't have butter or honey, right?"

"Right. Do you have some jam?"

Danny slipped a few slices of stoneground wheat bread into the positively antique toaster tucked into a corner atop the counter, then plucked a jar of preserves from the fridge and a spoon from the utensil drawer. "Help yourself," he offered as he plucked a big, cast-iron skillet from the overhead rack. He scooped a dollop of butter into the ebony cookware and heated it on the stove. By the time Wilson's toast was ready, a quartet of bacon strips sizzled around the pan's perimeter while a trio of eggs solidified from raw to over-easy. "So," Danny sprinkled a bit of pepper from a grinder into the still-cooking food, "you said last night that you think your suspects are on the rez?"

"Likely," Wilson nodded. "They have a few associates in that area. I have addresses for us to check."

Danny used tongs to turn the bacon. "We can head out after breakfast." He switched to a spatula and gently flipped the eggs. "Quicker we're on it, the quicker we're done."

Anita looked at the hairy bush that still adorned Danny's face. "Do you need more time to finish cleaning up?"

"My vacation resumes the second we catch your perps," he reminded his guest. "Besides, the less I look like that guy on the news, the better things are probably gonna go for both of us."

Special Agent Wakefield's trip to Montana was officially an expenditure of personal leave not cashed in since he took his assignment in D.C. Nobody in the Secret Service used the term 'Administrative Leave,' when they advised him to take some time off since the shootout on Arlington Bridge. Nor did he hear anyone say, 'lay low' before he left the Beltway. But everyone around him knew that he needed to put some time and distance between himself and recent events. A little cooling off period after something like that was perfectly normal, and Danny relished the chance to clear some ghosts from his head. If Wakefield's career was going to survive into the new year, his few remaining allies back at headquarters needed time to help the fallout blow over in the aftermath from his unorthodox handling of the Constitutional Killer situation.

When he dared face the truth of the matter, Danny had to admit he needed to re-center himself. He needed to blow off some steam away from prying eyes. He needed his mind and spirit to heal from the loss of his partner and lover. And if that meant living for a few weeks as a bearded mountain man far enough from civilization that he could shoot or scream whatever he wanted without worrying about anyone's judgement then so be it.

Anita cast a stern look at the collection of flesh sizzling in Danny's skillet. "If you were really interested in what was good for you, you wouldn't be eating all of that."

Danny glanced down at his big breakfast. "The body needs fuel," he reminded her.

"The human body can get all of the nutrients it needs without consuming flesh." She licked a bit of sticky residue from her thumb. "You know, eating stuff like that will drive your cholesterol through the roof. The bacon alone will probably give you a heart attack."

Danny replied with a look of warning. "Bacon is proof that Jesus loves me. Besides," he frowned, "the body needs protein."

"Which you can get through soy or jackfruit. Our bodies are naturally evolved for a diet of plants, not animals."

"Those pointy teeth in the middle of your jaw say otherwise," he countered. "They're designed for tearing into meat, not carrots."

Wilson shook her head and took a bite of jellied toast while Wakefield eased his food onto a plate and closed his eyes for a brief, silent prayer. When his eyes opened again, he noticed his Canadian guest clearly had something on her mind other than a debate on nutrition.

Anita blushed. "I know this is gonna sound stupid -"

"Not as stupid as the sound of someone not eating meat," he loaded his fork with still-smoking sustenance. "I mean, you've obviously got no problems maintaining a trim figure. What gives?"

"But," she ignored his half-compliment and pressed forward, "the only way my section chief would let me come down here was if I was unarmed."

Danny finished his bite and raised an eyebrow. "Your boss sent you on a potentially dangerous mission to apprehend a pair of known killers in a foreign country without a gun?"

"He made me check it at the armory before I left."

"Oh, Canada," he sang his own version of his northern neighbor's national anthem, "the home of naive cops…"

"Would you stop?" she chuckled. "I'm being serious here."

"Does he want you to get killed? 'Cause believe it or not, I know what that's like. I've got a boss just like that. We call him 'Nick the Dick.' Before I left Washington, the dude literally asked me to eat my own forty-five while I'm on leave."

"What kind of -" Anita stopped herself mid-gasp. "It's not that. I think he's worried that I might cause an international incident by shooting a foreign national while I'm in a host nation just because the bastard was my partner's killer."

Danny thought about her story for a second while he evaluated the food on his plate. *Partner's killer… no chain of command weighing you down…* It seemed to Wakefield that he and Constable Wilson lived lives like parallel tracks laid by the same tank. *What would she do?* he considered. *Hell,* he answered his own question, *what did I do?* "And do you *intend* to shoot anyone while you're here?" he inquired with the careful tone of someone who suspected they might later be compelled to remember the exact verbiage of their conversation while they gave a deposition.

"It's not what I'd prefer," she shook her head. "But, if it comes down to it... Well, you know how it is."

That's an understatement, Danny mused. He considered the situation, then pointed to the wooden racks built into the adjoining living room wall. Several lever-action rifles and sundry shotguns - his father's cowboy guns - were propped up vertically from the floor to about waist level. Maybe they rode a little higher on his petite guest. A second row started about midway up the wall and was filled with long guns of more modern designs. Those fine pieces comprised the bulk of Danny's collection of tactical and sport firearms. A set of wooden drawers ran horizontally between the two rows of guns. Shelves to either side of the rack held thousands upon thousands of rounds of ammunition - a healthy stock for each of the calibers represented in the Wakefields' private collection. A smattering of holsters and gun belts hung on a nearby coat rack.

"Alright, I can spot you something." Danny shoveled the rest of an egg into his mouth and savored the flavor before he returned to the cabinets and retrieved a fresh ceramic mug. "How do you like your coffee?"

"With rum," Anita quipped. "This early, though, I'll take it black." Danny poured her a cup, topped off his own hefty barrel, then returned to the table.

"What do you Mounties usually carry as a duty sidearm?"

"Oh, anything will be fine. I'll manage. I don't want to be a bother."

Danny waived his hand at the wall of guns. "Suit yourself," he invited. "None of these are trophy guns. We don't have anything here we don't shoot." He took a bite of bacon, then tossed the rest of the piece past his teeth and munched on the crispy morsel. "Pick something you're comfortable with."

They finished their food quickly. Wilson walked into the living room while Wakefield policed their dishes. When he was finished in the kitchen, he saw her looking at the shelves like a kid browsing the aisle at their favorite toy store.

"Is that an M-203 grenade launcher?" her voice rose with incredulity as she stared wide-eyed at the standalone tube launcher with the pistol grip and collapsible stock nestled between Danny's customized M1A and his favorite Kalashnikov-patterned rifle.

"No, officer," his bearded face announced dryly. "It's a *flare* launcher."

The Mountie looked at him with one black eyebrow raised. "Oh, really? And what, may I ask, the difference?"

Danny folded his arms across his chest and tilted his head to the left. "The two-oh-three is a forty-millimeter grenade launcher," he explained, "and a destructive device whose ownership, transport, and use is heavily restricted by law. *That*," his head shifted toward his right shoulder, "is a *thirty-seven* millimeter device, and since it's neither a grenade launcher nor a gun *per se,* it can be bought without any registration, license, or even the most rudimentary of background checks. Straight off the internet and mailed right to your door." A mixture of delight and mischief gave birth to a smile behind his beard. "I call it Aunt Brenda."

"Aunt Brenda?"

"It's kinda squat, not overly fancy, and is *not* to be underestimated. Just like my dad's little sister."

"I understand the ranch rifles, Wakefield. But what on Earth do you shoot with this thing?" Anita jerked her thumb at the standalone launcher.

"Well, since this is America," he Danny smiled at his Canadian counterpart, "I shoot whatever the Hell I want." He shrugged and crinkled his nose. "Mostly fireworks, though, when it comes to Aunt Brenda. Smoke. Flares. I've got some birdshot rounds for dropping groups of crows and other nuisance birds as they flock overhead."

"Anything more, *potent,* than that?" the Canadian cop asked pointedly.

Danny's voice remained neutral. "Of course not, officer. That would be illegal. Besides, stuff like that's not commercially available." His eyes defocused as he looked out the window on the far wall. "You'd have to mill out your own hulls from aluminum instead of the plastic or cardboard ones on the market." He ticked off his excuses on his fingers, "then pack 'em with illicitly acquired or homemade explosives - and you're more likely to blow yourself up trying to make that stuff than you are anything else. And you'd have to find a way to safely store the rounds without them self-detonating as the explosive decomposes. And you'd have to be pretty good at it, too, if you didn't want your homemade grenade to detonate in the tube when you shot it." Danny wore an expression of disgust as he shook his head. "That's a lot of hassle to break a perfectly good statute designed to keep good, law-abiding folk safe."

Anita did not appear to completely believe Wakefield's explanation, but she let the issue go and returned her attention to the cabinetry. She consulted one drawer, which housed a pair of cowboy revolvers. The second drawer she checked contained a common 9mm Glock that was perfectly adequate and equally unexciting. But when she opened the third drawer, her eyes lit like the Christmas tree in the living room's rear corner. Nestled in the drawer was a large caliber stainless steel revolver with a six-inch barrel. The big bore pistol was topped with a brushed nickel scope that ran almost the full length of the gun. "God bless America," Anita sighed.

"It's called the White Rhino," Danny explained. "I usually don't go for wheel guns myself, but that one fires out of the bottom cylinder instead of the top like a conventional revolver." As her host outlined the gun's particulars, Anita turned the hefty stainless-steel pistol over and examined every millimeter from the tip of the muzzle to the base of the wooden grip. *A girl that petite goes for a gun that big,* he mentally weighed, *and she either really knows her stuff or she's completely clueless.* "The design requires a slight modification to how you normally hold a revolver," he advised, "but it takes most of the felt recoil right out of it. Makes a three-fifty-seven round feel almost like a twenty-two long rifle."

Anita's face took on a new level of seriousness as she hefted the big gun. "Do you mind if I test it out before we leave?"

"I'd be disappointed if you didn't. Ammo's over there. We'll grab a box and some leather. Eyes and ears are on the counter on the way out."

CHAPTER 5

JAMES STOOD WITH his back to a metal wall as his older brother unlocked the door to a nondescript shipping container laid to rest on some innocuous looking storage facility's rear parking apron. The faded and chipped markings on the corrugated side belonged to a packing and processing plant fifty miles up the road. Justin forced the heavy steel door open with a *creak* as dirt popped out of its hinges. The elder Gage lifted his pistol - the same Glock his little brother took from one of their attackers last week - swung the door wide and stared into a big box of meat.

More than two dozen people were huddled together for warmth along the container's floor. Maybe half looked like they could walk. They were all obviously stoned - kept docile by a lack of water and minimal food, all of which was laced with the Sinaloa cartel's own special candy.

Selling drugs was easy money. But smart business leaders learned to diversify their markets. For some groups, that meant drugs plus stolen cars. For cartels like the Gage's bosses, the Jaliscos - or their competitors, the Sinaloas - that included human trafficking. Coyotes ran caravans and truckloads across the Rio Grande. Local boys like this Sinaloa *cholo* delivered human merchandise to sweat shops, sex houses, large scale farms… even some restaurants and hotels which used them as a cheap source of menial labor.

Justin swept the gun back and forth, just in case anyone's drugged-out brain managed to fire enough neurons to spawn any bright ideas. "Toss it in, Jimmy."

The younger Gage frowned, but he obediently dropped a pair of large pizza boxes as into the container and let them slide along the floor between the human cargo. "Still think we should'a sprinkled some powder on top, just to keep 'em quiet."

"They're no good to us dead, Jimmy. We'll wait for whatever they're on start to wear off." Justin closed the door again and secured it with a new lock. "Then we'll dose 'em again. If," he leaned back and smiled as he rubbed his corpulent belly, "there's still any of 'em left."

James dusted his hands clean. "Always thinkin'," he grinned. "So, what's next?"

"Crew up north said the Sinaloas were already paid for these girls." Justin tucked the Glock into his waistband and headed back to their truck. "The first kick in the balls for those little bastards'll comes when their little boy don't deliver 'em."

"Then what?"

Justin rubbed his plentiful pudge and smiled. "That there is free cargo. All we gotta do is find a place to offload it right quick. Whatever we make is one-hunnert-percent pure profit. That's money outta the Sinaloa's pocket and into ours."

"Balls," James howled in mock pain.

"Lock us in. I wanna be movin' again before these piggies sober up enough to start makin' noise."

"Where we takin' 'em?"

"Oh, there's always places," Justin's hands slid around in circles along the front of his bibbed coveralls. "Sinaloas wanna screw with our shipments? Let's see how they like a taste of their own medicine."

*   *   *

"Oh, baby," Anita breathed out. Under Danny's supervision, she emptied the White Rhino into the modest shooting berm for the fourth time.

"Too much for you?" Noise-cancelling earmuffs protected their senses from gunfire, but still allowed them to hear softer sounds like spoken words or even rustled grass with perfect clarity.

"Too much?" she chuckled and caressed the steel gun's six-inch long barrel. "My dear," she purred, "I think I want to marry it."

A double entendre crossed Danny's mind, but he kept his poker face firmly in place. *Best not go there yet,* he decided. *We don't know each other* that *well.* "I don't know if that's legal," he fell back on a safer joke, "even up in Canada. But I'll indulge the lady. Here," he plucked his cell phone from his parka's pocket,

"I'll get a quick glamor shot for you to take home or whatever."

"Oh, no thank you," she smiled. "I don't like having my picture taken."

Danny shrugged at the irony. *A hundred million ugly camera hogs out there polluting the internet with their mugs,* he tucked his phone back into its place, *and someone this pretty doesn't like to have her picture taken.* "Suit yourself. Shoot the rest of the box and we'll head out."

Danny was content to stand aside with his bronze and black 1911 tucked into its leather shoulder holster inside his dark blue winter parka. Constable Wilson seemed to enjoy having the range to herself. He watched the Mountie as she reloaded the White Rhino and went back to work. *Favors the bigger caliber,* he noted to himself. The big bore gun was able shoot either no-nonsense .38 Special or even beefier .357 Magnum ammunition, and they brought a box of each out with them for her to use. But Anita completely ignored the smaller, conventional cartridges and exclusively shot the more powerful magnum rounds.

Her marksmanship was better than average, but not quite up to the standard to which the former Special Operations Marine's was accustomed. Then again, Wakefield had to admit that when it came to marksmanship - as in so many aspects of his life - he held himself to a standard that was unrealistically high for most people. At seven paces, Anita consistently placed her shots well within the middle of an eight-inch paper plate - the National Rifle Association's traditional method of gauging whether a shooter could consistently hit an adult torso near the outer limits of what most firearms enthusiasts would designate 'realistic practical distance' for a pistol. After the first few rounds and a few minor adjustments to her grip, familiarity with the gun let Anita cluster her .357-inch holes within a neat little herd approximately three inches - about eight centimeters, as his northern neighbor would probably note - in diameter near the target's center.

At that same distance, Wakefield knew he could empty his 1911 into a silver dollar and turn it into a silver donut.

"Looks like you're getting the hang of it," Danny nodded after his guest emptied the revolver again.

"Thanks."

"Better than I expected."

"I *am* a cop, Wakefield," she reminded him as she cleared spent brass casings from the gun's cylinder.

"Yeah," he grinned, "and most cops display the worst marksmanship I've ever seen. But despite that little detail, you still managed to keep your rounds on the target."

"Nice," she dryly responded.

"Add to that the fact that you're Canadian," he smiled devilishly, "and I kinda figured I'd need to give you a hockey stick if I wanted you to actually hit anything."

Anita's face soured as she held the empty gun at the low-ready position. "I think the wind's starting to blow the target off the post," she dared him. "Why don't you be a dear and go hold it up for me?"

Danny ignored her mock challenge and looked up as clouds moved into the late morning sky. "Well, shoot faster so we can get on the road."

A quick reload later and Danny's headset muffled another string of six shots - this one delivered at a notably quicker cadence than the previous volleys. A stray ribbon of perforated paper at the plate's center flapped and flipped as the sextet of projectiles sailed through the target's tattered center hole. *So,* he mused, *she can shoot - when she's motivated.*

CHAPTER 6

"I'VE FIGURED OUT the real secret to weight loss," the radio host's disembodied voice proudly announced from the Jeep's speakers.

"And based on how that sweater is stretched across your frame," his cohost countered, "it appears that whatever the secret is, you've locked it away in a vault and are avoiding it like the plague."

"I'll have you know that I've lost almost twelve pounds since Halloween," the first voice indignantly replied.

"You - what?!? Didn't you just tell me during the last break that you've gained over fifteen pounds since the fall?"

"That's right. But I figured that it would be at least thirty by Christmas," the host explained. "So, since I didn't fatten up as much as I expected -"

"You're counting lower-than-anticipated obesity as a net weight loss?"

"Exactly."

"I don't think that's how it works, Lonnie."

"Pretty sure that's similar to how the government tracks the economy," the host countered. "It didn't shrink as badly as expected, so they're saying it improved."

"I still don't think that's how math actually works," the junior cohost countered. "Not in the real world."

"Well, that's how I want it to work."

"That may be the case, but the fact remains that there is a number on that scale, and the number today is higher than the one three months ago."

"That's your opinion, Fred."

"That's not an opinion!" Fred protested. "That's an observable, objective fact!"

"But I choose to embrace an alternative fact," Lonnie slowly countered.

"Alternative fact?" Fred fumed. "There's no such thing as an 'alternative fact!' There's fact, and then there's fiction."

"Well," Lonnie drew out, "not if you have a more evolved perspective."

"And what perspective could possibly override common sense?"

"The postmodern perspective," the Conservative talk radio superstar explained. "The perspective that I don't want to be fat anymore - or listen to any more of your fat shaming."

"Well, if that's the case," Factcheck Fred opined, "then maybe putting down the fork is a more viable course of action than self-delusion."

"If blind self-delusion and misinformation is good enough for Progressives in American universities and Congress then it's good enough for my waistline." The host's smug smile was visible even through the radio. "If the Alphabet Soup Troupe can just make crap up and we have to accept it -"

"Whoa, wait a second," the junior showman interrupted, "the 'Alphabet Soup Troupe?'"

"Right."

"Who's that?"

"You know," Lonnie hemmed, "the LGBTQRSY crowd."

Countless audience members followed suit as Factcheck Fred silently spelled his way through his boss' acronym. *L is for lesbian; G is for gay...* "Okay, I had you through Q for queer -"

"You can't say that word," Lonnie jumped in angrily, "that's *their* word."

"But it's a word."

"It's *their* word," Lonnie emphasized. "You don't have Q-word privileges."

"But it's been in the English lexicon for centuries. Granted, it used to mean something else -"

"And now that it doesn't, you can't use it anymore."

"Oh, for Pete's..." Fred growled. "Fine. We'll sort that out later. But for now, please explain to me what the R, A, and Y stand for."

"You don't know?"

"I don't know."

"I can't believe you don't know." Lonnie's shock grew more audible with each syllable.

"I haven't a clue," Fred flatly answered.

"Well, that just goes to show how out of touch you are."

"Clearly," Fred chuckled. "So, what do they mean?"

"Nobody knows," Lonnie admitted. "But they just keep adding letters to the name, making it more and more ridiculous every day, so they're bound to mean something by dinner tomorrow."

"If they don't already."

"Right? And, at the end of the day, since everything is subjective these days, anything can mean anything to anyone, and nobody can actually be called out for it, because there's no objective standard to anything anymore."

"Still," Fred moped, "there's gotta be an easier, less-offensive way to refer to them than 'Alphabet Soup Troupe.' I know! QUILT BAG!"

"Quilt Bag?"

"Queer, Undecided…"

Danny switched the Jeep's radio from satellite service to music and shuffled the songs on his iPhone. Free from the political ramblings and nonsense of the outside world, he pressed a few more soft keys and returned the touch screen to navigation mode. "We'll take Highway Ninety to Missoula," he explained as he locked in his Jeep's cruise control, "then circle into high country."

Anita's bags rode in the back of his sport utility vehicle alongside his own gear. Danny felt more comfortable driving his red 4x4 than riding in her cheap little rental car. The roads were mostly clear - which was an oddity for this time of year - but Montana's winter weather could turn rough fast. It was most prudent and practical for them to utilize a vehicle that was better equipped to handle snow and ice regardless of the current conditions. Just in case.

The Canadian constable zoomed out on the console's digital map and the outline of their route. "That's right on the edge of the Flathead Reservation. Why stop short?"

"That's where you said their bed down was."

"I'm guessing we can't just drive straight in?"

"We can," he nodded, "if we want to announce to everyone on the rez that we're there." Danny worked his jaw. "Tribal communities have a way of knowing when strangers come and go." Anita gave him a critical look. "It's not racist. It's the truth. Look, you've got a homogenous ethic group - a closed social circle - with its own distinct way of doing things, an intimate familiarity with the area, and a culturally reinforced distrust of outsiders." He cast her a sideways glance. "You think you're just gonna slip in there and piss in someone's Cheerios without anyone noticing, Pale Face?"

"I'd say your nation's history has proven the natives' distrust of strangers to be justifiably prudent," Anita opined. "Wouldn't you, Wakefield?"

"Not saying it's wrong. Not saying it's not justified. Just saying that it is what it is. Who's right and who's wrong for what and when don't factor into it. Not for us. Not today."

"So, what are we doing?"

"I've got an asset," the former Marine caught himself at the use of terminology from his previous career in military intelligence, "a buddy of my dad. He's got a cabin out between Glacier National Park and the edge of the rez. He and his wife live at their ranch back down south. Not too far from my dad's.

They rent the cabin to tourists during the warmer months. It mostly sits empty this time of year. I've been clearing predators off their family's land since I got here."

"Sounds cozy," Anita teased.

"I called them this morning before you got up. Cabin's ours for the time being. Gives us cover for placement - that's a plausible reason to be here."

"I know what the term means, Wakefield."

"Sorry." Danny's phone chirped. "Force of habit." He glanced down quickly enough to read a text from his father. "Mrs. Johnson - the wife - agreed to keep her eyes and ears open for me while she's in town today. Let me know if the local gossip includes anything that might be your boys bouncing around."

"Kind of her to do that."

"Hens cluck," he replied matter-of-factly. "Small, closed community like this? Women can't help but flap their gums about every little thing happening around them. You go to the store and some little old lady who doesn't know you from Adam just goes on and on about her latest, most painful medical issues while you're waiting on the cashier." He frowned as he recalled the all-too-frequent event. "In intimate, forensic detail." His nose wrinkled at the nightmarish memory, as if the lack of discretion or personal privacy had an odor that he still smelled. "I mean, I just wanna check out, and she keeps going on and on about draining some cyst -"

"I see," Anita cut in before he went into more detail.

Danny shuttered. "I feel like I need to sign a release or nondisclosure agreement just to stand in the checkout line."

"Lovely."

"Oh," he instantly brightened, "more good news. Looks like we're off the hook for any of the damages from last night's brawl. Seeing as how Dad explained to Kitty that you were just the poor, innocent victim of a sexual assault from those big brutes and all."

"That's a relief," Anita smiled. "Might have some problems explaining that particular expense on the trip."

"Yeah, well, you might wanna hashtag it or something next time you're online. Just to keep up appearances."

"I don't hashtag," she said dryly.

"Well, in that case, why don't you give me the make, model, and plate number for the Gage's truck so that I can call in an APB?" An All-Points Bulletin, or APB - sometimes referred to in law enforcement circles as a BOLO – or Be On the Look Out - would alert every cop from every department in the state that Wakefield and Wilson were looking for the suspects and their vehicle. If any officer anywhere saw the truck or its occupants, their location was immediately reported. It was a great force multiplier during manhunts, as it gave the investigators extra eyes everywhere. "You said you've got that, right?"

"I do," she nodded slowly, "but I don't want to go down that route if we can avoid it."

"What?"

"I'd rather fly under the radar for now. Don't want to announce our activities to any outside parties."

"You're kidding me. Look, Wilson, cop work works because there's a bunch of cops out there talking to each other, sharing information. Every trooper's a sensor - you know?"

"This isn't my first rodeo, Wakefield."

"Then you understand that bad guys can run from one cop, but they can't run from all of them. Not for long, anyway. Right?"

"Look, Wakefield, I know you don't want to hear it, but state and city agencies around here have too many leaks. You can't say that surprises you, either. We believe that the Jaliscos have a number of local officers on the payroll. It's just another reason why my superiors let me come to you for help. As a fed, so far as local law enforcement is concerned, you're an outsider. And I'm not here."

"That's just -" he seethed. "Fine. You know what? It'll make things that much harder for us and take us that much longer to get anything accomplished, but fine. It's your case."

"Thank you."

"Feel free to monkey it up as you see fit."

"I'm trying to keep a low profile," she countered as she lifted her phone. "I copied all of my investigative notes and anything that I thought might be relevant before I left. I have what we need."

"Fine."

"Don't tell me how to do my job, Wakefield."

Danny's time with the Department of Homeland Security basically amounted to a multi-year train of investigations where every case was its own railcar. As he looked back at his career, the line never felt like it ended. It just blended back toward the horizon to his time in military intelligence - which was, from a certain perspective, just another collection of cases, one after the other. And before that, having grown up with a cop as a father, it seemed like Wakefield's entire life was an endless series of investigations and inquiries.

Sometimes the job seemed to permeate every aspect of his life. Survival tactics that kept him alive on the battlefield became daily habits - things like always sitting with his back to a wall, never leaving home without a spare mag, keeping a good knife on his person at all times. The former Marine turned federal agent maintained a constant visual sweep that checked the hands, eyes, hands, hips, then *hands again* of every person within engagement range. He trusted rarely and verified often. And like the old warrior said: everywhere Danny went he was polite, professional... and maintained a plan to kill everyone around him.

Danny's job was an armored persona he wore. It kept him safe - safe from physical harm and, usually, emotional hurt. It penetrated his pores like a clown's makeup or the grease on an engineer's hands. It was what the world saw and how people identified him. Many days it was hard for Wakefield to tell just where the job ended and where he began... or who he would be without that carefully crafted identity to serve as his anchor in a tumultuous world.

And he knew exactly how he would respond if someone tried to tell him how they thought he should conduct an ongoing investigation. He knew it firsthand. The occasions were few, but there were times when he had to remind a fellow professional to mind their own business and let him run his own case as he saw fit. *I owe her the same courtesy,* he admitted to himself inwardly.

"The universe is just determined to ruin my vacation," he grumbled.

*   *   *

Miguel Jalisco - the cleaner, leaner of the brothers who ran the logistics side of the Jalisco cartel - sat on the veranda with his older brother and looked at the cell phone in his hand. "Verdad?" he demanded from the person on the other end of the line. "Hey, Hector! You hear this?"

His elder sibling pouted his lips in consideration. "Where's our money?"

"Like I said, *jefe*," Justin assured him over the phone, "there's a chop shop up here run by a guy named Salvadore. It's neutral territory. Totally safe."

"You're sure?" Hector probed.

"Nobody messes with Salvadore," Justin insisted. "He's like the Casa Blanca of Montana, man."

There was enough overlap in how many of the criminal organizations active on the streets carried out their operations that sometimes it was more convenient for all parties involved to share resources rather than go to war for the small stuff. Located nowhere in particular in northwestern Montana, Salvadore's Auto Repair was the Switzerland of stolen cars. They moved purloined automobiles the same way certain banks hid Nazi gold and hush money from the Vatican. Salvadore was completely independent. Everyone who needed to know about him knew his turf was openly available, but never aligned with any faction. He was a friend to anyone with money, but his allegiance could not be bought. And he did not tolerate rivalries to flare up on his turf.

"I hate old movies," Miguel spat.

"He's got a gated lot and a handful of dudes to keep it secure," Justin explained. "Your money is totally safe there."

"We don't want our money safe up there," Hector's voice carried through the open air and over the speakerphone, "we want it safe down here."

"Two days, tops," Justin assured the cartel boss. "We just need to get rid of the merch we looted from the Sinaloas. Get our payback for that scrape at the border."

"Two days," Hector insisted. "And no more delays."

"As long as we get our cut," Miguel chimed in. "You're buying our time now, *gringo*."

"Ten percent," Justin offered.

"Twenty-five," Hector countered. A wicked grin reshaped the thin beard that grew upon his rounded face. "Or, you could just bring 'em with you now. We could always offload them down here. Get some extra *putas* in place before the spring rush."

Every spring, *notreamerericanos* descended upon certain garden spots in Mexico to cut loose, blow off steam, and party. The annual revelry was a marathon of sex, booze, drugs, and other bad decisions that often made the last days of Sodom and Gomorrah look like a Baptist picnic. The gringos' vice-ridden appetites were as hedonic as they were predictable. And the Jaliscos were just one of several local organizations that were happy to cater to their wealthy northern neighbors' needs - for the right price. Their leg men supplied paying customers with a nearly endless stream of cheap marijuana, MeX, and plenty of *señoritas* to satisfy whatever needs they might have. For a few greenbacks, someone in the Jalisco network would gladly deliver the high life to you. "*Mi e mi hermano* take a percentage for our cut, then you guys keep the rest for your troubles last week."

"Fifteen percent," the elder Gage brother conceded with seething pain in his voice. "We're the ones who got shot at. And we're doing all the legwork."

"Twenty," Miguel interrupted, "plus, when you get back, we'll move you to the Chicago run."

Justin's smile positively beamed on his end of the phone call. James silently pumped his fist in the air at their turn of fortune. "You bet, *jefe*. This ain't really about profit anyway," Justin reassured his Mexican taskmaster, "it's about payback."

"Maybe not for you, *amigo*," Miguel allowed, "but it's always about profit for us. So you better not gyp us, *gringo*."

"That's right, *amigo*. You two really showed your *cajones* up there last week." Hector exchanged nods with his little brother. "We think maybe you're ready for the big hauls."

While there was a respectable amount of cash to be made distributing MeX up I-25 from Las Cruces to Lethbridge, that money was small potatoes compared to routes that serviced major metropolitan areas. The Chicago Run followed America's interstate system right up its spine, straight up the middle, with stops that included Midland, Oklahoma City, St. Louis, and ended in the Windy City herself -

whose denizens, inner city and suburbanite alike, gobbled up MeX like it was Skittles.

"We just need a couple of days to sort this out."

"So long as you don't need us to send anyone up there to clean up your mess," Miguel warned. "We need our supply lines to run smoothly."

"We've got this," Justin assured his handler.

"Do your thing, *gringo*," Hector waved away his hot-headed brother's concerns like the waft of smoke that drifted up from the fat cigar perched between his fingers. "But be sure to be back in time for your next run."

"Will do, *jefe*. An' you might wanna be prepared for any blowback on your end."

"*No me importa una mierda con Sinoloa putas!*" Hector spat. "Those *pendejos* try to jack one of our mules, they get what they've got coming."

"You're the boss."

"Let those motherless *bribóns* try that kind of *mierda* down here," Hector dared the unseen fates.

Miguel pulled the phone away from his brother and a bit closer to himself. "Teach them a little lesson, *amigo*. Just don't draw any heat from *la policía*. We don't need the attention right now. *Comprende?*"

"We understand, boss."

"And be quick about it," Hector insisted.

"Sure thing, *jefe*. We won't let you down."

"Be sure you don't, *amigo blanco.*" Hector deactivated the phone in his brother's hand, then leaned back in smug satisfaction and waved for one of the house maidens to bring him a fresh drink.

Miguel and Hector kept a handful of young ladies around to serve their needs - whatever those needs might be and whenever they might come. A brown skinned beauty clad in a white string bikini and a linen skirt tied around her waist - the standard uniform for all of the girls - deposited a small glass onto the small table between the brothers. As was always expected, the tumbler was filled to within a millimeter of its brim with Don Julio Silver.

The house maiden's life story was as unimportant to Hector as it was stereotypical of all of the brothers' girls: bought or taken at the age of eight or nine years old - which, based upon Hector's judgement of how she had grown up and filled out since, was about a dozen or so years ago - and raised to know no life other than one of perpetual service. When they were young, the house girls cleaned and did chores at one villa or another. As they grew up, the less desirable ones either continued the servile work, labored at a cocaine or MeX refinery, or were used as mules to carry product northward. Prettier *señoritas* usually found themselves turning tricks into dollars at locales favored by *notreamerericanos*. But Miguel and Hector were raised by an uncle who, like a good gardener or farmer, taught them to keep the most delectable fruit for themselves.

"Maria, isn't it?" Hector patted his lap and smiled invitingly, "please, join us." Years of servitude taught the house maiden to obey without hesitation, and to do so with the appearance of someone who was happy to oblige.

"Make mine a double," Miguel called over his shoulder toward the veranda's bar. A pair of smiling girls sauntered his way, ready to enthusiastically satisfy whatever request he made.

…

CHAPTER 7

"YOU'RE OUT OF your goddamned mind if you think I'm staying here, Wakefield."

Danny stopped midway up the snow-covered walk from the driveway to the rugged cabin's weathered front door and looked up in confusion. "What?"

"This place is a total dump," Anita fumed.

With his backpack slung over one shoulder and his all-weather parka tucked under his arm, Wakefield looked back and forth between the cabin nestled among the trees and the Canadian cop. "Well, I'll admit that it's not the Ritz..."

"Forget the Ritz. It's not even the Bates Hotel."

"Now, come on," he protested. "It's not that bad." He gestured to the cabin's hairy cedar logs and gray-brown roof. "I mean, sure, it's a little rustic -"

"*Rustic?*" she scoffed. "I feel under-vaccinated."

"It's Lake County, not a third world country."

"Nobody checks Sasquatch's passport when he kidnaps you," she countered. "They just look at the trees and wonder which one he ate you under."

"It's fine," Danny assured her. "The Johnsons are a good family. Decent people. And Mrs. Johnson gets out here to clean the place regularly."

"If she's up here so often, why are you having to plow through the snow just to get up the walk?"

"Oh, c'mon, Wilson. This is just a little dusting. We haven't had a real snow in weeks. I was just up here. This powder's only been on the ground three or four days. Now quit being such a baby."

"*Osti de tabarnak de calice, c'est pas possible comment que t'es cave,*" Anita growled. Wakefield was not fluent in *Quebecois,* but he caught the gist of her meaning, nonetheless. "If I get bed bugs, I swear to God I'm going to break your face." Her own preference to the contrary, she stomped up the walk behind him.

Danny snorted. "You'd think a Mounty would be accustomed to austere accommodations every now and again."

"I prefer heat and indoor plumbing," she replied through clenched teeth. "I have a credit card, Wakefield. *J'men calice des couverture ou placement.* There has to be a decent hotel in the area. If you're short on cash, I'll get us a room."

He shook his head. "I prefer a place where I have a little more visibility on the comings and goings than most hotels allow me." Danny retrieved a key concealed beneath a pile of fake dog droppings, kicked the snow off of his weathered boots, and let himself into the cabin.

Anita followed him inside, where her reservations about the cabin melted like the snow on her designer hiking boots. Just past the stone entryway floor where Wakefield deposited his damp footwear, beautiful hardwood planks flowed under an inviting leather living room suit and poured into an open kitchen and eat-in dining area. Not a speck of dust could be found atop the rich hardwood table or among the chairs, stools, or cabinetry.

"There's just one bedroom," Danny pointed down a short hallway between the couch and the refrigerator. "Feel free to drop your gear back there."

"Assuming a bit much, don't you think, Wakefield?"

"The only thing I'm assuming," he hung his parka on the coatrack next to the door, "is that if it takes us longer than a day to catch your boys, you'd prefer the bed to the sofa." He dialed the thermostat to a warmer setting. The idle heat exchange *huffed* to life in the background. Danny dropped his duffel bag onto the big couch and stretched tired shoulders within his thick wool sweater. "Now, Constable, once you unload your extraneous gear, I'd like to get straight to business. If it's all the same to you."

"Suits me just fine, Wakefield."

"Great. So, where did you say your suspects should be?"

*   *   *

Russel Gage fell back slowly and kicked one leg up onto the worn-out arm of his cracked pleather sofa. Though it was late in the afternoon, sleep fell upon him like a dark blanket. Failing northern sunlight filtered through broken blinds and faded to black as he surrendered to his body's need for a nap.

The door to Russel's trailer burst open, but the middle-aged man barely managed a startle. A pair of blurry silhouettes rushed around and yelled words that his tired ears muffled and garbled into nonsense. A strong hand grabbed Russel by the crusty flannel shirt he still wore from yesterday and yanked him up from his resting place.

"Where are they?" a woman's face came into focus just a handbreadth from his own nose. "Where are your boys, Gage?"

"Who?"

"Clear in back!" a deeper voice called from the rear of the trailer.

"Your sons, Gage!" the woman scowled.

"Hey," Russel rambled with a slimy smile, "you're hot. You wanna go?"

A wall slammed into Gage's back. He was barely sober enough to recognize the impact. The muzzle of a wicked looking revolver pressed against his temple and helped him awaken.

"You nasty, meth-mouthed motherf-"

"Wilson!" The other shadow came into focus and swept to the woman's side. "Be cool, Wilson."

"I-I-I..." Gage stammered through a blackened, crusty face grill that was missing more teeth than it still had left.

The second shadow - a dude, bigger than the woman, and all the scarier for it - flashed a badge. "We're looking for your sons, Mr. Gage. Justin and James. Where are they?"

"They ain't here."

"Where are they?" the bearded man grew louder, scarier. In Russel's eyes, he transformed into something like a grizzly - a tower of anger and hair that loomed over him and made his bony knees collapse.

"They ain't here, officer!" For all of its volume, Russ' voice carried the pitch of a whimper. "They ain't here!"

Wilson pulled the gun away, but bumped Russel against the flimsy wall again. "I don't care where they *aren't*," she growled. "Tell us where they *are*. Now!"

"I don' know... I don' know..."

"Bullshit!" she spat.

"Nah-nah-nah... They pulled out this morning."

"So they *were* here?"

"Yes'm. Last night. We were... uh..."

"Partying," the bear-man finished for him.

"Yeah. With friends."

"Did they get high last night, too?" the man-thing pressed. "Your boys. Did Justin and James get high here last night?"

"Nah." Russel shriveled up visibly. "My boys..." eyes that tried to shut out the light squeezed closed to hold in tears. "They don't use... They ain't messed up like me."

"Bullshit," Wilson sneered.

"They ain't!" Russel heaved against sobs that refused to subside. "They hate cristi."

The angry woman's grip lightened just a bit. "Christine?"

"Cristi," the bearded man-bear-cop corrected. "Crystal meth."

Fluid fell from every orifice in Gage's drug-damaged face. "They say I'm weak... That's why they left me."

"Last night?"

"Yeah."

"They couldn't've gotten far, Wakefield." Wilson shook Gage back into the moment. "Did they tell you where they were going?"

"N-N-No."

"Think!" her arm pressed Russel back into the wall hard enough that everyone in the ratty trailer's cluttered central room seemed surprised the smackhead did not go right through it and fall onto the gravel parking apron on the other side. "Where would they go?"

"I don' know... I don' know..."

"Worthless!" Wilson walked toward the door and left Russel against the wall.

The elder Gage tried to focus on the man - Wakefield, she called him - who remained. To Russel's drug-addled mind, the guy looked as much like a bear with a gun as he did a man with a badge. Maybe more so. The cop-bear's face went sour. "Is that your boy's blood on your shirt, Gage?"

"Nah. That's Ike's."

"Who's Ike?"

"My... He..."

"Your dealer."

"Yeah."

Wakefield holstered his handgun and huffed. "Your boys might not be into meth like you, Gage," a hand-paw wiped across the big blur's furry face, "but they *are* messed up. Maybe you don't think you're strong enough to help them, but we can. Now, if you know where they've gone -"

"I don' know..."

"We didn't come here for you, Russel. But that doesn't guarantee you're in the clear. I got outta bed early this morning, and *somebody's* going to jail tonight. Give us something better to do with our time. You hear me, Gage? Tell me where your boys might be, and we'll roll out of here. Even give you a lift to a place where you can detox."

"I don' know, man! They just got in the truck and took off."

"Which way did they go?"

Gage's left hand drifted up, then swung through the air in a wide arc that barely missed Wakefield's face. "I don' know!" he managed as the waterworks resumed. His face became a leaking mess, like some struggling art student's barely comprehensible project. Wakefield stepped back and let the addict crumble down the wall under the weight of his own decisions. A moment later, he stood with Wilson outside the trailer.

"It's a big state," Danny reminded her. "Don't suppose I can get you to rethink that APB?"

Anita shook her head. "Like I said before, Wakefield. We've got to do this on our own."

Danny donned his sunglasses and gazed down the highway. "Well then, I guess we're headed north."

"Why north? Gage said he didn't know where they went."

"Yep. That's what he said, alright." He gave her a deeply meaningful look. "With his words."

"And you think he was lying?"

"Of course he was lying. That's what drug addicts do." Danny shrugged. "Three things you can always count on from druggies," he counted on his fingers. "First, that they wanna get high."

"Obviously."

"Second," he continued, "that they'll beat on women." Anita's face bounced slightly as she wordlessly conceded the point to him without protest. "And thirdly, that they're lying."

"Thank you, Agent Obvious. So, how does that help us with him?"

"He's so high right now, I doubt he could think straight enough to come up with a decent story. Which is probably why he didn't say jack diddly."

"Maybe he genuinely cares for his sons," she countered. "Or just wants to cover for them."

"Okay, fine. It's *another* reason why he didn't say squat. But then again, maybe he was so strung out that he didn't realize he was lying. That, or he didn't realize that he was telling the truth, either." Anita looked at him in utter confusion, so he explained on their way back to the Jeep. "Look, Wilson, you can't believe a word that comes out of an addict's mouth. Especially when they aren't sober. Everybody knows that."

"Of course."

"But his body language," Danny said pointedly, "that speaks volumes." He stopped a few paces short of the Jeep and pantomimed Gage's hand movement perfectly. "I don' know," Danny mimicked. "Obviously a lie," he amplified.

"Obviously."

Wakefield resumed his method act and once more played the role of Russel Gage, junkie dad. "I don' know... I don' know..." he repeated. Each time he spoke the line, he married it to the same pantomime. "I don' know," and again for his partner's benefit. Just as before, the dialogue was perfectly synchronized with the choreography. It was a perfect impression of the junkie.

That time, Wilson caught it: the way his left hand came up and ran parallel to the short gravel road into the trailer park, then turned left in perfect synchronicity with the highway and travelled along the pavement's path.

"He subconsciously answered the question," Anita nodded, "even while he vocally denied it."

Wakefield swung around to the driver's door and hopped into the Jeep. Wilson matched his move and observed quietly as the American agent navigated a route which was startlingly congruent with the drug addict's addled gesture.

"Alright," Danny mused. "We're northbound on on Highway Ninety-three. The next major stopping point is Polson. Plenty of places up there a pair of troublemakers could hold up." He worked his lips thoughtfully. "You know, he may not have consciously realized with Gage that his boys went this way. Maybe he heard it, but it just didn't register in his conscious mind that they went this way."

Wilson consulted her phone's data. "Or maybe he was too high to care," she countered. "I mean, what kind of parent lets drugs take priority in their life over their own kids?"

"The terrible kind," Danny answered, "you know that. Surely you've seen it before."

"I have," she shook her head, "but that doesn't make it easier to accept." She turned off the phone.

"There are no known associates or areas of interest along this route."

"Maybe not for the Gages," he allowed, "but what about for the rest of the Jaliscos?"

"Nope. But," Anita tapped her mobile device, "there's a Sinaloa mule with a suspected BDE up by the lake."

BDL - or Bed Down Location - was a term Wakefield knew very well from his time in the Corps. Whether you lived somewhere or not was often a matter open to a degree of interpretation. Conventional wisdom held that one of the best places to find a person was at their home. Opinions as to what, precisely, established 'residency' varied greatly from place to place and person to person. Did a target live at a place if their clothes were there? What if they slept there? What if they bought groceries or paid a bill, but their name was not on the lease or mortgage? Was that home?

The United States Navy defined a 'temporary' stay as up to and including 179 days in the same location. On day 180 the location in question became a permanent residence and, under the strictest interpretation of regulations, required change of duty station - even if being there started as a temporary duty assignment. Sailors were assigned to ships, not ports, so this heuristic made a certain sort of sense within that peculiar culture. Wherever the ship was, that was the Sailor's home... regardless of where their family slept or their car was parked. And since the Marine Corps was part of the Department of the Navy - *the men's department,* as the old joke went - the former jarhead was accustomed to viewing life from the perspective of naval regulations.

The Army's rule of thumb for residency was a year, but they specifically excluded deployments from that guideline. Even well into the war and with years for the Department of the Army to get its act together, it was still common to find a Soldier who had been in the desert for fourteen months or more, all while his wife and kids - well, presumably *his* kids - were thousands of miles away back Stateside at some base hundreds of miles from their own hometown. One of his roommates in Iraq had a simple rule: *Home is where the X-Box is.* An Air Force colonel he knew once told Sergeant Wakefield that if he ever got confused as to where home was then he could just check his voter identification card - sound advice for troopers who racked up so much time in-country that they qualified to run for a seat in their host nation's parliament.

Danny chewed the inside of his lip. "You said the Sinaloas were behind the attack against the Gages?"

"Yep."

"Well, maybe the boys dropped by to settle the score."

"We should check it out."

"And soon." Danny looked down at the Jeep's clock. "Now that we've made our presence felt, it won't take long for everyone around here to know that law enforcement is hot after the Gage boys." He shifted up a gear as they glided through a turn. "You really think they'll rabbit?"

"Likely as not," she shrugged, "if they get spooked. They *are* truck drivers."

Danny shifted again and accelerated. "Just so you know, Wilson," shift, "if this manhunt of yours crosses state lines, I'm billing the Canadian government for mileage."

"Homeland Security's checks not clearing?" she teased.

"Oh, they clear." Shift. "They're small, but they clear. By the way," he gave her a meaningful sideways glance, which was obscured by his polarized sunglasses, "you should probably know that I get paid the same whether I'm working or not. Not that I'm not having fun and all filling my days with druggies, murderers, and fugitives. But if this donkey cart chase drags out then I'm gonna mentally resume my vacation. On the clock."

"No stamina for the long jobs, Wakefield?"

Danny thought back on how the last year went for him, both professionally and personally. Most of the calendar was spent focused on only one case: the hunt for the Constitutional Killer. The closest thing to productive work that he had done since he laid Sandra into Arlington's cold ground was to research the most obscure, least demanding positions within the Department of Homeland Security's nebulous clemency. There were a startling number of places a fellow could easily put himself and disappear until he was retirement eligible. And from where Wakefield sat, invisibility was an attractive career prospect. "Let's just say that after the last few months, I'm prepared to embrace my inner dirtbag."

CHAPTER 8

"THREE FIFTY EACH ain't much," James grumbled from the semi's passenger seat as his brother maneuvered their big blue truck out of the hospital's rear loading area.

"No," Justin corrected a tricky turn and up-shifted, "but, it's cash in hand that we didn't have two hours ago. And where else are we gonna dump a bunch of unwanted bodies off?"

"Some hospital this is," James shook his head. "Whadda they need people for? Don't they have enough patients there already?"

"They ain't payin' for 'em as patients, Jimmy," the older brother shook his head. "They're using 'em as parts. Spare parts. They got stuff that'll flush the last of the dope from their system. Keep 'em sedated and each of 'em is liver, some kidneys, a heart… The right doc in the right place with the right skills can make a lotta bank harvesting needed parts from unwanted folk and selling 'em to those that can afford 'em."

"Must be nice," James scoffed.

"Well, I guarantee these folks ain't goin' to the cops to complain, either. You heard the dude. There's always more folks in need than donors. Desperate folks."

James nodded. The Gage brothers did not ask for their buyer's credentials, but he seemed to know what he was talking about - and the cash he brought to the loading dock was all that really mattered to Justin and James. Enough crisp portraits of Andrew Jackson tucked into a plain envelope meant more to them than a hospital badge.

"So," the younger Gage patted his denim jacket pocket and the paper wrapped bills inside it, "what do we do with the ones he didn't take?"

The elder Gage brother thought about the possibilities from behind the oversized steering wheel. There were still about a half dozen people in the trailer. No young women, no children… nobody of any real value to the Gages or most of their prospective buyers. Sure, there were a few construction outfits or commercial farms who would probably give a few bucks each for semi-skilled laborers, but Justin could not risk the chance of a runaway or that he might make an offer to the wrong stranger. One undercover cop with integrity could really throw a wrench into their lives. "To Hell with them," he decided. He angled the truck for I-90 and the quickest escape from the edge of Missoula. "We'll pull off the highway on the way back to Salvadore's and dump them off the side of the road."

"We can't just leave 'em wandering the countryside," James reminded his brother. "It's too risky - even in this cold. They might get found and finger us."

"Duh," Justin sang at length. "That's why I have you. Now, pull Hector an' Miguel's cut from that wad. We'll pay Salvadore an' split the rest like always."

James Gage withdrew the envelope of money, peeled off a few bills, then folded them neatly and stuffed them into his left hip pocket. The rest went back into the envelope and his jacket's inner breast cavity. Then he fingered the clip that held his karambit securely inside his right jeans pocket. *Makin' cash and bleedin' sheep,* he bobbed his head to the music from the dash. *Not a bad day at all.*

CHAPTER 9

DANIEL WAKEFIELD WAS no stranger to harsh realities. Before his career in the Secret Service, Danny was a Marine Force Recon sniper. His time in that particular career was cut short by injury, but it was still long enough to expose him firsthand to the truth about man's cruelty toward his fellow man.

The latter part of Wakefield's time in the Corps was spent as a Tactical Human Intelligence operator - TACHUMINT for short. It was a trade with an often-overlooked tendency to delve into the depths of human depravity and vice. TACHUMINT guys, it was whispered, ate other peoples' sins. They kept their superiors' hands clean in the service of more virtuous priorities than objective truth. They did the dirty work, the high-risk/high-reward stuff most intelligence personnel only dreamed of doing.

A lifetime before the Corps, Danny was a kid who watched his mother die from cancer. At every turn, Wakefield's life seemed to be a road littered with opportunities for God to show him just how horrible human beings were. And all too often, Danny had to question whether the people he was exposed to were really worth saving.

A young woman sat in front of him with her head in her hands. Jennifer Redelk - Jenny, to those who knew her - was just another girl from the reservation. At least, she was until she met Carlos, the smooth-talking Sinaloa runner who promised to lead her out of the frozen, dead end life up north and take her somewhere as warm and beautiful as she was - someday. She knew how Carlos made his money. The danger associated with him and the other *chollos* he rolled with was part of what made him so alluring to the naive young woman.

By the time Jenny figured out that there was never quite as much money as promised and that Carlos' fiery latino passion came hand in hand - and sometimes fist in face - with a hot temper, she had already given up on school, left her family, and moved into the Sinaloa mule's trailer. Now it was too late to change her choices, too late to change her mind, and too hard to change him. Like the cartel brand inked across her back, she was where she was. And she was there to stay.

Jenny was probably nineteen, maybe twenty years old. It was hard for Danny to tell for sure just by looking. She was at that magical stage in life when the Native American blood in her veins made her look exactly as old - or as young - as the beholder chose. She could be almost thirty... or barely over twelve. Wakefield tried not to think about how often Carlos and his homies probably had her pretend to be at either end of that spectrum as they played whatever games suited them.

Jet black hair fell in front of Jenny's forward-canted face like a dreary waterfall. Tears flowed out of her palms and rained onto the mobile home's cheap, grease-stained linoleum floor. Quick breaths were interrupted periodically by a haunted, creaking sound that seemed to come from a soul that tried not to break under the strain of its own despair.

"Which one did it?" Danny inquired. *Not that it matters,* he grumbled inwardly. *The deed's done.*

"I don't know their names," Jenny shook her head. "The skinny one."

"James," Anita confirmed. "When did it happen?" she asked as she patted the crying girl on the shoulder.

"This morning," Jenny managed between sobs.

"And what happened when you told your boyfriend?" Danny asked.

"He," the young native girl sniffed, "he hasn't been back yet."

"So Carlos doesn't know?" Anita hummed. The crying girl's shoulders heaved as she shook her head.

"Look, we need to -"

Wilson cut Wakefield off with a quickly raised finger. "And then what happened?" she pressed. "After they left."

"I just laid there."

The girl seemed to have inherited abuse. By the look of her, she was at least half Native American, but at least partially white - a pedigree that did nothing to help her overcome either people group's historic prejudices toward the other. And as if the eternal red/white divide did not make her life hard enough, her own Salish ancestors suffered greatly at the hands of their Chinook neighbors and other cousins. Her boyfriend was a habitual felon and lifelong dirtbag who came to the States solely so that he could perform odd jobs for his bosses south of the Rio Grande. And the fact that this young girl was shacked up with an openly felonious loser instead of at school, working, or hanging out with friends gave Danny an indication that life around her parents' place was probably no picnic, either.

"Did they do anything else?" Wilson continued. "Where they were going? Anyone they might be meeting up with? Did they say anything?"

"I don't..." her voice tapered off.

"Was there anyone else who might've seen them?"

Jenny shook her head. "I don't think so. Nobody comes by here. Except to see Carlos, anyway. They just left. Then I took a shower," more tears fell from her eyes as she rubbed her hands down her body, but it was clear from where Wakefield stood that no amount of scrubbing could make this unfortunate girl feel clean today.

Damn it all to Hell, Danny's right hand balled into a fist. *Now we can't run a rape kit.* His left hand pushed itself through his beard as he contemplated their next step. Administered by a doctor or nurse specialist, a rape kit would have given the police physical evidence invaluable to levying charges against the offender. Forensic proof linking James Gage to the crime would have made things different for everyone. It would have given Wakefield and Constable Wilson an excuse to put out an APB without tipping local law enforcement as to their original purpose. And it would have given Jenny the ammunition that she would eventually need to prosecute her assailants. Now they were all left to their own devices - Wilson and Wakefield with a shrinking list of locations where they might find the brothers, and Jenny with nothing more than her word against his. Unfortunately, victims like her did not always get justice under such circumstances.

"Look," Danny reluctantly grumbled, "we're gonna need to hand this off to local law enforcement. I'm sorry, Jenny, but if you could just gather your things -"

"No," she shook her head. "No cops."

"I beg your pardon?"

"No cops," Jenny insisted. "Cops won't do nothing. Carlos will take care of this."

"Carlos will take care of what?" a man called as he burst through the door into the mobile home. He was about a head shorter than Wakefield and had skin that was about the same color that good coffee turned after someone added way too much creamer to it. A penciled-in wannabeard traced his jawline and something that might someday grow into a real mustache darkened his upper lip. Despite the freezing cold outside, the only clothes the latino spitfire wore were a pair of ill-fitting jeans and a cheap checkered shirt buttoned solely at the collar and left opened to reveal a skintight wife beater and a few chains that almost passed for real gold. "Who dafaq are deez people up in *mi casa*?"

"Carlos?" Danny held his hands up in a calming gesture, "we're not looking for trouble, but there's been an incident. Let's just sit down and -"

"Baby, what happened?" the *chollo* demanded from his live-in girlfriend.

Anita leapt up from her position next to Jenny and crossed the mobile home's tiny main room in the blink of an eye. Her fists were filled with the newcomer's gingham patterned shirt and slammed his back against the nearest wall. "What did they take?" she snarled.

"Who?"

"Justin and James Gage," Danny explained. "We're looking for them. Seems they were here."

"I don' know no-" *slam!* "Bitch, Imma slap yo' cracker-" *slam!* "Okayokayokay! Geez, lady. Chu' got some real iss-" *slam!* "Okay! Look, I swear, I don't know who you're -" Anita brought her knee up into the brown skinned man's solar plexus hard enough to double him over in her hands and make him revisit his lunch. The fresh puddle of vomit did nothing to improve the trailer's overall bouquet - but it did not make the place smell any worse, either.

"They were here," she insisted as she shook him like an unwanted baby. "We know that. So why? What business would a pair of Jalisco runners have with a low-level thug from a competing cartel? Were you buddies at school or something? What?"

"They were here?" Carlos wiped spittle from his mouth. "Must'a been after my stash."

"That's a lot of trouble for a couple of ounces of weed," Danny mused aloud as he looked at the traumatized young woman in the chair. "Just how much drugs did you have here?"

"Not here," Carlos clarified. "I don' bring my bid'ness home. That's just plain stupid, mang." He jerked his head toward the door. "The parking lot up the road. The one at the abandoned gas station." Danny recalled a decrepit lot a few miles back where they turned off of the main highway and onto the cracked and pot hole riddled road that led them to the trailer park. "Truckers use it all the time. Stop there to sleep. Or to drop off or trade out their trailers." He coughed and choked his breakfast back into his belly. "We bring the goods in an' outta there." He coughed again as the pain in his midsection swelled once more. "They must'a been after that."

"That's not all they were after." Anita twisted Carlos' shoulders so that he could see his disheveled girlfriend. A fresh spring of tears started to well up in Jenny's eyes. "Things between the Sinaloas and the Jaliscos have gone sour, Carlos. Who's up here that can bring the heat? Who's in charge?"

"Baby," Carlos cooed. The thug became a case study in sensitivity. "What did they do to you?"

Jenny's face twisted with the memory, but only Wilson spoke. "Where's your boss, Carlos? We're not here for some piddly little Sinaloa mule. Where do I find someone with enough clout to carry out a hit?"

"Baby," the gangbanger repeated. Suddenly, his legs acted like they did not work. Anita let Carlos fall to the trailer's grungy floor. "Baby, what did they do?"

"They made me -" Jenny's voice trailed off as she wrapped her hands around her face and sobbed. "They made me…"

Danny steeled himself. Silently, he saw Anita do the same. They had just gone over Jenny's story with her a few minutes ago, but this was the first time

Carlos heard the news. For his own part, Wakefield did not want to hear it again. And though the not-so-toughguy kept asking, Danny knew male psychology enough to know Carlos would not want to hear it at all.

"Make you what?" The Sinaloa mule melted out of Wilson's clenched fists and crawled over to his girlfriend. "Made you what, Baby?"

Leather creaked as Danny's gloved hand squeezed into a ball, then opened, then squeezed closed again. His jaw clenched. He desperately wanted to hit something - or someone. *Please, dear God,* he silently prayed through clenched teeth, *let this little sonofabitch man up.* His fist shook as he fought back his own rage. *Let something good come out of this.*

"The key," Jenny sobbed. "They said they wanted the key." She sniffed. "And when I didn't give it to them…" Her lips twisted into a gruesome shape and eyes skewed shut as the memory threw her once more into an uncontrollable fit.

"*Lo juro por Dios,*" Carlos tenderly took Jenny's shoulders into his hands, "Baby, Imma make this right."

"Make it right?" Anita spat. "How are you gonna 'make it right,' Carlos? You can't undo what they did to her! You can't change the fact that they did it because of you!" Danny shot her a look that silently screamed, *Tone it down.* The Mounty evidently caught onto the idea that they needed to make allies and friends if they were going to find their fugitives. She adjusted her tone slightly. "But you *can* tell us where this stash was so that we can catch up with them." In light of what Jenny suffered at the Gages' hands, it was small hope. But outside of police involvement and filing formal charges - which Jenny had clearly refused - such was all that she and Wakefield had to offer. And at least it was something.

"*Vete a la mierda...*" Carlos seethed with anger as he shook his head. "We'll sort this out. Now, get outta here, *bura*," he hissed, "while you still can."

"Look, Carlos," Danny offered in his most reasonable tone, "we're not after you here. We want the Gages. And we want justice for Jenny. You've got things to worry about right now - maybe some decisions to make." It burned Wakefield to be cop blocked by some thug's pride, but there were times to play hardball and times that required a softer approach. "Believe me, man. We're your best chance at seeing this gets done right. Help us help you. What's this key go to?"

"Chu' t'ink I want help from *la juda?*" Carlos scoffed. 'Get dafuq outta *mi casa*, mang! 'Fo I start stacking crackers in da yard."

So many parts of Danny wished that the *chollo* would actually swing on him. Or produce a weapon. Or make his hand disappear from clear view for the barest of moments. Or even complete the threat with more direct language aimed at either himself or his partner. Wakefield wanted an excuse - any excuse - to put the Mexican gangbanger in his place. But for all his hot air, the hispanic half pint was all show and no throw.

Wilson looked like she was well beyond 'fighting mad.' Danny had enough sense to know when to let a little dog with no bite just bark. He decided the smartest - though not necessarily the most satisfying - thing to do was to walk the good guys away from a bad decision.

Wakefield produced a business card and held it in his outstretched hand. "This is my number. Call me when you wise up."

"Getdafuqouttahere."

Danny dropped the card on the table. "In case you change your mind." He shook his head. "I know you think you wanna do this on your own, Carlos. But there's a right way to do things and a wrong way. *Comprende?*"

"Trust me, gringo," Carlos fumed, "*mi e mi amigos* know how to take care of our own problems."

CHAPTER 10

DANNY SAT AT the cabin's small table and twisted his mostly empty glass with quick little flicks from his left hand. The aftertaste of barley aged in an oak casket lingered on his pallet. Its scent lingered in his nostrils as he silently sat and let the sedative seep into his bloodstream. One molecule at a time, the self-administered medication began to dilute the day's disappointments.

The last few ounces of caramel colored fluid in the tumbler sparkled like a liquid jewel as it refracted the firelight. Cool, tawny whiskey and orange hot flames danced in his sight and bracketed the soft, blonde hair that filled his thoughts. Somewhere between the wintery air outside and burning logs in the hearth inside, his numbed mind dared to think back to earlier in winter - a lifetime ago - when Sandra would have been waiting for him under the covers in the cabin's bedroom.

He conjured an image of her soft, milky skin between the crisp linens. The ghost waited for him to join her for the evening. The memory of Elbee's voice wordlessly echoed across space and time as it called to him like a siren. A coy smile and twinkling eyes beckoned him with tantalizing promises which would never be spoken aloud again.

"Well, that's all the hot water," Anita announced from under a towel as she exited the bathroom. She stood in the doorway, backlit by the only lights switched on in the whole cabin and rubbed her hair dry. "I'm afraid you'll need to wait a while for the tank to recharge."

Danny hoisted his glass. "I'm warm enough. Thanks."

With a towel wrapped around her petite frame, Wilson padded across the bearskin rug draped atop hardwood floors and plucked the half-empty bottle of whiskey from the small dinette table. She consulted the label, pressed the bottle's lip to her own, and threw back a healthy gulp. Her brow furrowed as she pulled the bottle back and held it at bay. "Was this in the refrigerator?"

"I like my whiskey cold," Danny took the bottle from her.

"So use ice like regular people."

"Ice takes up valuable space in the glass," he countered.

"What else would you need to put in there?"

"More whiskey," he noted as he refilled his tumbler. "Besides, when the ice melts, it waters down the booze."

Anita plucked his glass up from the table and flashed her eyes. "So drink faster." She demonstrated by draining most of the fluid from his cup, then returned the vessel to its perch. Satisfied, she snatched the bottle again and topped off Wakefield's glass in repayment for the pilfered liquor. "Penny for your thoughts?" she teased.

"I," he hesitated. *Don't. Elbee's too special. And she'd never understand, anyway.* He shook his head. "I was just trying to figure out our next move if Carlos doesn't call."

Wilson snickered as she sat in the chair on the other side of the little table. "You really expect a Sinaloa drug runner whose live-in girlfriend was raped by members of a rival gang to call an American federal agent for help?" She shook her head and rolled her eyes. "Trust me, Wakefield. That ship has sailed."

"I'll make a call to some friends in the morning," he shrugged. "See if we can't use him anyway. Whether he likes it or not." She gave him a quizzical look, so Danny relented and held up his phone. "While you were debriefing Jenny, I cloned her phone into partitioned memory on mine. Contact list, messages, and such are all in my cell."

"You can catch her calls?"

"If we need to," he sniffed. "But I've already sent all of that to a buddy back east. He'll pull Carlos' number from there. We'll be tracking the little twerp's phone by breakfast."

"If there's one thing I figured I could count on," Anita grinned, "it's the American government's ability to spy on its own people."

"Okay," Danny stabbed a finger in her direction and noticed that she began to wave back and forth slightly, as if she sat on a boat which rocked in the open ocean. *Either she's dodging my finger,* he noted to himself, *or the booze is starting to kick in.* "First off, that wetback ain't one of our people. He's a dirty illegal and we both know it. And 'Merican rights don't extend to hostile foreigners who brake the law to get here so that they can break more laws. So I don't wanna hear any crap about his so-called 'right to privacy.' He forsook that when he snuck across the Rio Grande."

"Forsook?" Anita peered down her nose into his half-drained glass. "You drinking a thesaurus there?"

"And point B," he continued unabated, "you Cannucks are the experts on surveillance on Americans." His bold statement elicited a confused expression from her face. "The Canadian Security Intelligence Service spends more money each year spying on America then it does any other nation. In fact," he smiled smugly, "you spent more money last year spying on America than any other country did. More than Russia, more than China. *I* should be asking *you* a thing or two about surveilling Americans."

"I don't know what you're talking about."

"Oh, really?"

"Yeah, really. Look, Wakefield, I'm a Mounty. I don't work for the SIS."

"That's not a denial," he pressed. "Our friendly, innocent little neighbors up north," he ran his middle finger around the rim of his glass, "only, not always so friendly and innocent, are you?"

"Surely you didn't sit here moping about foreign policy the whole time I was in the shower."

"Just remembering stuff. That's all."

"Really?" she positively beamed. "Like what?"

"Private stuff," he dodged.

For a long moment, nobody said anything. Nobody moved. The only sound came from the crackling fire. The only motion in the room came from the rocking floor and dark shadows as they danced along the walls. "Look, Wakefield," she resumed more somberly as she slid onto the seat next to him at the undersized table, "I'm sorry to mess up your vacation. With any luck, we'll bag the Gage brothers in the morning and you can get back to it."

Danny raised his glass in salute and toasted the sentiment. A combination of warmth and numbness flowed down his legs. His body continued to process the first half bottle of whiskey, but his metabolic rate could not keep up with his rate of consumption tonight. "You said the Gages killed your partner," he probed. "Were you two close?"

The Canadian woman's big brown eyes fell. "Yeah," she breathed. "Probably closer than we should've been. Back toward the beginning, anyway. Before we knew better." She shook her head as if to cast off the memory. "It didn't work out the way we thought it would."

"I bet that made things harder," Danny sympathized. "Working together, I mean. After."

"It did." She helped herself to another pull from the whiskey bottle, then put it back on the table. Her sullen face refused to leave the decanter's label. "For a while. Eventually, we moved on and things got back to normal." When she finally looked back up at him, Danny saw a softness in her that he had not seen in the tough agent before. "What about you,

Wakefield? I heard you lost your partner, too. Were you two... close?"

Danny hesitated. He ran his finger around the edge of his glass. *She's being honest,* he thought. *Vulnerable. You owe her the same courtesy.* The now-expired romance that was born out of his partnership with Elbee was not common knowledge, but his instincts told him that there was no risk in sharing it with Anita. "Yeah," he admitted. "You know how it is. You keep it on the down-low, but when you spend that much time with someone and things just click..." He consulted Dr. Whiskeyglass again for an opinion, but found his usual therapist to be less effective than normal. "Anyway," he hissed as the cool drink burned its way past his peripheral nerves and into his core, "what can you do? They're gone."

Here, in the stillness of a cabin nestled in the heart of the mountains, there was no boss for the Special Agent to appease; no staff shrink for him to convince; no reason for the former Marine to lie about how he felt. For a quiet, simple moment, he was just Danny - honest, human, and hurt.

Anita rose from her seat, slipped her smooth right leg over him, and straddled him in his chair. She cupped his neck in her hands and kissed him - gently at first, then more deeply. Danny left his glass on the table and let his hands do what came naturally.

Her towel fell to the floor. Anita plied her unwrapped body like a bandage across his wounded psyche. She rose from their kiss and seized him by the shoulders. Her bare legs snaked around his waist and pinned him to the wooden chair. She ground her pelvis and teased him with her hips while her wild eyes locked onto his with a gaze which was nothing short of spellbinding.

Danny felt her taught muscles as his hands slid up her legs and found purchase around her firm waist. The fireplace, it seemed, was not the only source of heat in this small cabin. Anita kissed him hungrily. She devoured his lips and traced the muscles in the back of his neck with her fingertips. Her lips and tongue carried a subtle flavor - an aftertaste of the whiskey they shared.

When she came up for air again, he used his mouth to trace the line of her jaw down her neck. He lost himself around her collarbone.

Anita's fingers dug through Danny's hair while his kisses fell down to her sternum, then her excited breasts. She seized his brown locks, pulled back sharply, and kissed him again with such vigor that the chair legs beneath him creaked, then snapped. The impact from them crashing onto the floor broke the chair's back. They landed with a muffled *huff* and rolled out of the wrecked chair pieces still entwined with each other. She ended up on her back with him atop her and locked her ankles behind Danny's spine like a wrestler in a classic guard position. One hand kept ahold of Danny's head while the other slid down his muscled chest.

The petite woman stared up at him with those big, brown eyes, then pulled frantically at his clothes. Freed from his loneliness as well as his garments, Danny fell into her. The couple added their own heat to the radiant fireplace's output as they drove the cold, lonesome night away with reckless abandon.

Those familiar enough with coitus knew that there were different kinds of sex - not just in terms of performance mechanics, but different emotional flavors to the act. Wakefield and Wilson partook of each other in the kind of intimacy which served primarily as therapy. There was no real romance between them, but they each felt a different kind of desire in common: a need for someone with whom they could share their loss - someone who knew what they felt because they felt it, too. They shared a need for the understanding that each could offer to the other. It was a need for release which could only come from the unique closeness that special kind of understanding provided. That sameness shared between them bound them together. It echoed back and forth between them as it recognized itself, each in the other. Common need built previously nonexistent ground they could share and explore. It was a space where each of them was safe from the outside world's judgement, where each could find strength in the other. It was a moment when their entwined weakness created power.

*   *   *

Gravel crunched under their boots as the Gage brothers approached the container doors. As the evening set in, Justin had backed the truck up to the fence in the rearmost part of the truck yard and left the engine running. It was a big lot near a major interchange, the kind of place where truckers left their rigs or trailers parked in between runs. Coincidentally, that also made it the kind of place where one more nondescript shipping containers which might appear sometime after hours would go unnoticed for a good, long while.

"Sure wish that guy at the hospital could'a taken more of these folks," James shook his head as he unlocked the door's cold steel handle with gloved hands. "Seems like a waste."

"I told you," Justin traced a great circle route around his rotund midsection, "too much crud in the system to harvest anything worth anything. Shoot," he turned his head aside and spat into the night, "he said that they're so crapped up right now that he couldn't even use their blood." He peered at his younger brother. "You ain't gettin' cold feet, are you?"

"No," James shook his head, "it's just, you know, there's folks waitin' for livers and kidneys and shit. Seems like a waste not to snatch up every one of 'em that we brought him." He flicked his knife open and held it discreetly behind his back as he stood outside the container door like a runner about to start a race. "You got your watch ready?"

Justin scoffed incredulously. "You want me to time you?"

"Gotta make it challenging somehow."

The older brother shook his head in disbelief, but cycled through his watch's settings until he found the stopwatch function. "Ready when you are."

Justin exchanged quick nods with his brother,. When he heard the faint *beep* of the watch button, the younger Gage opened the container's steel door just wide and long enough to rush through it. The first shriek from inside the container was covered up by the groan of steel on steel as Justin closed the heavy hatch the rest of the way behind his sibling.

Outside the big steel box of death, the elder Gage scanned the lot and the surrounding area for signs of any witnesses or passersby. After a momentary mixture of shuffles, slams, and short screams from inside the container, a rhythmic pounding rapped against the door. Justin hit the button on his watch again, then opened the door for his brother.

James wiped his knife on a scrap of cloth that used to be somebody's shirt as he slipped out of the container. "How'd I do?" He caught his breath as he cleaned his karambit.

Still gloved, Justin unwrapped a new lock, fresh from the package, and bolted the container closed. Just for good measure, he ran a disposable alcohol wipe along each of the handles to remove any fingerprints he might have left on the lock or door. Then he glanced down at his watch. "You're slowing down, Jimmy."

"I'm getting stiff from the cold." James sniffed a nose full of wintery evening air and swung his arms to aid in circulation. "Let's get someplace warmer."

CHAPTER 11

"WE'RE MAKING GOOD time," James noted as they passed the latest road sign. "

"You heard Hector," Justin reminded his younger brother. "We do *not* wanna be late getting back down to Juarez." He drummed his thumbs on the big truck's steering wheel in excitement. "The Chicago Run! The big time, Jimmy!"

"Yeah, well, just try 'n keep from getting caught speeding. I don't wanna get pulled over."

"Relax, Jimmy. The rig's clean. Ain't nobody gonna find those bodies anytime soon, either. Not where we left 'em." Justin shook his head. "Probably freeze solid out there like that. Won't even start to stink until the spring thaw."

The drive from this part of Montana down to the Mexican border usually took a solid twenty-one hours. Driving in the dead of night left most of the major highways empty of civilian traffic. The solitude usually allowed long haul truckers like Justin and James to bend the speed limit a little bit more than daylight driving did - as long as they avoided speed traps and overzealous highway patrol officers. They still had to pay attention, though. The reduced casual traffic increased the probability that any set of headlights on the road that did not belong to another big rig marked some cop with a radar gun looking for something to do.

Still, they made better time and burned less fuel running bobtail - the trucking term for driving without a load. Even an empty trailer added weight and wind resistance which, in turn, slowed the truck and cost more fuel. But the Gages had no need to drag dead weight all the way across the country. The Gages ran dope for the Jaliscos for years. Justin and James knew their employers' schedule. They were accustomed to each other's methods.

"If I know Hector," Justin glanced down at the dashboard clock, "he's already got guys packing up our load. Sooner we get across the border, the sooner we're rolling northeast."

A shadow crept out of the darkness from behind the Gages' truck as they barreled down the highway. The invisible shape gave off no light and ran much more quietly than the diesel-powered rig. "I don't know about you," the younger Gage brother smiled, "but I kinda hope we get down there before they're ready for us. Jalisco's always got some *senioritas* trolling around the compound."

Justin never saw the dark disturbance in his rearview mirror as the smaller, faster vehicle slipped into the lane next to his truck and settled into position just under the driver-side window.

James slapped his brother on the shoulder from the passenger seat. "I wouldn't mind getting me a little trim in between runs."

Justin rubbed his bulbous belly and looked at his younger brother with a serious warning in his eyes. "You know, Jimmy, if you ain't careful, the food down there ain't the only thing gonna make you feel a burning sensation." He laughed and slapped his brother's lap -

- and at that exact moment, a spiderweb punched into the driver's window with a *crack-snap!*

Justin slumped into the space between the seats. His hand dragged on the wheel and the truck lurched to the right.

James hollered as he pushed his brother back up. "Are you hit? Are you hit?" he frantically checked.

"I'm fine, Jimmy!" Justin regained control of the rig, then stole a glance out through the shattered window just in time for a *scree-pop!* to rip a hole in his door barely an inch afield of his torso. The engine idled and the truck slowed as Justin pressed himself as deeply into his seat as the cushioned back allowed. "We got trouble, Jimmy," he nervously announced. He held the wheel low and steered one-handed from the six o'clock position. His eyes darted to the door's ruined window and the useless mirror.

James kept low as he reached into the back of the cab from his seat. He retrieved the Glock from his bag, then crouched low and rolled the passenger side window down. "I'm ready, Jay."

Justin pulled on the bottom of the wheel. The truck, still coasting, slipped into the left lane. A buzzing drone sounded from their left as their attacker's tires rolled over a rumble strip carved into the highway's inner shoulder while the Gages were still in the middle of the road. Suddenly, a blacked-out sedan swung around the rig from the driver-side blind spot and accelerated forward.

"There!" Justin barked at the car, awash in his headlights. James was already in motion. He braced the Glock against his window's outer ledge and fired once, twice at their attacker.

The sedan's rear window shattered and rained into the car's back seat. Justin activated his high intensity beams and pained the darkened sedan with bright light. The little car's interior glowed with unwanted illumination. He jockeyed the truck to keep his lights trained on the little car, which swerved as it accelerated up the road.

James fired, aimed, fired, took more careful aim, then fired yet again.

"Take 'em out, Jimmy!"

bang! "I'm trying, Jay." *bang!* "Drop the hammer!"

Justin downshifted and stomped the accelerator hard enough that it almost went through the floorboard. The truck's massive Cummins diesel engine howled angrily and the rig launched toward its target. Despite his best efforts to keep up, though, the sedan shrank in the headlights as it pulled further away from them. No matter what they did, the Gage brothers could not change the fact that the smaller vehicle was lighter and faster than the big truck. But James had something that was smaller, lighter, and faster than any car.

The younger Gage hung his head and shoulders out of his window. Cool night air bit and blasted into his face as the truck rushed along the highway. He stared painfully down the Glock's sights at the fleeing car.

bang! Nothing. His eyes dried. *bang!* His face burned as cool air rushed past it. *bang!*

The brothers were rewarded to see the sedan lurch to the left. The car rolled past the shoulder and barreled into the divided highway's sunken median at full speed. There was no guard rail or guide wire on that side of the road. When the front tires dropped into more dense terrain, the difference in drag between the forward and rear tires forced the little car to flip sideways, roll upside down, and skid along the frosty ground on its roof.

Justin hit the brakes and executed a serpentine turn. He reined the truck in and stopped right next to the blacked out wreck. He and Jimmy leapt out of the rig - Jimmy with the Glock, Justin with a six inch Smith & Wesson .38 in hand. They approached the crashed car a dozen paces apart from each other.

Upside down, the door nearest to them worked itself open far enough for the sedan's passenger to fall out of the wrecked car. He slumped onto the ground, then scrambled to his feet and shuffled across the frozen tundra as fast as his dazed feet could carry him. As he rounded the car's front bumper, he turned back and fired a quick shot at the brothers with a suppressed pistol. Distance, movement, haste, gangbanger marksmanship, and a probable concussion forced the shot to pass harmlessly between the brothers. Still, they each took an instinctive step out of the line of fire and ducked.

Justin answered with a single, steadily aimed shot from his revolver. He was rewarded to see his target stumble to the ground, then recover as he fled. The elder Gage brother jogged after the attacker. The younger one slammed into their prey at a dead run and knocked the guy back to the ground. Their attacker's gun flew from his hand and landed in the frozen turf.

When Justin caught up to them, his brother had their quarry pinned to the ground. James held the injured man down with his knees atop the other guy's shoulders and rained punches onto the guy's head and shoulders. Justin knew he had a minute, while his brother softened their attacker up, so he paused long enough to pick up the stranger's discarded pistol on his way to the interrogation.

"Who are you?" James demanded. His fist hammered into the brown nose again. Blood exploded all over the dude's gray hoodie and James' jeans. "What do you want?"

"Jimmy!" Justin barked as he scooped up the gangbanger's dropped pistol. "Give him a chance to answer."

"*Vete a la mierda…*" the gangbanger coughed.

"Oh, really?" Justin saw the bloody spot on the guy's leg where his .38 must have struck. "Look, *pendejo*," he stepped on the bullet hole and drove his work boot into the wound. The *pandillero* squirmed and howled. "We ain't gonna ask again. Why are you beaners gunnin' fer us?"

The brown skinned man struggled more against the pain that jolted up his leg than he did against the captor holding him in place. "*Hijo de puta,*" he growled, "You raped my girlfriend! You're gonna burn!"

"I mean before that," Justin clarified. "At the border."

"*Lo se,*" the trapped thug shook his head slowly. "What do you mean?"

"Sinaloas," Justin spat. The elder Gage lowered his gun. "Jimmy," he prompted.

James tucked the Glock into his waistband and reached for his pocket. He whipped out his karambit, flicked the blade open, and slashed the cartel triggerman across the throat. The knife's wickedly curved beak ripped a savage, bubbling wound through the man's life pipes. The younger brother pushed up off of his victim before any more ichor flowed onto his clothes and watched as the man flopped on the ground and gasped in vain.

"Hey, Jay," James chuckled as he cleaned his gory blade on the dying man's pant leg, "wetback bastard's doing the fish."

Justin surveyed the inside of the overturned car, then stepped away and rubbed his arms. "Driver's dead," he confirmed. "Let's get back to the truck, Jimmy. It's cold out here."

James joined his brother, but a flood of adrenaline in his system staved off the cold. "That's twice we've run into Sinaloas in a week, Jay," he sniffed. "Reckon we oughta do something about our little immigration problem?"

"I reckon so," Justin surveyed the damage to his door. "Somethin's crawled up somebody's ass." He shook his head as he climbed back into the truck's cab.

"How you wanna play this?" James sunk into the passenger seat, but he was far from settled.

Justin held his newly acquired handgun up in illustration as he settled into the driver's seat. "Whaddaya make of this?"

The younger Gage took the gangbanger's gun from his brother and examined it under the cabin's dim lights. "Plain ol' Glock nine mil. Just like mine." James shrugged. "Fifty bucks on the street."

"Nothing special about that, Jimmy. But," he pointed to the pistol's suppressor as he continued, "no serial number or markings on the can, so that's homemade. Pretty good job of it, though. Made a big difference when the dude was shooting at us."

"It *was* quiet," James admitted.

"I'll call Hector," Justin released the brakes and goosed the truck into motion. "Best take care of this up here."

"What about the Chicago Run?"

"We'll get the next one, Jimmy." Justin tried to remember where the nearest truck repair station was. "Looks like the other night wasn't a fluke after all. Sinaloas've got a hard on for us."

"Jaliscos must be cutting into their business." James tucked the Glocks into his duffle bag. "Rival cartels. Whaddaya expect?"

"Yeah, well, the brothers ain't gonna like it too much if we roll down into Juarez with this sort of heat hanging on us."

"Kinda makes you wonder if any other runners are dealing with this shit right now."

"I ain't worried about other runners right now," Justin shifted the truck angrily, "this is starting to feel personal."

*   *   *

Danny's bare arm hung out from under the fluffy blanket wrapped around him as he slept heavily on the living room couch. Though they had quite a heated dalliance earlier, Wakefield was not yet comfortable sharing a bed with his new partner. Though nobody said anything, it was obvious to both of them that it was still too soon for him to display that sort of intimacy or level of vulnerability with a new woman. And so he bid Anita adieu and watched as she retired to the bedroom before he assumed his current position an hour ago.

Such a contradiction, the brunette mused as she silently watched him from the room's shadows. *Such self-denial. I wonder if he does it because he thinks it's the right thing to do, or if he assumes it's expected?* Wearing only a loose-fitting sweatshirt on her body and a curious smile upon her face, the petite woman silently slinked back into her temporary bedroom, carefully closed the hatch, and pondered the psychological maze that seemed to be Wakefield's mind.

Door or no door, locks or no locks, some things were best done when one was the sole conscious person in the building. It was the only way she could ensure her privacy. It was the only way to keep from being caught. And so she had to wait until Captain America was passed out before she could continue.

Careful not to make any undue noise, she plucked her cream-colored vest from the back of a chair. She knew she would wear it once more tomorrow, so she withdrew a Walther P22 from a small pocket concealed within her rolling bag. She loved that gun. It was one of the more compact semi-auto pistols on the market, and its light weight and easy concealment made it the tool of choice for several wet work operators she knew in the CIA and

Mossad. As was her preference, she attached the accompanying suppressor she kept hidden within her hygiene kit and slipped a magazine loaded with hollow point bullets into the gun. She stuffed the weapon into a pocket discreetly sewn into the vest's inner lining and secured it in place. Then she quietly unzipped another compartment in her bag - the pocket that held her tightly folded panties - dug through the undergarments and withdrew another weapon.

It was less like a knife and more like an aluminum spike with a ribbed grip. The Deathridge Toothpick, it was called, and it sported a loop of paracord threaded through a hole in its base to aid in retention. The athletic brunette turned the weapon over in her hand a few times, then stuffed it into a pen-sized pocket hidden among her puffy cream vest's seams and stitching. Satisfied, she hung the garment back on the chair and padded to bed.

Anita checked her phone once more. There were no new messages, emails, or missed calls; no updates of any kind. Under the circumstances, that was the best news she could have received. *Everything is going according to plan,* she deactivated the device and let her head sink into a fluffy down pillow. If her luck held, she was a few hours of sleep away from what promised to be a very productive day indeed.

CHAPTER 12

DANNY SHOVELED another fork loaded with peppery scrambled eggs into his mouth. He savored the warm breakfast, drank in the smell of perfectly crisp bacon on his plate, and hoisted a mug of steaming, fresh roasted, jet-black coffee.

"This is the best breakfast ever," he joyfully declared. "Thanks again, Mrs. Johnson. You really didn't have to do this."

"Oh, I'm happy to, dear." The cabin's matron smiled as she wiped down her cast iron skillet. "Though I am a little disappointed with that broken chair over there."

"Sorry," he sheepishly grinned at the stack of fresh, polished kindling next to the fireplace. "Didn't realize my bag was that heavy. I'll totally replace that. You have my word."

"Oh, I know you will, dear." Dressed in dull work trousers and a white knit cardigan over a multicolored floral blouse, Old Man Johnson's silver-maned wife was the picture of stereotypical agrarian grandmothers, right down to the reading glasses that hung from a chain around her neck. She even hummed a bit, quietly and under her breath, as she worked her magic in the kitchen. "Might need the extra firewood, that storm comes in like they say it might."

"They've forecasted a snowstorm every night for the last week and a half," Danny skeptically shook his head. "And so far, it's been the mildest winter anyone can remember."

"Just means we're due, is all."

Wakefield winked at the matron. "Well, I can't really argue with a woman who makes such a delicious breakfast now, can I?" He had no idea how his hostess managed to prepare a full meal in a single pan in the time it took him to pull on a clean, gray-and-black quarter-zip top and dig a fresh pair of gray, fleece-lined trousers tucked away in his three-day pack. He had even less insight into how the spry grandmother washed every dish and cooking utensil clean before they even cooled from their use atop the stove. But he did know what happiness tasted like, and he counted himself truly blessed for the unexpected treat.

"You said you've already been to town this morning?" the agent brought their conversation back to point. "What's the word?"

Old habits died hard, and honed tradecraft made for strong habits. TACHUMINT was a skill set that, once adopted, was hard to surrender. And after all his years in the Corps and in the Secret Service, tradecraft such as running sources and setting up networks of informants wherever he went was second nature to Danny. He did it as naturally as ducks swam - and as effortlessly as Mrs. Johnson maintained a kitchen.

"Well, dear," Mrs. Johnson grinned at the chance to engage in some good, old-fashioned gossip, "Sharilyn down at the Post Office told me that she heard from her sister that one of Jessi Griffin's boys has fallen back into the drugs again. Oh, it seems it's always one thing or another with kids these days. Always smoking, eating, huffing, or injecting something they shouldn't just to try to get high." She frowned at him. "You know, back in my day, we didn't do any of that. I mean, the worst thing you ever heard of people doing was sometimes smoking cigarettes in the bathroom at school. Now it seems all the young kids just want to get high, get pregnant, and get welfare."

"Cigarettes are pretty bad," Anita opined as she padded out of the bedroom. Her thick wool socks were pulled up high and overlapped her warm black leggings. A fitted, silvery, merino top was unzipped enough to leave her neck free to move. Her jet-black hair was pulled back in a sporty ponytail. "They kill more people in America and Canada than guns and drunk drivers combined."

"Mrs. Johnson," Danny recognized the look of judgement on the matron's face when Anita came in, "this is Constable Wilson with the Royal Canadian Mounted Police." The introduction did nothing to melt Mrs. Johnson's judgemental glare. "My partner," he clarified. "On the case."

"Of course," Mrs. Johnson dried her hands on a dish towel. "How do you do?"

"Well, thank you. And thank you for the use of your cabin. I apologize for any inconvenience."

"Oh, it's no inconvenience at all. Danny here was kind enough to clear some predators off of our land this last week. My husband, Roy, was awful worked up over the beef we lost this month. But at our age, it's hard to spend hours hiking in the cold and waiting in a hunting blind."

"Glad to be of help, ma'am," Danny smiled. "But I never imagined I'd get such a fine breakfast outta the deal."

"It's my pleasure, dear. Speaking of which, you didn't tell me about your partner." She fetched the cast iron skillet, still warm from the wash, from the dish rack on the counter. "Let me just whip something up for you real quick, darling."

"Oh, no thank you," Anita waved. "I've got some yogurt in the fridge."

"Suit yourself," Mrs. Johnson's attention turned back to Wakefield as she replaced the frying pan. Thoughts of much more than just bacon and eggs cooked up behind her wise eyes. "Roy and I were hoping Danny'd be able to come out to the main house and help with a few things, but I guess if you've got a case…"

"I'd love to," Wakefield smiled. "Just as soon as we've got this wrapped up. Shouldn't be more than a day or two. It isn't anything urgent, is it?"

"Oh, no, dear. That'll be fine."

"You know what might actually speed things up?" Anita fished a spoon out of a drawer. "I couldn't help but overhear something about a kid with a drug problem. I don't mean to pry, but if we knew where his dealer was, it might actually help our investigation."

"Really?" the older lady sang in utter fascination. "Big federal agents after little Tommy Griffin?"

"Not Tommy," Danny corrected, "but his dealer might be able to point us toward the people we're looking for."

"I'm after a pair of truck drivers. Caucasian males, about thirty years old. Brothers. Grew up in these parts."

"Justin and Jim Gage," Danny clarified.

"The Gage brothers?" Mrs. Johnson guessed. "Oh, are those boys still around? I haven't seen them in an age," she wistfully sighed as her mind flipped through a lifetime of memories. "Oh, those boys were always up to no good." She looked at Danny. "You don't know the Gage boys?"

"Never heard of 'em before the other day."

"Oh, well, no, I guess you wouldn't," the kindly old lady resigned. "Bozeman's far enough off. The older one, Justin, he's about your age, though. I just thought you might've crossed paths." She waved her hands and gave a *hoot*. "Them boys were always up to something. All their lives. Of course, their father's a real piece of work. He was one of my students, back when I used to teach at the grade school. Seems that boy spend half his time with his nose in a corner, and the other half doin' stuff to get it put right back there."

Anita popped the seal on her yogurt. "Yeah. We've met."

"Do the Gages have any other friends, family, or associates in the area?"

Mrs. Johnson pondered the question. "Their father. Russel Gage. Last I heard, he lived in a trailer just a few miles up the road as the crow flies."

"We've met," Wakefield grinned. "Real charmer, that one."

"What about their mother?" Anita asked.

"Shanon? Shanon Rogers was her name. Well, back in the day, anyways. Suppose she could be going by anything these days."

"Running from trouble?" Danny inquired in between bites.

Mrs. Johnson *hooted* again. "Oh, that girl ran off long ago. Sad story. She was a wild one, that girl. Tessa Wilkins told me that she got pregnant with each o' them boys trading favors for drugs from Russ."

"Classy," Anita snarked.

"Well, Connie Anderson's boy, Stuart, fell for that girl hard. Married her and took them boys in like his own. And he was doin' alright for himself." The old gossip leaned closer to Anita to explain. "The Andersons run a butcher shop out on the edge of town. Best meat you'll find for sale. Much better than that stuff you find at Walmart. Processed in house and fresh cut to order. A lot of local hunters bring their kills in to have them cleaned right there." Once she was satisfied that her anecdotal footnote had brought the outsider up to speed, Mrs. Johnson returned her attention to Danny. "Anyway, that girl just up and disappeared one day. Lori Hicks told me her boy, Samuel, the EMT, got called out to their place and found those boys were left all alone one day. Shanon had evidently shaken them pretty bad. Bounced one of 'em off the wall. Then she took

Stuart's Camero and ran off. Disappeared in broad daylight. Left that man and the boys and ran back into the rez somewhere. Stuart called the ambulance as soon as he saw them boys, cryin' and bruised."

"Did anyone report her Family Services?" Danny asked.

"Didn't get nowhere with it," Mrs. Johnson shook her matronly head. "She was part of the tribe, so there was no way they were gonna give her up to the white folk."

"You sure she didn't go back to Russ?" Anita inquired.

"Oh, there's no way she'd do that, honey. Not once she was free of him and tasted a better life."

"Things between them were that rough?" Wakefield inquired.

"Oh, Danny. He laid into her so bad some days. You know, my hairdresser, Glenda, she told me that she always thought Russ had his indelicate way with her when he'd had a bit too much to drink or such. 'Course, hear tell these days it ain't just the booze. You ask me, there's a demon of abuse and addiction just nestled right into that whole family."

"Mrs. Johnson," Anita continued, "is there any chance the Gages would be with their mother?"

"Oh, dear," the older woman shook her head, "I'd be surprised if they even knew who she was. They weren't but little'uns when she left 'em - two and three. Justin might'a been four. Even if they knew where to look, I doubt they'd recognize her. But they used to try."

"What do you mean?" Danny probed.

"Stuart was always good to those boys. Raised 'em like they were his own. He was every bit the daddy that anyone could have hoped for. Even tried to teach them the family trade." Saddened by the memory, she shook her head. "But those two never took to him. The Andersons never told them who their father was, but the boys knew that Stuart wasn't him. Don't take a special schoolin' to figure out that if Daddy don't look like you and folks look at you funny, somethin' ain't right. More'n a few times, they tried to run away and find their mamma. Then, when they was teens, they found out who their biological father was and tracked him down."

"I bet that went really well," Anita smirked.

Mrs. Johnson sighed. "The last thing those boys needed was a bad influence in their lives. But once they fell in with Russ, they took his name - and some of his habits."

"Yeah, well, we struck out at daddy's trailer," Danny scratched his chin. "And whatever things used to be between them, it didn't look to me like they were in a hurry to head back."

"So we're left with the dealer," Anita spooned her breakfast from its cup. "It's not that big an area," She explained to the older woman. "There's not enough of a market to support too many sources. If we're talking about the same type of drugs, odds are good that Tommy's dealer - whoever that is - is pushing street candy hauled in by the Gages."

"Either way," Danny offered, "it's worth a look. So, who's pushing dope around here these days?"

Mrs. Johnson looked positively offended. "Well, I wouldn't know myself, dear." Her offense transformed into shame. "But I think I might know who does."

Danny waited patiently while the old woman knitted her fingers. Her hesitation, however, was nearly maddening. Anita's eyes went wide and her face started to tremble with impatience as if her rattling eyes could pry the story out of their suddenly reluctant hostess like a jackhammer.

Mrs. Johnson finally resumed. "You know as well as anyone how hard the war has been on some of our boys." Her previously vibrant face was darkened with sorrow. "So many come back broken. And not just their bodies, Danny."

Wakefield understood the general direction in which this story was going, but he politely nodded in silence until the old woman could give him the missing details. Sure, he needed the information. And that meant playing the game and adopting the quiet listener role until he got it. But he also knew that what she said was true. And sometimes truth needed to be heard.

"We were so proud of Adam when he enlisted," she continued. "Our grandson," she added for Anita's benefit. "He was so brave, so excited when he found out he was going to Iraq." The old woman's momentary pride disappeared. "But he came back different. We let him stay here a while after he left the Army, but he just -" Her voice cracked and sputtered as she choked back tears of shame. "He'd just sit around the cabin all day. Sometimes he'd stay inside for weeks. Other times, he'd disappear into the woods for a few days, but when he came back he'd say it was nothing. I had to bring him groceries for nearly six months. He wouldn't even go to town. He just stayed up here smoking things and drinking things." She patted

Danny's forearm. "Not normal stuff, mind you. Dangerous things."

"What did you do?" Anita asked.

"It wasn't healthy for him," Mrs. Johnson declared. "Living like that. He couldn't hold down a job - not that I think he ever looked," she huffed. "Finally, we decided we were just enabling his bad decisions. We told him he had to leave. Grandson or no, Roy and I just can't abide that kind of nonsense under our roof."

If Mrs. Johnson was looking for judgement, she was not going to find it from Danny; not for her, not for her grandson, and not for the situation. *Still,* he resigned, *he might lead me where I need to go.* "Where's Adam now?"

"He's got a place just on the other side of the valley." Mrs. Johnson's expression grew into open concern. "Now, you're not gonna get him in trouble, are you?"

"Not if I can avoid it," he shot Anita a silent warning, then gave Mrs. Johnson his most reassuring look. "Can you text me his address?"

"Sure thing, dear." The old lady shuffled over to the counter to collect her purse.

"And keep your ears open for me while you're in town?"

"Of course." Hands that were so confident in the kitchen fumbled as she clumsily stabbed her phone's screen.

Danny smiled. "I'd appreciate it."

Wakefield grew up in the general vicinity, but years away made him a stranger. And when an unfamiliar, athletic, white male came snooping about, there were few people who did not automatically assume that he was a cop. Even though that assumption was not technically true, it was close enough to reality to keep him from getting the information he needed from suspicious strangers.

Worse yet, if anyone in these parts actually recognized Danny then they would probably know his face from news reports about the fiasco in Washington. In his opinion, those reports had not faded fast enough from the public eye. For days, the news loop continuously flashed his face and identity - Special Agent Daniel Wakefield of the United States Secret Service - every few minutes, interspersed with video coverage of the shootout in Arlington and file footage of the Constitutional Killer's various victims. After a few weeks, things had finally started to calm down. People had a short attention span. The public's collective eye needed something new on which to focus - and eventually they would get it. But in the meantime, working through intermediaries like Mrs. Johnson afforded Danny the opportunity to lay low until folks finally forgot about him.

Mrs. Johnson looked triumphant as her text finally transmitted with a *whoosh*. Danny figured the technology probably got the better of her about half the time... and circumstances conspired to make this day one of the worse times. "Well, I'd best be going," She shuffled to the door. "I just came for a moment while Roy's at the feed store. If I don't get back with the truck soon, I'll catch an ear full."

"Thanks again for everything," Danny squeezed the old lady's shoulder in a one-armed hug. "I appreciate it."

"Now, you're gonna eat at the restaurant tonight, right?"

Danny drew a hungry breath through his nose. The Johnsons ran his favorite eatery in the area and stocked it with beef harvested from their own herds. Herds that had, up until recently, been prey to the very big cat he harvested from their land. Keeping game animals alive was good conservation, but every head of cattle lost to the mountain lion was money out of the Johnsons' pocket. *I can't wait to taste my investment,* he smiled. "That's the plan."

The matron patted him on the torso. "Well, in that case, I've got something special in mind. What time do you think you'll be eating?"

"Probably around six thirty," he shrugged, "maybe seven."

"I'll just have it ready for you then," she smiled. "But don't you risk the roads if the weather they're talking about comes in. Better safe than stupid."

"We'll be mindful," Danny assured her halfheartedly.

"Thank you, Mrs. Johnson," Anita repeated. "It was lovely to meet you." As soon as the older woman closed the door, Wilson turned to Wakefield. Her face was a case study in sweetness and charm. "Well, she seems nice."

"Dirty old girl copped a feel," Danny quipped, deadpan. "Did you see her grope me just then?" Anita snorted at the accusation. "Seriously. She just fondled my peck. If I grabbed some gal's glands on the way out the door, they'd throw me in jail."

"So, your local informant is a seventy-year-old grandmother?"

"She responds to tasking," he joked in reference to one of the intelligence trade's criteria for evaluating sources and snitches. *The difference between a random witness and a good source is that the source gets you what you need,* his instructors used to preach.

Anita's eyes dashed over to the dishes drying atop a towel on the countertop. "Did that tasking include a short order breakfast and a weather update?"

Danny blew a raspberry with his lips. "There hasn't been more than a handful of powder fall at a time all winter. But a few years back it fell pretty bad - worse than usual - and now if anyone sees more than a hint of dandruff on your shoulder, they get flashbacks to 'the big one.' Now, as for breakfast," he held up his hands defensively, "I had nothing to do with that. She was here when I got out of the shower. I walked out of the bathroom in my skivvies and she was already in the doing her thing in the kitchen. It *is* her cabin, after all. She came out to check and see if we needed anything - just in case this mythical snow comes - and just started whipping up some grub on her own volition."

"How sweet," Anita's honey words were met with a sarcastic tone. "I couldn't help but notice that she only made breakfast for one, though."

"You're a vegan," he countered. "I knew you wouldn't want any of what she was cooking. And I didn't want to offend her by sounding ungrateful asking for something else. Besides," he gestured innocently toward the bedroom, "you were still racked out. Didn't want to wake you just yet."

"You're so lame," she scoffed.

Danny shrugged. "I think she wants to set me up with her niece," he explained.

"Typical."

"And," he further confessed, "when I told her that my new partner and I needed to use the cabin, I might have forgotten to mention that you're a woman."

"Oh," Anita sang in a long tone. "I see." She licked the last dollop of yogurt from her spoon, then flicked the clean cutlery toward him as if she was cueing a symphony. "And is that how you see us? Partners?"

"Well," he rubbed the back of his head, "I mean, I know you're just here for a few days, but... Well, we *are* working together. So, as long as you're here, yeah."

Short exposure sometimes made for fast relationships.

Danny's phone rang from the end table next to the couch that doubled as he bed. *Probably Mrs. Johnson,* he assumed. His mood sobered instantly at the caller identification notice on his screen. "Go for Wakefield," he answered.

"Agent Wakefield," a humorless voice rang out from the other end of the connection, "this is Trooper Dietz with the Montana Highway Patrol. How're you doing this morning?"

Alarm bells sounded in the back of Danny's head. "How can I help you, Trooper Dietz?" Anita stiffened a bit at the half of the conversation she could hear.

"I'm out here at your father's place," Dietz answered. "I was hoping to get a word with you."

Danny's stomach dropped. "Is Dad okay?"

"Your father's fine, Agent Wakefield. But we need to ask you some questions. We thought you'd be here, but obviously you're not. Can you come in to the station sometime today? We need to have a talk."

"About what, exactly?" Danny's momentary panic began to subside, but he was far from relaxed.

"Carlos Gonzalas," Dietz answered plainly. "We found him dead a few hours ago out on the highway. We went to his home and your card was there. We just need to clear up some details. Where are you right now, Agent Wakefield?"

Danny's mind was a whirlwind. Questions, concerns, and caution battered against each other within his skull. "St. Ignatius," he lied as his brain scrambled for a suitable rendezvous point. But St. Ignatius, Montana was not a big place, and it was only really known for one thing. "How soon can you meet me at the Mission?"

"I can have a trooper pick you up in about thirty minutes."

Danny was no stranger to police-speak. *Pick you up* might have sounded nice and cordial to ignorant civilians, but in law enforcement terms it meant, *We're keeping you until you tell us what we want to hear.* "I'm working," Wakefield dodged, "so I'm not coming in. But we can meet face to face this afternoon. After I take care of a few things."

"You got something going on that I need to know about?" Dietz inquired.

"Nothing I wanna talk about over the phone." Danny did not like the patrolman's tone in the least bit. He consulted the watch strapped to the underside of his left wrist and calculated drive times. "I'm free for lunch," he invited.

"Eleven thirty," the trooper answered. "I'll see you there."

Danny deactivated his phone and looked at Anita. "Jenny's boyfriend," he relayed. "State Troopers found him dead."

"That's too bad," the Canadian sympathetically hissed. "You think he went after the Gages?"

"Probably." Danny consulted his most recent text, then slipped his shoulder holster over his knit shirt. "Let's hope Mrs. Johnson's grandson gives us more than Carlos did."

CHAPTER 13

"LOUISIANA SENATOR Chandra Lee Evans, elected just a few months ago in the wake of the assassination of her husband - the late 'Duke' Evans, who sat in the seat for decades - made an appearance in the Beltway today." The radio personality sounded like he was particularly amused at the announcement.

"That's right, Fred." Factcheck Fred, the junior-most member of the popular radio program's trio, allowed his cohort to carry the conversation for a moment. "Now, Senator Evans survived the White House bombing last month - which I think is just awful, by the way -"

"Wait, Kyp," a third voice interrupted, "do you think the bombing is awful, or the fact that she survived is awful?"

"Well," Kyp wavered, "definitely the first one. And maybe the second. I mean, she's only been a senator for a month, so I'll wait to reserve judgement until she proves herself to be just another evil, power-hungry Democrat."

"That's big of you."

"Thank you. And she's already off to a great start on that front. Like Fred said, she just made her first public appearance since the attack, and she's walking around with her arm in a sling -"

"So she was injured in the attack?"

"Well, Lonnie," Kyp answered, "that's the thing. See, we got mixed reporting after the attack - you know, because of the confusion and everything."

"They call it the 'fog of war.'"

"Right. And then we start hearing from people who were there, you know? Folks checking in and saying, 'Yeah, we were in this room, and then ka-blam!, but we're fine.' And while we have heard several times from Senator Evans' spokesperson that she was fine, we haven't seen her until now."

"Where was she when the bomb went off?" Lonnie pressed.

"That's another point of confusion," Factcheck Fred offered. "But it seems, based upon most of the credible statements, that she was in the main dining room, which is where most of the other people were."

"That's where President Whetherby was," Lonnie affirmed.

"Right. And there were no serious injuries reported that night by any of the guests in the main dining room," Fred explained.

"But now," Kyp continued, "all of a sudden, Chandra Lee shows up a month later in front of the cameras with her arm in a sling."

"And this injury is alleged to have resulted from the bombing?" Lonnie inquired. "It's not, like, I don't know, tennis elbow? A hockey injury? Something like that?"

"Not a lot of millionaire grandmothers from the Deep South playing hockey," Kyp countered.

"That's true," Fred offered.

"So," Lonnie resumed, "you're implying that Senator Evans is milking this for sympathy with the voters?"

"Sure seems that way to me," Kyp concluded. "Either that, or maybe she was injured in a separate incident and nobody wants to talk about it to the public. But voter sympathy is the most likely, if you ask me. Which you did."

"But she already won the election," Fred added. "That's another thing that's just weird to me. You know? I mean, she just got elected. So why the grandstanding?"

"I don't know," Lonnie's voice modulated in such a way that it conveyed an audible eye roll, "but it wouldn't be the first time that a politician lied about danger in an attempt to impress the public. And I'd like to talk about that some more after the break. You know, here at the Lonnie Chase Program, we know it's important to keep -"

Danny muted the Jeep's radio. He was less interested in the upcoming commercial block than he was in the mobile home that rested on cement blocks near the gravel road just ahead of him.

"I'd rather focus on what we can get from the scene of Carlos' death," Anita opined from the Jeep's passenger seat.

"I heard you the first time."

"Yet here we are," she fumed.

Danny parked in front of the mobile home that belonged to the address Mrs. Johnson sent him. His eyes were unreadable behind his sunglasses. "We've got time." *There's always time for a vet,* he left unsaid. "Listen, Wilson. I need you to go soft in there, okay?"

"What do you mean?"

"Yesterday," he reminded her. "You were pretty high impact."

The Canadian cop scoffed. "I was playing 'Bad Cop,' Wakefield. I assumed you knew what to do."

The Good Cop/Bad Cop routine was a time-honored police tactic where one officer - the Bad Cop - utilized aggressive or downright hostile behavior to intimidate a suspect so their partner - the Good Cop - was afforded the opportunity to present themselves as the perfectly reasonable and sympathetic ear into which the perp could confide. The approach was so well known that it had lost its impact with more savvy criminals. Still, the fact that the technique worked after so many years stood as a testament to its effectiveness.

"Pretty damned convincing," Danny remarked. "I thought you were gonna throw Russ Gage through that wall."

"Would've served him right," Anita gave a wicked grin. "It wasn't much of a wall anyway, really."

Danny held a finger up in warning. "Go soft," he insisted, "or stay in the car."

Wilson rolled her eyes and hopped out of the Jeep. "Don't ever tell me to stay in the car," she grumbled. "So," she mused as she slipped her puffy vest over her shoulders, "giving it a go with granny's little boy, eh?"

"We'll try him first, yeah." Wakefield pulled his big blue parka onto his frame. Even the short walk from the Jeep to the trailer was long enough for Montana's cold winter air to bite clear to the bones. "Let's see if I can reach him. Connect with him. Vet to vet." He made sure to beat his companion to the trailer's rickety stairs. "Did you bring snitch money with you?"

"Snitch money?"

"Cash," he clarified. "To pay informants."

"A bit," she nodded.

"American currency," he pressed. "Not that Canadian Monopoly money."

Anita glared. "Of course."

"How much you got?"

"That's none of your business."

"Ballpark," he insisted. "Hundreds? Thousands? Tens of thousands?"

Wilson's eyes darted back and forth. Her hands fidgeted. "I've got a couple of grand in cash on me," she admitted. "Mostly hundreds. A few small bills."

"Good," Danny resolved as he knocked. There was no extra room in front of the mobile home's door. Anita had to wait on the gravel parking apron. Danny knocked on the aluminum frame a second time, louder than the first.

After a long pause, the inner door opened a few inches. A pair of squinting eyes strained against the morning sun and peered through the gap. "What?"

"Adam Johnson?" Danny asked in a confident but calm tone.

"Who're you?" the eyes growled.

"Sergeant Daniel Wakefield," the Agent replied with just a little grumble in his voice. "Third Reconnaissance Battalion. At least, I used to be. Can I come in?"

The eyes jerked in a nod, then disappeared. "Come on in."

"Coming in," Danny announced. The *coming in/come in* exchange was a tool taught to door kickers downrange. Walking into a room unannounced while clearing buildings was a stupid way to get shot by your own people, so guys were taught to call ahead, *Coming in,* when they suspected armed friendlies had control of a target space they wanted to enter. If it was safe - which, in this context, meant that fingers were off of triggers and nervous troopers knew to treat the new face as friendly - someone on the receiving end would answer back, *Come in.* It was a simple soldier solution to a serious soldier problem. The exchange was so prolific that it could sometimes be heard in the wardrooms and showers of units who frequently deployed. And in mixed or unfamiliar company, it also served as a subtle way to separate experienced warfighters from posers and wannabes. Most armchair warriors, Fobbits, and rear echelon voyeurs - unindoctrinated to war's real work - were utterly clueless about the exchange. So so many things about war's hard learned tradecraft, they did not know what it was, how it worked, or why it was important.

Wakefield pulled the cheap screen door open and beckoned for Anita to follow him. He stepped slowly into the darkened trailer, pushed his boot's toe through a collapsed pile of empty beer cans, and pulled off his sunglasses. He took a few more steps into the darkened trailer and held a nonthreatening - but tactically sound - position on the far side of the main room's covered window with his back to the corner.

The odor of unwashed laundry hung in the air. The caustic miasma mixed with the distinctive tinge of lingering smoke that definitely did not come from commercial tobacco products. Adam flopped into a nesting space made out of a rumpled pile of blankets, shirts, and jackets heaped upon a threadbare couch. An air conditioner hung haphazardly in the window kicked on and fought to push warmth into the room against the cold air that followed Wakefield through the door.

Wilson cleared the hatch quickly, then instantly regretted it. "Damn," she squeaked as the room's bouquet ran up into her nostrils. She obviously wanted to open every portal she could find and vent fresh air into the stinky shack. Still, she quickly closed the inner door against winter's chilly bite.

The malnourished Caucasian male sat in a discolored wife-beater shirt and faded, tattered jeans. His uncut mop of hair looked like it rarely saw its way more than two-thirds through an endless routine of style-sleep-shower. Patches of hair grew on his face in a wannabeard that reminded Wakefield of '90s grunge singers. "S'up, Sarge?"

"You *are* Corporal Adam Tyler Johnson," Danny clarified, "correct?"

"I was," Adam corrected him. The younger man reached past his nest, flipped open a wooden cigar box, and plucked a tightly rolled party favor from his stash. He slipped the joint into the corner of his mouth and fished within his pockets for a lighter. "Not anymore."

Danny pulled a Zippo from his own pocket and tossed it to the veteran. "Welcome home."

"Thanks." Adam availed himself of the lighter. Once his joint was lit, he gazed at the eagle, globe, and anchor symbol engraved into the stainless-steel case. Then he snapped the device closed with a flick of his wrist and sent it sailing through the air back to its owner. "So, Marines, eh? Pretty hardcore, man. Where were you?"

"Here and there," Wakefield shrugged. "I was a scout sniper. You know how it is." In truth, the bearded former Marine did start off his time in uniform as a sniper. But he elected not to share the details of his intelligence background later in his career. Not with a stranger, anyway - especially one who practically had 'Jaded Ground Pounder' tattooed across his forehead. Many troops had mixed feelings about military intelligence, and some outright hated it. *Meet on common ground,* he reminded himself. *Build rapport so he'll wanna talk to you.* "What about you?"

"Eighty-eight Mike," Adam nodded. "Recruiter told me I'd be driving tanks. Ended up driving an up-armored Hummer most of the time," he sneered. "Running convoys in and outta Baghdad for fourteen months."

"That's a long time driving up and down IED Alley."

The Improvised Explosive Device - or IED, for short - was the bread and butter of Sunni insurgents and the bane of American ground troops during the war. *Driving up IED alley* was soldier slang for the requirement of logistics personnel and motor technicians to utilize ground transit in order to transport men and material along high-risk freeways. This near-daily motor traffic was comprised almost entirely of large, slow vehicles that seemed designed to draw fire and expose their occupants to danger.

It was no surprise to Allied leadership that the Iraqi Army folded at first contact with Coalition Forces at the onset of the 2003 invasion. With the notable exception of the Iran-Iraq War, history indicated that the only time the Iraqi Army would raise its weapons and fight was if their AK-47s were pointed at unarmed civilians - usually their own citizens. But after Hussein went on the lamb and his cronies fled across the sand to Syria, loyalist holdouts and insurgents raided local weapons stockpiles for unused military ordinance. They fabricated their own bombs from leftover artillery shells, blocks of Iranian C4 flown across the border, or whatever Russian munitions they could find. *Jihadists* took great pleasure at the opportunity to cobble these resources together in boxes packed with nails, gasoline, or whatnot and leave the little packages along the roadside, concealed within a donkey cart or stuffed inside some beat up car's trunk or a dead animal carcass in wait for a Coalition convoy to come down the road. They also took great pride in the attacks results - despite the fact that they were usually too scared to be present during the actual blast - and blamed any civilian casualties that resulted from their own cowardly acts on the so-called 'invading infidels,' or *kufiri*.

During the course of modern warfare, Coalition troops almost never engaged the enemy in the kind of stand-up gunfight for which most soldiers trained. Most Coalition casualties during the Iraq war came from weapons abandoned in civilian areas and left there by an enemy too afraid to show their own face. IEDs could be anywhere. They were found everywhere. And they left their mark on many, many troops.

"Tell me about it, man." Adam held what remained of his left hand up for Danny's inspection. The last three digits and a significant amount of the palm were notably absent. "Piece of shrapnel punched right though my door." A line of twisted, wrinkled scar tissue marked the border of the butcher's bill. "Doc saved my booger hook," he wiggled his left index finger. "If I'd've been driving just a little faster, the blast would've decapitated me."

Danny shook his head at the all-too-familiar tale. "I'm sorry, little guy."

"Good thing it was my left hand, though," Adam snickered. "Otherwise, it'd've wrecked my love life."

"Did you see how it ended?" Anita asked.

"Oh, I never passed out or nothin,'" he answered with tired pride. "After the blast, we just blew through. You know? Kicked the tires and laid down fire. We were in a mounted Humm-Vee. My gunner got his bell rung, but he said he got the guy recording the attack. Probably the same dude who had the remote."

"Probably," Danny nodded. As much as he wanted closure for the younger Soldier, though, he knew well enough that there was no reason to believe that Johnson's crew actually killed the person who built, deployed, or detonated the IED that hit them - if there was a person at the switch at all. *It could easily have been triggered by a pressure plate,* Wakefield kept to himself, *or a cell phone remote.* But he knew better than to give life to any idea that might compromise the disabled veteran's tenuous grasp on closure. *Let him believe what he needs to so he can get by.*

"So, what brings you here, Sarge?"

"Honestly," Danny shrugged, "your grandma asked us to come check on you."

Adam took a puff from his magic dragon and grinned. "'Us' being you and..." his bloodshot eyes looked up and down Wilson, "the hooker?"

"'Us' being me," Wakefield chuckled, "and the Mountie." Adam did not appear fazed by the prospect of a Canadian cop in his living room, even while he helped himself to what was either a controversial homeopathic treatment or a brazen felony. "And truth be told, little guy, it's not Sergeant anymore. It's Special Agent."

"Congratulations." Johnson offered up a cheese eating grin and practically dared Danny to arrest him for self-medicating. "I've got a prescription."

"Your grandma told us you've been having a rough time," Danny continued. "Said she was worried."

Adam rolled his eyes. "If she and gramps were really worried about me, they wouldn't've kicked me outta their cabin."

"She said that you were hitting it pretty hard," Anita countered from next to the door.

"Look, brother," Danny continued, "we're not here for you, and I ain't gonna judge. Not for the herb," he admitted. "Hell, you and I both know that it can do a lot of good for folks who need it. A lot of our dudes get 'scrips for it, and a lot more who need it can't get the VA docs to help. That ain't why we're here. As a matter of fact," he held a handout toward Anita, but kept his eyes on the broken soldier on the couch, "Constable Wilson here is even gonna help with your treatment."

"Really?" Adam shook his head in disbelief.

Wakefield gave him a disapproving look. "It's Montana, little guy, not Chicago. There aren't so many people here that there could possibly be a lot of dealers. We need one in particular," he confessed.

"Must be a slow day for the feds if you're shaking guys like me down for our weed."

"Actually," Anita smiled, "we're looking for something a little harder. Ex. MeX, specifically."

"Tell us who's pushing it and we leave you to party with our friend Benjamin." He flicked his fingers impatiently behind himself until Wilson finally slipped a crisp note into his hand. Danny extended a hundred-dollar bill toward the other veteran.

"I ain't doin' nothin' wrong," Adam insisted. "I ain't botherin' nobody. Nobody cares about me an' I don't make waves." He took another pull from his joint.

Danny pulled the cash back toward his shoulder. "C'mon, Adam. You know the drill. We need to have a chat with the local MeX pusher. Who is it?"

"I ain't no snitch."

"We're not after your marijuana guy," Anita clarified. "Unless he's also got what we need," she pulled another bill from her pocket. "I mean, if I wanted to score, you could point me in the right direction, couldn't you? Anonymously."

"You're not doing Ex," Danny quizzed him, "are you, little guy? 'Cause that stuff'll mess you up."

The medical and law enforcement communities commonly referred to marijuana was a gateway drug. Readily available, relatively inexpensive, and seemingly benign, the green goddess served as an introduction to the highs offered by narcotics and often led people to try harder, more dangerous substances. For many people, the streets to hardcore drug use were paved with Acapulco gold.

Danny tried to keep an open mind about the issue of marijuana use. Unlaced, it was a natural herbal remedy for a number of ailments and conditions. Scientific studies seemed to show it was far less harmful than some commercially produced substances. It was legitimately used to treat glaucoma and cancer patients like his mom before she died - though back then medical cannabis was not available in the US. These days it was also prescribed to a growing number of veterans who struggled with pain management and Post Traumatic Stress Disorder.

As an educated man, Wakefield could not deny the argument presented by a mountain of medical evidence. But he could also not turn a blind eye to the serious health problems that resulted from wanton drug abuse: medical conditions and damage to the body, other criminal activity often associated with the drug trade, the potential risks to bystanders posed by people who were stoned out of their gourd, and so forth. And while these concerns were usually associated with synthetic narcotics like cocaine, heroin, and methamphetamines, they were not totally absent in the seemingly innocent community of marijuana users, despite the group's vocal protests to the contrary. And even if Mary Jane was just the gateway to a dark path, rather than its conduit, Dany felt that the risks were just too high for the reward.

"I ain't no snitch," Adam insisted.

"Suit yourself." Danny gave his bill back to Anita. "You were right," he admitted to her. "I was trying to hook a brother up, but I bet Tommy will tell us for less." He pointed to the door, which Wilson gladly opened. "I mean, he'd sell his own mother for a buck."

"Wait," Adam called from the couch. "Tommy Griffin? Wait a second, dude." Young Johnson might not have been the kind to talk, but the disabled veteran's sudden sense of urgency told Wakefield that the younger man apparently held a different opinion of the Griffin boy. Danny held short of the door and looked back over his shoulder. "You're right." Danny waited for a moment longer while Adam seemed to struggle with his priorities. "Fine," he nodded, "fine."

"You got something for me?" Danny took the second bill from Anita and made the bills dance in the air to tease the guy on the couch.

Adam's face looked like he wanted to swear, but nothing came out of his mouth but a drawn-out hiss. "You ain't wrong about Tommy, man. I mean, if you're gonna be out the cash anyway, we might as well keep it in the family. Right?"

Danny waved the bills again. "I'm waiting."

Adam swallowed and made up his mind. "Okayokayokay. C'mon back in, man." Danny was much less hesitant to acquiesce to Adam's invitation, but they both returned to the young man's living room - and its odorous bouquet. "For four bills, I'll tell you what you wanna know."

"Four?" Anita choked.

Danny looked at the cash held between his fingers. "One Mississippi..." he pointed as he counted, "two Mississippi..."

"Man," Adam whined, "you can't expect me to risk steppin' on a guy like that for two lousy c-notes. I mean, you say 'anonymous,' but these things have a way of circling back."

Wakefield's face lit up as if his mind was suddenly struck by an epiphany. "You're right. Let's make it three. Constable Wilson?" Both men looked at Anita expectantly and waited. She stood frozen for a moment, then rolled her eyes and relinquished another c-note.

"I'll give you three names," Danny declared, "and then you'll give me one." He dropped a hundred-dollar bill onto Adam's lap. "Ben." Then he dealt a second bill. "Jammone." And a third. "Franklin." Then he dramatically laced his arms across his chest. "There. Three names. That's what I've got. What'chu got?"

Adam pinched his joint in the corner of his mouth and collected the cash with his half-a-paw, then closed his eyes and blew a jet of air from his nostrils. "D'licious."

"You're welcome," Anita huffed. "Now, the name?"

"That's the dude's name," Adam clarified. "Dee-Licious. He's the heavy at the Gray Wolf."

"The Gray Wolf Peak Casino?" Danny inquired, "just up the street from your folks' restaurant?" Adam nodded. "Cool. Thanks, Johnson." He thought about leaving a card with the younger veteran, then remembered the issue with Carlos. He reconsidered and turned toward the door. Halfway through his turning step, though, his conscious struck him in the back of the head. *Screw that,* he resolved as he doubled back. *Never leave a buddy hanging.* "Look, brother. Here's my card. If you need anything, if you think of something, or you just need to talk… Don't hesitate. Alright?"

Adam accepted the card, but he never gave it a first glance - let alone a second. "Yeah, man. Whatever."

CHAPTER 14

DANNY CHECKED THE Jeep's clock as he pulled away from Adam's sad little mobile home and navigated back to the main road. Anita watched the decrepit little box shrink behind them in the rearview mirror. Once the trailer was obscured from her line of sight, she turned to the driver.

"Pretty generous with my lunch money," she snidely remarked.

"You bring snitch money, you pay for snitches."

"I don't know how you do things here in America, but the going rate for a rat in Canada is a lot lower."

"Yeah," Wakefield turned onto the paved roadway, "well, those are Canadian dollars you're using up there. You lose a bit in the currency conversion." Danny could tell without looking that his new temporary partner was not amused. A familiar voice sounded in the back of his head with words that echoed from months ago, spoken miles away, by a woman kept away from him by a white marble headstone: *You're soft on vets.* Danny shook the criticism out of his head and buried the comment back under six feet of Arlington soil. "Look, Wilson. You were there. What'd you see?"

"A stoner," she coldly replied, "plain and simple."

"Right. Well, I saw a kid who tried to do something with his life, only he got blown up in the process. Why? Moving a truckload of X-Boxes from one base to another? Or some other bullshit? It's a raw deal, Wilson, but the truth is that most guys in his place don't eat it on a mission to go catch bad guys or secure an enemy position. They get hit moving stupid crap from one FOB to another because *this* Exchange is running low on movies, or *that* one needs some more potato chips in the chow hall." Indignation crept into his voice. "They don't lose a leg, or a hand, or a buddy on their way to liberate a town. They leave their blood, body parts, and brothers in the dust driving armored bulldozers through a combat zone on their way to build a soccer field that some pinhead far removed from the fighting thinks might make the local barbarians like us enough to rat out their own friends and family." Wakefield was unaware of the fact that his tone had hardened and his volume had increased. "I saw a young man with authentic battle damage, struggling with a Veteran's Administration that works real hard to ignore him. I see a guy in pain, just trying to get by in a community that won't give him a job. And maybe, just maybe, I see a guy who's already written a check to this country and has earned a break."

Suddenly aware of his tirade, Wakefield ended his rant. *Elbee'd probably say something psychological right now,* he noted to himself. The two of them rode for a tense moment with no sound but the Jeep's engine and the road as it rolled along under them. Danny flicked on the heater to warm the cabin and forced himself off of the soapbox. "Sorry," he said more quietly.

"Look, Wakefield, I get it. Okay? And maybe you're right. Forget I said anything." She scanned the highway and checked the clock on the navigation display that dominated the Jeep's dashboard. "We're on our way to see the Trooper?"

"Yep. And then we'll mosey up to the casino and check out the bouncer." Just then, a set of musical notes played over the speakers and the words *Incoming Call* appeared on the Jeep's big dashboard display. Danny pressed the soft key that activated the cabin's speakerphone and carried the phone call over his truck's Bluetooth link. "Go for Wakefield," he announced into the Jeep's voice pickup.

"Hello?" a familiar voice answered. "Am I on speakerphone? Take me off that stupid thing."

Danny kept one hand on the wheel while he fetched his phone from the center console and switched the call over to his handset. "Can you hear me now?"

"Much better," the older voice declared. "Don't ever put me on speakerphone, Wakefield." Danny's mind conjured the image of a disheveled, white-haired man in a herringbone jacket, seated in a high-backed leather chair and huddled over a rich, mahogany desk: Dr. Jonas Wiley, his boss back in Washington D.C. "You know I hate that thing."

"I'm driving, Father." Danny countered. "It's safer."

"Compensate, Danny boy." Dr. Jonas Wiley was Wakefield's mentor as well as his supervisor. Danny shared a bond with the wizened, Jesuit-educated man whom he referred to in their more cordial moments as *Father*. "Listen, I got something for you, son."

"Send it."

"I'm sorry to disrupt your vacation, but that was a helluva Leave bomb you dropped after –" *After you shot that guy*, Danny expected him to say. "Well, you know. Anyway, what's up with your phone? I've been trying to reach you since this morning."

"It's Montana," Wakefield countered. "Cell service sucks. It's part of the state's appeal." Danny let his snarky comment hang in the air for the appropriate length of time. "Why? What's up?"

"There's a bit of a situation, son. I've got a Canadian officer here who needs help with a case that's strayed into your turf."

Alarm bells sounded in Wakefield's mind. Suddenly, he was thankful that the call was not being broadcast into the Jeep's cabin over his stereo, then locked onto the road ahead of him. "What?"

"Sorry, Danny boy, but the Mounties are here after a couple of nasties, and my hands are tied."

Wakefield felt his stomach drop. "Say again?"

"You really do have coverage problems up there," Wiley remarked. "Look, son, this is just the way things are. So don't give me any macho *'I don't need a partner'* crap. I know you're still raw from what happened with Elbee, but you're a professional and this is the job. You're just gonna have to sort it out.

Anyway, her name's Wilson. I'm flying her out to Helena to link up with you. She's got the details."

What the Hell is going on? Behind his sunglasses' lenses, Danny's eyes flashed over to the petite brunette that sat next to him. "Sir," he fought to hide the suspicion from his voice, "Constable Wilson and I just left a source meeting." *Think fast!* "I think the snitch's information might pan out. Before we check it out, we're on our way to link up with a local Trooper who might also have a line on our suspects." *That's right. Act like we're all having the same conversation.* "We'll be a long way out from Missoula. And we've got a line on another source I wanna check out tonight."

Dr. Wiley was the head of the Secret Service's Analysis Division. A lifetime ago he had served with distinction as a naval intelligence officer - one of legendary capability. *Surely*, Danny hoped, *he picked up on the hint.*

"Constable Anita Wilson?" Jonas asked slowly.

"Yes, sir."

"From the Royal Canadian Mounted Police?"

Wakefield covertly watched for any indication that his passenger could hear even the slightest bit of the conversation happening within his ear, but she gave no sign that she was clued into the exchange. "That's affirmative."

"Son, she's standing right in front of me. Here in my office. In Washington."

"That's doubtful, sir," Danny shook his head, "but we can try." He mentally kicked himself. Unlike DHS Headquarters back in D.C., out in the middle of nowhere he had no access to JPAS - the Joint Personnel Adjudication System - to check his visitor's identification, clearance, or other credentials when he met her. He had no way to verify who this woman in his passenger seat was. *Not that I even bothered to ask...* Wakefield's mind raced as he worked the problem at hand. *Rookie mistake,* he fumed. *Can't undo it. Gotta fix it.* And now a strange woman sat a foot away, leading him around for unknown reasons.

And she was armed with one of his own guns.

"Alright, son," Wiley's voice grew quieter. More measured. It was a voice all too familiar to Danny. It was the kind of tone people in the military adopted when they found themselves immersed in a situation that unexpectedly became confusing, out of control, and deadly serious. "We'll sort this out and get back with you. Keep your phone handy. And in the meantime, just stay frosty."

"Thanks for the heads up, sir." Danny's mind explored all of the options available to him at the moment. There were not many, and he did not like a single one. "If there's nothing else?"

"Nothing now. I'll be in touch."

"Out." Danny deactivated his phone and returned the device to its normal resting place on the center console. He cycled a slow breath to calm his nerves. His fight-or-flight instinct screamed for him to grab the imposter next to him around her lying throat and squeeze until she told him who she really was and what she really wanted. His counterintelligence training held him in check and cautioned him that any hasty action on his part might burn a potentially valuable source for information.

"Is everything okay?" the woman he knew as Anita asked.

Be cool. Be cool. "Plan A is humped," he shook his head. "We'll have to go with Plan B."

"Which is what, exactly?"

Hell if I know, Wakefield mused. *I was a Marine. We don't plan. We adapt, improvise, and overcome.* Hidden behind his beard, Danny gritted his teeth. *But for the time being,* he decided, *I'll keep you off balance. At least until I can figure out exactly what is going on.*

"Weather threat seems a little more solid than I thought. Local forecaster is pretty much guaranteeing a big snow tonight. Dad suggested that we call it an early evening and get back to the cabin before the front has a chance to roll in."

"How bad a snow?"

"Never saw a Canadian winter firsthand," Danny admitted, "but I can't imagine they're mild. Well, we're about four feet behind our annual snowfall so far this winter. And the crap that's supposed to roll in tonight could easily make that up."

Unconsciously, the woman who called herself Wilson pulled her vest a little tighter around her torso. "Well, we best not take any chances then, shall we?"

"Safety first," Danny shook his head. "Safety first."

*   *   *

"*¡Me cago en la hostia!*" Justin Gage winced reflexively. He knew some curse words in Spanish, but as his Mexican boss sounded off a string of rapid fire vindictive that went on and on, he decided he would have to look up a few of the phrases for his own future use.

"I'm sorry, *jefe*," Justin explained, "but we can't drive eleven hund'rd miles to Chihuahua inna truck shot full of holes. We'd get pulled over fifty times before we even cleared the Tetons."

"Time is money," Hector fumed. "Do you have any idea how much these kinds of delays cost us? We have people we answer to, *gringo*. Just like you do. And if you put us in bad with them -"

"You gave us two days," Justin reminded him. "It's just comin' on day two. We'll be in Sanders County by sunrise. Salvadore's crew works fast," he assured Hector. "We should be back on the road in twelve hours. Tops. Then it's a straight shot back down to you. You'll have your money tomorrow night, *jefe*. I promise."

"*Noche de mañana,*" Miguel chimed in, "*o estas muerto.*"

Justin cast his attention to the locked trailer full of cash hitched to his truck. He always thought the Jaliscos just kept their money in a warehouse in Juarez. Maybe the higher ups spent afternoons swimming in it. Before this moment, he never considered that Hector and Miguel might actually have debts of their own to pay. Whoever the Mexican brothers' bosses were, though, Justin figured they had to be powerful players - the kind of hard creditors who did not take delays lightly. "Count on it, *jefe*. And thanks again, Hector."

James eyed his older brother as the latter deactivated his phone. "That went well," he announced sarcastically.

"Better than I thought it would," Justin adjusted himself in the driver's seat. "We'll have to hot-seat it all the way south if we're gonna make it."

Justin propped an elbow on his door and rested his cheek upon his hand. "Nothin' we haven't done before."

"Yeah." The elder Gage dropped his phone onto the center console and traced a circle around his belly with is freshly freed hand. "This run's turnin' into a real pain in the ass."

The younger brother pondered their predicament from his own side of the truck's cabin. "You know," he offered, "there's an obvious solution." He let his words hang in the air for a moment, but when Justing did not acknowledge them, he continued. "We could just take the money an' run."

"Jimmy," Justin shook his head, "you know how much cash is stuffed into those boxes back there?"

"I dunno," James shrugged. "Like, twenty mil, right?"

"More like thirty," Justin corrected his younger brother. "An' fer losing 'em that kinda money, the brother's'd send folks after us."

"So we go off the grid."

"There's nowhere we could hide. Trust me. I've thought about it. You've seen it yerself. Cartels've got cops in pocket. They've got their own politicians, bought an' paid for. On both sides of the border. And beyond." Justin sighed in resignation. "No, Jimmy. We play this straight. These ain't the kinda guys you get wrong with."

"Doesn't stop the Sinaloas," James countered.

"Problem's up here," Justin rubbed his belly thoughtfully. "We gotta sort it out. Long enough to get down the road and away from local hang-ups." He gave a humorless smile. "If I know Hector, they're probably gonna pay the local Sinaloas a visit down south, too."

"Okay. So, how do we find a Mexican drug cartel in the middle of friggin' Montana?"

"Who's the only one who knew we were in the area?" Justin quizzed him.

"Other than that dead wetback?" Justin thought aloud. "Just - No. You don't think?"

The older brother drove as quickly as he felt the pre-dawn morning hours would allow. "I don't know, Jimmy. But it's worth a look while the truck's getting patched."

CHAPTER 15

ST. IGNATIUS MISSION was a building in the middle of nowhere. As Danny drove up to it, he was struck by the way the red brick stood in stark contrast against a lingering blanket of downy snow that covered the grounds and evergreens around the building. His eyes traced the church's clean lines, so simple and elegant against the majestic backdrop of the jagged National Bison Range: human craftsmanship beside God's own handiwork, each adding to the other's beauty.

And nested in front of the heavy wooden beams that made up the Mission's welcome sign sat a shiny black Dodge Challenger with reflective gold stripes.

"Looks like your trooper buddy is early," the brunette in Wakefield's passenger seat quipped.

"He's not my buddy," Danny turned in a wide arc to pull up beside the police cruiser, *and neither are you.* Wakefield wondered what to call the woman with which he had spent the last few days. *Wiley says he's got the real Wilson back in Washington,* he mused. *What's that make you?*

Danny brought the red Jeep to a halt with the driver's door mere inches from the black Challenger's window. He slipped the truck out of gear and let the engine idle as he lowered his own portal. The cruiser's driver did the same. "Trooper Dietz?"

The man inside the cruiser wore the kind of thick, heavy mustache that fell out of fashion in mainstream America decades ago. It was the kind of lip wig favored by cops and porn stars, and it only accentuated the officer's displeased demeanor as he glared at Danny from behind his aviator-style sunglasses. "Mr. Wakefield?"

"*Special Agent* Wakefield," Danny corrected. "How can I help you, Trooper?"

"Maybe we should go inside," Dietz suggested.

"I'm working a case right now, Trooper."

Even through the reflective lenses of the cop's aviator shades, Wakefield detected the Highway Patrol officer's judging gaze. "You Homeland Security guys don't shave on duty?"

"You didn't call me out here to bitch about my grooming habits," Danny tersely replied. "Now, you said earlier that you found Carlos dead?"

"And your business card at his trailer," Dietz affirmed. "Was Gonzales part of your investigation?"

"We're not at liberty to say," the woman who called herself Anita answered.

Dietz's sunglasses shifted a few degrees as his vision locked onto the brunette. "And you are...?"

"Not at liberty to say that, either," she countered.

"I put in an RFI with Homeland, the Justice Department, and local authorities." Dietz's lenses re-centered on Danny's face. "Neither the Attorney General's office nor any of the local sheriffs have any knowledge of an active federal investigation by your office. Whatever you're doing, Wakefield, you're doing it without authorization."

You're so full of shit that I bet your eyes are brown, Danny smiled. No force in Heaven or Earth could get an official Request for Information - or RFI, for short - submitted and processed with even one of the entities Trooper Dietz just listed and in the amount of time the cop had available, let alone all of them. Nobody at any level in the government was that efficient. And Wakefield knew it. *But let's see how far he'll carry his bluff before calling him on it.*

"Without *official* authorization," Danny amended. "Surely, trooper, you recognize the difference."

"I recognize bullshit when I smell it, Wakefield. And this whole thing stinks."

The thought occurred to Danny that his hesitation to share information with this cop was largely due to a request for discretion made by a woman who he did not trust in the slightest. *Still,* he weighed, *just because she's a liar doesn't mean she's wrong. And,* he realized, *if she doesn't know that I know she's up to something, it might help me figure out who she is - and give me a way to get rid of her.* "Look, Trooper, I'm trying to find a way to help you here. Ask your questions. I'll answer what I can."

"Gonzales and his associate, George Martinez-Rojas, were found dead this morning. Their car flipped over on I-15 just outside of Monida."

"Car crash?"

"Not exactly. The car crashed, but that's not what killed them."

Of course not, Danny nodded. "You got photos?"

Trooper Dietz pointed to the computer terminal mounted above his center console. "You wanna take a look?"

Danny's mind dwelt upon what typically happened to non-cops who went into police cars - especially when it was not their own idea - and decided that he would rather stay in his cozy, handcuff-free Jeep. "Can you email them to me?"

"Same email address as the card?" Danny nodded, and Dietz punched a few buttons on the terminal. "Sent."

Wakefield retrieved his phone from the console and cycled his inbox's icon until the new message appeared. He opened the attached files and thumbed through the images. "Looks like a bullet pattern on the rear glass." Swipe. "Entry and exit wounds look like the driver - is that Rojas?"

"Yep."

"Looks like he got clocked in the back of the head." Swipe. "Carlos was ejected from the vehicle?"

"Not ejected," Dietz corrected. "Footprints show that he got out and walked. And he wasn't the only one." The trooper looked back and forth meaningfully between the Jeep's occupants. "We found two other distinct sets of footprints in the snow, mud and such in and around the median." The cop made no effort to hide the suspicion on his face as he looked back and forth between the Jeep's occupants.

"He was chased," the alleged Anita pointed to the tracks in the picture on Danny's screen. "Look at that wound on his neck."

"That ain't seatbelt rash," Dietz declared.

"It's a knife wound," Wakefield's companion leaned in close and whispered. "James."

"If you say so." Danny gave a slight nod, barely discernible, but remained quiet as he flipped through the crime scene photos. The Gages had, for whatever reason, already demonstrated a grudge against Carlos by what they did to Jenny. *And Wilson - or whoever - said that Jim killed her partner with a knife. Still, it could be confirmation bias; she could be jumping to conclusions that fit what she wants to hear. Or,* he had to admit, *she could be stringing me along.*

Before he could continue, Danny's phone rang. The number on his screen was a familiar extension at the office back in Washington. *Wiley's desk,* he recognized as he glanced back and forth between a pair of people he did not trust with the truth. "Excuse me," he held his hand up to Dietz, "I have to take this." The trooper jerked his head in assent as Danny rolled up his window and fumbled for his phone. His arm movements, shifting body, and shoulder shrugs caused his passenger to sit back in her seat. *That's right.* Danny inwardly confirmed as he accepted the call. *Give me some room. Just like I need you to.* "Go for Wakefield."

"Danny. It's Jonas Wiley here. You got a minute?"

"Barely," Danny looked through his tinted window at the officer who spoke into his radio's microphone. "Whatcha got?"

Danny dialed the cabin's fan up a notch. The increased heat compensated for the warm air he lost while the window was down, but he really just wanted the extra background noise to drown out anything that might leak from between his ear and his handset.

"I'm not on speaker, am I?"

"Not yet."

"Listen, Danny Boy," Jonas kept his voice low, but Wakefield did not dare turn the volume on his phone up any further, "we ran the security checks three times on our end, checked her identification twice, and even called the Mounties to confirm from their end. We've got the real Constable Wilson here."

"Cool," Danny said flatly. "So, what's the plan?"

"Clearly, you've got an imposter, son. One with the skills and means to impersonate a federal officer. Well, a Canadian one, anyway. And Wilson has begrudgingly conceded that her investigation has been compromised. Not officially, of course. But that changes things a little bit."

"You know me, Father. I'm adaptable."

"Good. Here's what I want you to do. We need to figure out who this broad is, what she wants, who she works for... everything. Think you can use some of those super TACHUMINT skills to play the disgruntled employee? Let her lead you astray far enough to figure it out?"

Danny chuckled. "You have no idea."

"That's my boy," Dr. Wiley praised. "Now, whatever's going on here has the real Wilson's panties in a wad. She's catching a flight out to Bozeman tonight. Whoever your imposter is, you've got until the real Wilson gets to you to figure it out. Once she's there, my hands are tied. She takes your girl into custody and we lose all visibility on this."

"Got it," Danny flatly acknowledged.

"I'm giving you a long leash on this one, Danny boy." Wiley's response was even quieter than normal. But Danny could not risk turning up his phone's volume and allowing his passenger to overhear the other side of the conversation. "See where she leads you. My gut tells me this could be huge."

Wakefield pursed his lips and raised his voice just a bit. "So, they didn't turn on my travel card?"

The US government-issued travel and impact card was one of the most beloved perks of being a federal agent. The simple credit card was used to pay for everything from hotel rooms and airline tickets to meals, cash advances at ATMs, and sometimes not-entirely-official purchases made while ostensibly conducting official business. The cards' purchase limits were defined by the organization's own travel office; each department was responsible for their own budget, but stories floated through the federal service in which agents purchased automobiles, paid for penthouses, or even leased private airplanes, all in the name of official government business. The cards were supposed to only be used for specific authorized purchases, but the history of federal service was filled with examples of people who used them to pay for personal artwork, bail money, prostitutes, and breast enhancement surgeries for young women who were not listed on their taxes as legal dependents.

As a rule, individual travel cards were maintained with whoever handled travel and logistics at a respective organization and kept inactive as a default. Due to the fact that his investigations frequently resulted in travel - and, in his most recent case, short notice trips at that - Danny's boss let him keep his travel card on his person. It was always in his wallet. That way, Wakefield only had to call the travel officer and have them activate his card should the need arise, then deactivate it when the trip or mission was finished.

Danny knew Jonas was smart enough to already have talked to the travel office. But feelings of mismanagement and money problems were common causes for workplace conflict, and Danny needed to make sure that the seeds were planted in his target's mind that all may not be well in the DHS Analysis Division in Washington, D.C.

"I'll get that squared away with the travel office," Dr. Wiley assured. "And I'll see if what other resources we might be able to throw your way. Let me know if you need anything."

"Well, I only have so much cash. So we'll see how things go." Danny deactivated his phone and turned to his passenger. "Sorry about that, Wilson. Logistics and finance. You know how it is."

"I know that laceration across Carlos' throat wasn't caused by windshield glass," she countered. "And I looked at the map. Monida is well south of here. On the border with Idaho. They're headed back to Mexico."

"Looks like it," Danny lowered his window. "Hey, Dietz. I don't suppose you guys recovered any guns, drugs, large sums of cash, or anything else interesting from the scene?"

"Nope. But I just got off the horn with the station. Blood work showed your boys had traces of drugs in their system at time of death."

I bet they did, Danny nodded. *Probably more than 'traces.'* "We have reason to believe that Carlos might've been a Sinaloa mule," Wakefield offered. "You know anything about that?"

Dietz shook his head and pursed his lips under that big mustache of his. "Not me. No. Why? Is that what you're investigating? The Sinaloas?"

"Still not talking about it, Trooper. Did his girlfriend say anything about it?"

"What girlfriend?" Dietz shrugged. "Never met any girlfriend."

"Oh," Danny bounced his head between his shoulders. "She must've stepped out." He looked at the underside of his left wrist and the watch worn inverted as a matter of habit. "Alright. Well, look, Trooper Dietz, we've gotta get going. Is there anything else that I can do for you?"

"Where're you staying?" the officer pulled out a pen and notepad. "It ain't your dad's place. He said you're in and out. And I checked the motel in town to see if I could catch you, but there's no room listed for Wakefield."

Good job, Dad. "Ninepines."

"Up in Kicking Horse? Yeah, I know it. Nice place."

"Dad doesn't have Wifi," Danny joked. "Plus," he dipped his head toward the looksome brunette in his passenger seat, "you know."

A wide, toothy grin bloomed under Dietz's lip blanket. "Yeah... I know."

"Stay safe, Trooper." Danny raised his window, dropped the Jeep back into gear, then gently pulled out of the church's parking area.

"That's it?" his mysterious passenger demanded.

Wakefield staved off her objections with a finger held aloft and spoke into the Jeep's voice pickup. "Call Derek," he ordered. The navigation system, tied once more into his phone, obediently dialed the assigned number. It only rang once.

"DHS," the voice hurriedly answered, "Agent Martin speaking. How may I help you?"

Derek Martin was probably - no, was *definitely* - the smartest person Wakefield had ever met. The younger analyst was a rarified genius, gifted researcher, and one of the few people Danny trusted with absolute certainty. Little D would get Wakefield the answers he needed. He knew it.

"Little D. I need you to do something for me."

"Hey, man! Sure thing."

"I need real time tracking and position updates on a vehicle. Montana State Highway Patrol. Cruiser. Tail number one-four-two-nine-two-five. Plate number Mike, Hotel, Papa, three-one-one. Backdoor into the state Department of Transportation to get the government tag already in place."

"So," Little D hummed, "I'm guessing this is an *ex officio* request?"

"We won't be bothering with a warrant today, Little D. Local agency's got too many leaks. And I think my mark is a dirty cop."

"Alright." Agent Derek Martin was Danny's best friend in the Analysis Division - and probably his best friend in the world. He was also a certifiable genius whose skills were arguably wasted in government work. For Derek, whom Wakefield had affectionately nicknamed 'Little D,' the use of a federal system to hack into local law enforcement networks to set up a remote uplink with the GPS systems installed in every police car for command, control, and in case the vehicle went missing was just another day at the office. No matter what technical skills the job entailed or how questionable his ethics might be to others, Wakefield knew he could count on Little D to get it done for him. Laws or no laws, Martin had shown time and again that he would move mountains for his buddy.

"How time sensitive is this?" the younger Secret Service analyst asked.

"Sooner is better than later," Danny answered.

"Give me a few minutes. I'll do what I can."

"Thanks, Little D. Out here." The call ended with a *click*.

"You're tracking the cop?" the alleged Anita asked.

"You said yourself that the Sinaloas have connections with local law enforcement," Danny reminded her. "Plus, you saw how he denied knowing about Jenny."

"Yeah. Well, maybe she wasn't home when they checked the trailer."

"Agent Wilson," Danny kept the sarcasm out of his voice, "twenty hours ago, you and I had a talk with that girl in that trailer. She said that she was just raped in there. Yet she preferred to stay in that place over anywhere else that she could be - so much so that she wanted to stay after all of the Hell she'd been through. And now she's just *gone*? Her clothes, toiletries and hygiene products, pregnancy tests in the trash. All gone? Even the worst cop on Earth would've noticed at least *some* of that and drawn the obvious conclusion."

The brunette nodded. "So, you think Dietz was lying."

"I *know* Dietz was lying. Question is: *What was he lying about?* Well, that, and *why*."

"Suppose he talked to Jenny and she told him about us - only he didn't believe her? Maybe he wanted to find out what we know. Validate his source?"

"More likely he talked to Jenny, didn't like what she had to say, and she's holed up in some Sinaloa lowlife's place until they find whoever killed Carlos."

"The Gages."

"If she's even still alive," Danny continued.

"So, you want to find Jenny."

"I want to find the Sinaloas," he corrected her. "And I'll bet you dinner tonight that Trooper Dietz will lead us straight to them. Wakefield's dashboard chirped with a text alert. Danny checked the screen and saw that his onboard navigation system displayed a map of the local area. A blue geotag indicated the Jeep's position on westbound Highway 200. And a red one, labelled MHP311, travelled north on Highway 93 - toward Kicking Horse. Danny pulled his wallet from his jacket's breast pocket and peeled his government credit card out with his thumb. "Do us a favor. Look up the Ninepines Lodge and book us a room."

"I think I see where this is going," the brunette smiled as she searched the internet.

Let the games begin, Danny smiled.

CHAPTER 16

NIGHT CAME QUICKLY in Montana's mountains during the winter. By six o'clock in the evening, the sky was a black blanket. Most folks were already settled in for the evening. Conventional wisdom encouraged folks to huddle up inside during the long nights - to go where it was warm and to stay there unless one was forced out into the bitter cold.

A pair of figures clad in black fatigues and knit masks crept slowly up the dark path between buildings at the Ninepines Lodge. The shadowy figures moved in tandem and communicated only with hand signals as they stalked up to the designated room. On the other side of the ground-level abode's dimly lit window, a pair of voices - one male, one female - carried a heated discussion. Based on a standard room layout, the voices came from or near what should have been the dinner table.

"What about the past couple of days?" he demanded. "They happened, you know?"

"I know that they happened," she replied with barely contained tears, "and they were wonderful. But they were also very irresponsible."

A rustle sounded within the room, like overturned furniture. One creeping figure - the leader - held up a hand to halt all action for a moment to evaluate whether or not they could proceed undetected.

The woman spoke over the commotion. "I have a fiancé waiting for me at a hotel who's gonna be crushed when he finds out what I did -"

"So you made love to me," the angry man cut in, "and then you go back to your husband?"

The leader waived a gloved hand to signal his partner to continue.

"Is that your plan?" the incredulous man continued. "Was that a test that I didn't pass?"

"No!" the woman roared. The men in black crouched low next to the rented room's door. "I made a promise to a man," the woman inside explained while silent shadows outside each screwed illegally fabricated suppressors onto their identical Glock 9mm hosts as she ranted inside the room. "He gave me a ring and I gave him my word."

"And your word is shot to Hell now, don't you think?" the man spat. Even in the shadows and hidden by a mask, the sneaky leader's wide-eyed nod virtually screamed, *Dude's got a point.*

"I don't know," the woman's voice defended. The leader jerked his head toward the door. "I'll find out when I talk to him."

"This is not about keeping your promises," the guy inside countered. The second man in black gently placed one gloved hand on the door handle. The leader held up three fingers. Both assassins held their pistols at the ready. Then two. "And it's not about following your heart." Then one. "It's about security."

The gunmen crashed through the door. Splinters from the frame flew across the small room and the only area large enough for two people to sit and eat together. The black-clad duo hurled themselves into Wakefield's room. Their pistols aimed at the source of the voices they heard from outside -

- and straight at the vacant eat-in kitchen.

"What is that supposed to mean?" the familiar woman's voice sounded... from under the table. The lead gunman lowered his aim and saw the television set as it flickered between a pair of unoccupied chairs.

"Money!" The image of a romantically disheveled actor yelled from a picturesque porch in a scene depicted on a television set.

"What are you talking about?" an equally idealized actress squeaked.

"He's got a lot of money!"

The twin gunmen looked at each other and shrugged.

"Now I hate you," the actress fumed, "you smug bastard!"

The lead hitman fired once into the television just to silence the argument which had distracted him and his partner. Then he fired again, just for good measure.

"Here ya go, sweetie," Mrs. Johnson's youngest niece was only a few years older than the grandson Danny met that morning. That put her maybe a couple of years younger than Danny himself - well within the range of socially acceptable dating ages for a man his age. She was no supermodel, but she was what he referred to mentally as *Montana pretty* - good enough looking to do the job out here where women seemed few and far between, but not pretty enough for him to usually bother pursuing back in D.C. unless she had an unusually agreeable personality. And after the day he had just endured, Wakefield was more interested in the steaming plate she delivered than whatever promise any woman's smile offered.

"Now that," Danny's teeth began to sweat, "is a proper Beef Wellington. Thank you, Clarissa."

"Can I get you anything else? More sweet tea?"

"That'd be great. Thanks."

"And you, hun?"

Across the table, the woman without a name offered a dry, humorless smile. "I'm fine. Thanks."

Clarissa did not make it two steps away from Danny's table before the mystery woman's face went flat. She forked another leafy bite from the garden on her plate.

"How's your salad, Wilson?"

"Why are we here, Wakefield, when we could be following your supposed lead?"

"First off," Danny sliced into the breaded concoction and deep into its meaty core, "your intel is shot to Hell. The Gages have no clue about their mom and there's obvious friction with the dad. So whatever your sources, you got nothing on my info."

He tossed his bite into his mouth, then set to work carving another. "Secondly," he managed around a mouthful of savory meat, "there could be weather tonight." Most of the locals commented rather matter-of-factly that a rough front was about to move into the area, but Montana weather could be unpredictable. Wakefield was, in all honesty, ignorant of what the evening's actual forecast was. He avoided checking any weather reports ever since he brought it up out of fear of having his bluff revealed. But if the locals were convinced, it was easy enough to sell himself as a believer. "So we should definitely not go anywhere tonight that we wouldn't want to get stuck." *If this dry spell continues,* he hid his face with his glass as he took a long drink from his sweet tea, *I can always just blame the weatherman for crappy reporting.* He lowered his glass. "And third, we're gathering data on the Trooper's movements and patterns. It's called a stake out." He finished carving his bite and pulled the morsel free. "Get it? Stake? As in -"

"I get it."

"And another thing, Constable." Danny gestured with his fork so that she could see his food's warm, pink center. "I was on vacation - before I was so rudely interrupted, mind you." He sank his teeth into the perfectly prepared entré and let the complex flavors roll across his pallet. Fresh Angus beef culled straight from the Johnsons' own herd, slow roasted and delectably tender, melted like butter as he chewed. Sweet breading flaked and disintegrated in his mouth. And between the two, a mortar made of gourmet mustard and spices held a layer of prosciutto was held in place.

It was a tricky ploy, but Danny had to stonewall any actual progress on What's-Her-Name's alleged investigation without actually looking like it was on purpose. So he adopted the persona of a disgruntled government employee who only begrudgingly did his job. And he played his part with Golden Globe-worthy *élan*.

"So you keep reminding me," the false Anita rolled her eyes.

Still, Danny reminded himself, *I don't wanna overplay my hand. Better keep the fish interested.* "Alright. So, you said earlier that Carlos' killing had all the earmarks of the Gage brothers, right?"

"It was them," she nodded. "I bet anything."

Wakefield carved himself another bite. "During the wee hours last night?"

"Evidently."

Danny dipped his dollop into the delectable steak's copious sauce and soaked even more flavor into the meat. "Leaving the state."

"So it would seem."

"And thus," *time to make her work for it,* he gestured toward her with his steak-tipped fork as if it was a magical wand, "taking with them the only reason for me to be on this case." Danny smiled greedily and made his bite disappear. "Sounds to me like I'm back on Leave."

The strange woman at his dinner table glared at Wakefield's announcement. "What about your orders?"

Danny's smile remained as he chomped and gnashed his morsel. "My orders," he declared around the food still in his mouth, "were to assist you with a manhunt up here due to my knowledge of the local area, network of helpful contacts, and geographic convenience." The tender meat slid down his gullet. "Your suspects are no longer in the local area. You said so yourself just now. So, my assistance is no longer required."

Wakefield bet heavily that his companion's vegan beliefs - if they were indeed true - would prevent her from stabbing him with the fork clenched in her hand. But a good con required the mark to take charge. If Not-Wilson had any sense at all, she should grow suspicious if he became overly interested in her or her case. He needed her to need him. If he was going to build the rapport necessary to finally start getting some answers, he needed her to keep reaching out to him. And the way Danny figured it, the best way to start learning the truth about this woman with a false name was to start testing her lies. How much of her story was true? What lengths would Not-Wilson go to just to string him along - and to what end?

It was a calculated gamble, but one which in Danny's mind held only winning outcomes. Either the counterfeit Anita was prepared to let him walk away or she was not. If she did not play along, Wakefield's official services truly were not needed. The Case of the Mysterious Mountie would go away, unsettled, and fade with no concern… at least, none from him. *I've got no skin in this game,* he concluded. *Now's as good a time as any to end it.*

"Wakefield," the word came slowly. Measured. The charlatan hid her obvious anger behind a façade of calm that was more thin, fragile, and weak than the paper towels next to their plates. "I need your help."

"Why?" he reeled her in, just a little. Danny dared her to tell him another lie. Or the truth. His every sense was tuned to her: the trembling she fought to keep out of her hands, the angle of her spine and its distance from her chair, the speed and depth of her breathing, the angle at which she canted her head, the expressions she tried to hide from her face... he read every word and micro-expression with covert clarity. The best interrogation training on planet Earth coupled with years of practice bored and pried at her story like a stubborn nut whose shell concealed precious meat.

Wakefield saw conflict in her eyes. He could almost visualize the synaptic crossfire as a dozen or more unspoken thoughts fought against each other. Clearly, this false woman struggled against her own mind as to what exactly she would allow herself to say.

"You're very good at what you do, Wakefield," she confessed. "If you weren't, I wouldn't've come to you."

"Well," *she's quite not ready to spill the beans yet,* he waved his fork, "I think that entitles me to a certain amount of operational discretion."

"Is that what you call eating a fifty-dollar steak? Discreet?"

She thinks this only costs fifty bucks, Danny chuckled to himself. *Not even in Canada, sweetheart.* "It is tonight," he carved himself another mouthful. "Call it 'culinary therapy.' Since they didn't get my government travel card turned on yet, maybe that's the universe's way of telling me I'm not really working tonight."

"You owe me for the hotel room," not-Anita scowled. "Especially if we're not actually gonna use it."

Clarissa appeared next to their table with a pitcher of fresh, sweet tea in hand and a pleased smile on her face. "How is it?"

"Heavenly," he chewed. "Thanks." Danny retrieved his wallet from the cargo pocket on his right thigh and plucked his personal credit card out from the leather billfold. "I've got dinner," he offered to his mysterious companion as he handed the card to Clarissa.

"Take your time," Clarissa insisted. "I'll ring you up and bring this right back."

"Thanks," Not-Wilson stabbed a baby carrot with her salad fork.

"Least I could do," Danny waved. "I owe you from this morning, too." As he drew his steak knife through his meaty meal, a thought occurred to him. *Normal people don't talk about such things at the table,* he remembered, *but then again, you're not normal, are you, Miss Whoever-You-Are?* "You said you recognized Gage's handiwork from the knife wound on Carlos' throat?"

The brunette chewed her vegetables until her mouth was cleared. "Yeah." She swallowed again. "James Gage loves to use a knife."

"Is he trained?"

"You heard Granny," his dinner companion looked at him dryly. "He was raised by a butcher."

"One he rejected as a father," Danny reminded her, "in favor of the dirtbag sperm donor. So where'd he learn to use a blade? Was he in the Army?"

"Oh, no. Nothing like that."

"So, some martial arts school?" She shook her head again. "C'mon, Wilson," he chided, "I don't know that there's official stats out there on this sort of stuff, but a lot of guys train somewhere. I mean, if we count the caged cockfighting they call Mixed Martial Arts, it's a fair bet at least one in ten dudes in America has some formal martial arts background."

"Gage isn't trained," she paused between bites. "At least, not in the traditional sense. Not that I've been able to determine. He's an animal. He fights purely on instinct. And his instincts are bloody."

"That pic earlier," Danny insisted, "the slash was purposeful. Practiced."

"It wouldn't be his first." Not-Wilson surrendered her salad fork. "Neither Gage brother's hands are clean," she explained, "but based on what I've seen, James is the real killer between the two. Justin's more pragmatic. Out of the pair, he's the thinker. But his little brother is a savage. James Gage likes to hurt people. He likes to kill. And he won't stop. Not until he's stopped by someone else." The nameless woman steepled her fingers. "What do you know about knife killers?"

"I know that my Colt has better range," he carved another bit out of his steak.

"They rely upon surprise or savagery," she explained. "They like to stalk or deceive their victims. And when that fails, they just plain overwhelm them." She found her glass once more. "Usually, they're sexually frustrated, too."

"Like, incapable?" he asked as he shifted in his seat with visible discomfort.

"Like, unsatisfied. Unfulfilled." Her eyes defocused as she appeared to recall a memory. "For most of them, the knife attack is a substitute for sexual desire. The proximity, the phallic weapon, the penetration, the fluids…"

Danny paused as he looked down at the steak knife half buried inside his own dinner. Then he shrugged and finished cutting his bite. "So, they get off on it," he concluded.

"On the thrill," she nodded, "yes. Many killers who choose to use the knife are also either rapists or wannabe rapists."

Danny hung on her every word. He analyzed every gesture. She was a deceiver, that he knew, and he had to be able to discern the truth from her lies. *She means what she says,* he inwardly noted. "You seem to know a lot about this stuff."

"It's part of my job," his mysterious dinner companion sat back in her chair.

"Is that *all* it is?"

At that moment, Clarissa reappeared beside their table. "I'm sorry," she frowned in sympathy as she held Wakefield's Visa in hand, "but your credit card was declined."

"Figures." He rolled his eyes. "I'm sorry, Wilson, but looks like you'll be springing for dinner, too." While Danny enjoyed the irony of forcing a vegan to buy him an expensive steak dinner, he really just wanted to see the name on her credit card. That was why he emailed Little D back at DHS and asked his buddy to put a twenty-four-hour block on his accounts. *Treasury Department has rules about monkeying with other people's money,* he reasoned, *but there's no harm in blocking my own.*

But instead of plastic, his unidentified dinner date pulled a wad of bills from her pocket. "How much is it?"

Clarissa's mood dropped a bit at Danny's *declasse* display. "Here's the check."

Not-Wilson's jaw dropped when she saw the number bottom of the ticket. "I should make you wash dishes for this, Wakefield." She frowned and peeled a few bills from her folded currency and stuffed the rest back into her pocket. "Keep the change."

Clarissa nodded and left.

"Sorry about that," Danny sheepishly shrugged. "Guess I overspent on Christmas presents. Of course, if the travel office had just turned on my card..." He stopped himself. "Sorry. It's my fault."

"Your people drop the ball like this a lot?" not-Wilson asked with what appeared to be genuine sympathy.

"You have no idea." For a guy who made a living investigating financial crimes, Danny was pretty unfaithful when it came to balancing his checkbook. That said, he generally had a good feel for about how much money was in his account, and one pricey dinner was not going to hurt him too badly. But players within his own department - and Wakefield knew this was the work of Little D and Father - were perfectly able to freeze his accounts and leave him reliant upon the kindness of strangers... and to make him look like a guy whose apparent financial problems might make him vulnerable to manipulation, if not outright exploitation.

"Maybe you should consider a more profitable line of work," his enigmatic dinner companion suggested, almost too subtly. "That, or a second source of income."

Maybe she is CSIS, Danny considered. His earlier remark about the Canadian Security and Intelligence Service's constant solicitation and elicitation of information from American sources echoed in his mind. *Trying to pimp me out for secrets? Turn me into a mole?* Wakefield rubbed his hand across his face in a show of muted dismay. "Still, maybe if I cancelled our room up the road, it'd free up some cash on my personal card." He recalled a recent number and dialed his phone.

"Thank you for calling the Ninepines Lodge," a woman's disembodied voice answered from the other side of the handset. "How may I help you?"

"Hi there. This is Daniel Wakefield in Room One-Oh-Four. I think there might be a prob-"

"M-M-Mister Wakefield!" the receptionist stammered, "you're okay?"

"Of course I am," Danny frowned. "Why wouldn't I be?"

"There was a shooting, sir. In your room. There's cops all over the place."

Danny perked up. "Was anyone hurt?" His dinner companion stiffened at the question. He could tell Not-Wilson was trying to dial in and catch details.

"No," the receptionist replied, "nobody was hurt. But they say your room's a mess. They won't let us go over to the building. And everybody's lookin' for you."

I bet they are. "We'll be there shortly." He deactivated his phone and waved for Clarissa's attention. "Can we get a couple of takeout boxes, please?" Their hostess acknowledged.

"Problem?" Not-Anita guessed.

"Looks like Trooper Dietz was in a hurry," Danny nodded. "They already hit the lodge."

"That didn't take long." His enigmatic companion reached behind herself and slipped her arms back into her puffy vest. "I told you local law enforcement was compromised."

"Just once," Danny looked down at his plate in sadness, "I wish I could enjoy a proper meal in peace."

CHAPTER 17

JUSTIN GAGE PULLED the blue Peterbilt tractor unit up until the front end was a mere handspan from the oversized door to the mechanic's service bay. He shut down the truck's lights and motor, then signaled James. "We'll need 'em to let us into the back lot to park the trailer again," he reminded his younger brother.

Blessed with healthy doses of mechanical skills and business savvy, Salvadore Garcia Hernandez worked himself out of the grease pit of the local tire-and-lube and into ownership of his own auto maintenance shop. But in a thin market with narrow margins, he figured out that there was more money to be made if he kept an open mind - and an open bay - to fixing up vehicles that might not belong to their drivers in the strictest legal definition of the word. In many ways Montana was still the Wild West, and when automobiles replaced equines as the predominant mode of transportation, bands of horse rustlers transformed into gangs of car thieves. But most thieves - whether burglars, horse rustlers, or car boosters - did not steal what they wanted for themselves. They stole what they could sell. And when a four-wheeled product needed to be moved it usually required a clean set of numbers. A little cosmetic alteration went a long way, too, when trying to pass a hot car for a perfectly legitimate one that just happened to be the same model. Given sufficiently plausible deniability, many people's eyes stopped being curious.

The secret to success, Salvadore learned early on, was to provide his widely needed service to self-sustaining population and to maintain a sense of neutrality among his potential clients as he did so. His crew worked on automobiles of every make and model, regardless of whose name was on the registration or which gang colors the driver wore. He took sides with nobody and did business with everybody. But his house had rules - the first and foremost of which was: *Nobody violates neutrality here.*

"Be sure to keep your hands to yourself," Justin reminded James as he led his little brother through the shop's front door and into the customer service area. The younger Gage's smart mouth and hot head served him well on the street, but any act of violence at Salvadore's shop was met not only by the owner's own crew, but also by members of every other gang, faction, and outfit who patronized the establishment. That was Salvadore's second rule.

The waiting area was not a large room - just a few hundred square feet - but it was a place people who came here on perfectly legitimate business could sit and read a magazine while they waited on an oil change or tire rotation. A miasma of motor oil mixed with stale cigarette smoke hung in the air and penetrated every surface. A few racks and shelves were stocked with a modest selection of minor parts: air filters, the latest bulbs for common headlights, aftermarket upgrades for street racers... those sorts of things. A display showed the difference between a brand-new cabin filter and one which looked more like a dingy sweater than anything else. A security camera tucked into an upper corner was angled at an ideal vantage point over the room.

A door behind the unmanned service counter swung open to reveal a gracefully aged Latino gentleman who looked like he belonged in a nightclub more than a garage. A tasteful gold chain hung across his black mock turtleneck. There was not a stray hair on his head and his pencil-thin beard and mustache were perfectly trimmed. A cool smile spread across his well-maintained face. "Good evening, gentlemen," he clasped his hands in front of his chest. "Back so soon?"

"Salvadore," Justin nodded, "our truck needs your, ah, *special* attention."

"Mind if we park our load out back again for the day?" Justin asked.

"Don't worry about it," the suave patron assured his guests. "My guy'll tuck it in for you. Keys?" Justin obligingly slid the truck's keys across the counter. Salvadore scooped them up while they were still in motion.

"This one you're keeping, or one you're passing on?" *Passing on* was a street euphemism for a vehicle, usually stolen, which was being sold to a third party. Car thieves passed their ill-gotten goods on to auctioneers, dealers, private collectors... whoever was paying on that particular day. Chop shops like Salvadore's specialized in swapping VINs - Vehicle Identification Numbers - from of stolen cars and trucks for numbers from autos with clean histories.

There was an urban legend spread amongst the criminal networks about how once, a few years back, a nice silver-haired couple brought their new-ish Cadillac Escalade in for routine maintenance. Salvadore's crew took great care of the luxury sport utility vehicle and did right by the couple. About two weeks later, the same SUV rolled up to the bay door - this time driven by a teenaged *chollo* and with an oversized screwdriver jammed into its ignition. In exchange for reasonable stall tool rental fees, Salvadore let the street rat change the Escalade's vehicle identification number. For a few dollars more, he even provided a convincing set of license plates. The *chollo* and the Caddy disappeared within thirty-six hours, and when the cops finally came around to ask the usual questions, they found the shop's security cameras only monitored activity rather than record anything.

So the story went, about a month later a black Cadillac with the same hot plates rolled into the shop with a half dozen fresh bullet holes in its side and a twenty-two year old black man behind the wheel. Another tool rental and stall fee. Only this time, it took several days to repair the damage, change the numbers, and replace the interior - after all, leather might resist coffee spills, but blood stained forever; new seats and upholstery plus a modest upcharge on the parts were all still a bit cheaper than the price a fellow paid if he was caught with a car full of forensic evidence by some detective with a ten dollar black light. The black guy even went the extra mile while the Escalade was opened up and installed a new stereo and speaker package bought from Salvadore's own shelves and sold with a modest cash discount.

"This one's ours," Justin explained as he rubbed his pot belly. "And we'll be needing it back on the road ASAP. No later'n tonight."

"That's pretty quick," Salvadore hissed through clenched teeth. "Can't guarantee a showroom finish on that kinda time crunch. Matching orange peel is an art form. You know?"

"Close enough's good enough for us," Justin assured him. "The clock's ticking on this one. You got a loaner we can use while your boys get 'er back up for us?"

"What kinda wheels you lookin' for?"

"You got something nice?" James inquired.

"Of course, *amigo*. My crew just finished a couple of slick tuners, if you wanna ride in style."

"Actually," Justin interjected, "I think it'd be best if we kept it to something that won't draw attention." He cast a warning gaze at his little brother, who in turn frowned in disappointment.

"Alright alright," Salvadore's voice remained chipper. "Staying local, I take it?"

"Yep."

"Follow me," Salvadore ushered them through the door into the maintenance bay. A few steps inside the cavernous area, he handed the Gages' keys to a lackey and gave an order in rapid fire Spanish. The minion rushed to the door - presumably to move the Peterbilt immediately and begin work on the truck. Salvadore continued onward and led the Gages through the bay with a spring in his step. "Now, this ain't exactly Alamo," his spotless taupe slacks and alligator skin boots moved with a light grace that was half-dance, half-walk across the concrete floor beneath his feet, "but let's see what we've got out back for you."

Salvadore grabbed a coat from his office along the maintenance building's back wall and led the brothers out a rear exit. The back parking area behind Salvadore's shop was completed enclosed by an eight-foot chainlink fence topped with rows of barbed wire angled to discourage climbers. A covered carport along the right-hand side of the fenced area contained a collection of about a dozen or so vehicles of different makes, models, and class. A metallic orange Toyota Supra with lime green splash effects down its sides and an oversized spoiler sat next to a purple and silver Honda Civic whose turn-of-the-millennium body was accentuated with an aftermarket ground effect kit and transparent hood to highlight all of the performance upgrades crammed into it.

"That one," Justin pointed to a white Ford pickup truck sandwiched between a polished black Honda Accord and a hunter green Jeep Cherokee which looked like a mobile catalogue for an off-road parts magazine. "We'll take that one."

"Good choice," Salvadore smiled. "You did say you wanted inconspicuous, eh?"

James looked longingly at the orange tuner. "C'mon, Jay," he mewled, "can't we have a little fun?"

"We don't want to draw attention," Justin reminded him sternly. "We just need to look around a bit while Salvadore's boys patch up the truck."

"Well, *amigo*, every *gringo* and their brother drives an F-150 around here. You'll be just another grain of sand on the beach. Four-wheel drive, too. You know. Just in case."

"It's a solid set of wheels," Justin hummed as he pulled a folded set of bills from his pocket. "You'll call us when our truck is done?"

"Of course," Salvadore smiled as he plucked the hundred-dollar bills from Justin's fingers. "Just leave your number with the boys on your way out."

* * *

"Not exactly doing 'subtle' tonight… are they, Wakefield?"

Amidst the sea of flashing strobes and rotating lights, Danny found an empty parking slot at the Ninepines Lodge. "No," he conceded, "they are not." Wakefield hoped for a bit more time to figure out who the imposter was who rode with him, but circumstances were far beyond his control.

Danny had barely even withdrawn the key from his Jeep's ignition before his window was filled by a uniform so stuffed to overflowing that the officer who wore it could not zip his winter coat closed.

"You Wakefield?" a voice demanded from behind a blinding light that suddenly appeared in Danny's window.

"Do you mind?" Danny shielded his eyes.

The police light lowered, but did not disappear. "Trooper Dietz is lookin' fer yah."

"I bet he is," Danny's passenger huffed.

"S'cuse me?"

Danny craned his neck for a view, but the line of sight to the bungalow they reserved was blocked by police vehicles and folks milling around the scene. "What happened?"

"Would you come with me, please, Mr. Wakefield?"

Danny resisted the temptation to remind the officer that the correct manner of addressing him was *Special Agent,* and not *Mister.* He wanted to see how the show before him played out without the added melodrama of a jurisdictional measuring contest. So he blinked his eyes clear and allowed the trooper - whom he suddenly saw was stereotypically rotund - to escort himself and his enigmatic accomplice to the room reserved in his name.

The woman that still pretended to be Constable Wilson did not show the slightest discomfort among the collection of cops despite her obvious subterfuge. She simply walked a step behind Danny and observed the officers. "Kicked the door clean off the frame," she noted as they entered the ground floor room. Inside, she clucked her tongue against the roof of her mouth. "Look at this mess," she sighed. "They are *so* going to hit you up for damages."

"Well, well, well... Nice of you to join us this evening, Wakefield."

"Trooper Dietz," Danny scanned the room quickly, "I assume by the mess and the party outside that there's been some sort of incident?"

"Indeed there has," Dietz rested his hands on his hips. "Afraid we'll have some more questions for you, Wakefield. Lots. Now, I'll need you both to come with us up to the station. You and your partner - I'm sorry, I forgot your name."

"That's because I didn't give it to you," Danny's mysterious companion quipped.

You and me both, pal. Danny briefly entertained the idea of letting the troopers interrogate the brunette. Even the Montana State Highway Patrol should have been up to the task of a basic background check to discern her true identity. But Danny dismissed the thought just as quickly as he seized upon it. *Father wants me to play her,* he reminded himself, to *see where she leads. And that'll be nowhere if these guys interfere.*

"Let's start here with the basics," Wakefield deflected Dietz's inquiry. "What do you know?"

"At least one unidentified individual entered the room earlier this evening," Dietz needlessly narrated. "Fired a few shots. Looks like they tossed the place. Probably looking for whatever you're working on."

"The only work we did in this room," not-Wilson countered, "was to move the telly under the table and put a movie on loop while we were gone."

"Any luck with the hotel's security cameras?" Danny probed.

Dietz shook his head. "It's a pretty bare bones surveillance system. Not a lot of coverage outside of the lobby and the parking lot. Whoever did this knew well enough to avoid getting recorded."

Danny offered Dietz a hard look. *C'mon,* he recalled the location trace Derek's backdoor access had provided him, *we both know that you were here when it went down.* "Huh."

"Which is why we need you to come with us," Dietz persisted. "You know the drill, Wakefield. Help us do our jobs so that we can catch the troublemakers."

"Or," Not-Wilson offered, "we could just check the footage from the attack."

"He told you," their overweight escort countered, "the hotel cameras missed it."

"I'm not talking about the hotel's cameras," the brunette slipped over to the small table next to the door and opened its main drawer. "I mean ours."

"What?"

The petite brunette let the troopers mentally catch up with her words as she slowly withdrew a digital video recorder from one of the dresser's drawers. "Pinhole camera," she explained. "Peeks into the room through a hole no bigger than a framing nail. Which, as it happens, appears to have gone unnoticed within the scrollwork on this drawer's hardware." She made sure everyone in the room caught a clear view of her as she stopped the device from recording. "There's another one stuffed inside the heater on the other side of the room. That one's aimed right at the door." Danny stood by and grinned as both troopers' heads spun toward the heat exchange system mounted high in the room's far corner. "Between the two of them, I'm sure we'll get something useful about our would-be assailants."

Dietz jerked his head toward the heater. "Rip it open," he ordered. The rotund trooper wasted no time, but was not as fast as Danny's female companion, who had already sprung into motion. Still, the heavy trooper retained about three times the gal's mass. He deflected her away with a swipe before she could reach the heater. Dietz stabbed his left finger toward Danny and laid his right hand to rest upon the Glock on his hip. "Don't move!" he ordered.

"Draw," Wakefield smiled madly, but otherwise remained motionless next to the room's busted entrance. "Please," he teased as he slowly placed his palms together and raised them in the universal gesture of prayer. His fingertips climbed ever-so-slowly higher until his hands came to a halt directly in front of his breastbone. At such close proximity, the special agent was confident he could close with Dietz and neutralize the antagonistic cop before the trooper's Glock ever cleared leather. And after a few days of interrupted vacation, Danny was eager for an excuse to tussle with anyone who crossed him.

The counterfeit Canadian constable came to a stop in the corner along the room's far wall opposite the heater. She watched as the fat trooper pulled the heater's cowling free. Porky the Policeman clumsily dug through the device's innards with his chubby fingers, checked inside the unit's vents, then looked to his superior and shook his head in frustration.

Not-Wilson casually reached right behind herself and above the sliding glass door that provided the room with a panoramic view of the nearby mountains. "I'm sorry." Her diminutive height forcer her up onto tiptoes as she dug behind the curtains that slid along a sturdy track and covered the door at night. "But did I say the heater?" Her hand came back down with another digital recorder, fiber optic cable, and miniature optical camera. "I meant the drapes."

"Gimme that," Dietz leapt at her, "now!"

The brunette tossed both recorders to Wakefield before the troopers made it to her. Dietz, fixated on the devices, managed to stop a pace short of impact, but the more corpulent cop barreled into the brunette and bodily knocked her into the wall. It was like a child's game of monkey-in-the-middle, only the monkey was an angry cop who might as well have worn a t-shirt that read, *'I work for the Sinaloas'* on it.

Danny caught the devices and quickly stowed them in his parka's outer pockets. "What's wrong, Dietz?" he pulled his heavy parka off so that everyone in the room enjoyed an unobstructed view the .45 holstered under his left shoulder and the shiny Homeland Security badge clipped to his hip. Everyone in the room stood silent and still, so Wakefield refrained from drawing his gun. "You afraid of whose face we might see on this recording? Maybe yours?"

"That's evidence from a crime scene!" Dietz growled as he rebounded.

"Indeed," Danny nodded. "One where the intended victim was a federal agent," he poured a healthy dose of warning into his voice, "who was, I'll remind you, engaged in an active investigation." The time for niceties was over. "And since my badge has an eagle on it and yours has a plow, that means my very real case has jurisdiction over your bullshit fishing expedition. So you can suck my balls."

"This ain't over, Wakefield."

"I imagine it isn't." A smirk crossed Danny's bearded face, and the thought behind it prompted him to pull out his cell phone. "I want a picture of this," he announced with aplomb as he aimed the device toward Dietz - then covertly shifted his aim ever so slightly so that the picture included a clear view of the brunette in the corner, "to commemorate our special evening together: me and my new best friend, Trooper Dietz." Danny gestured toward the open doorway to signal their exit to his companion. "Oh, and Dietz," he warned, "if anyone comes out to my pop's place again without phoning in a warrant notification first, they're just gonna get shot. Understood?" Wakefield's travel buddy joined him at the portal. Not-Wilson scooped Danny's jacket into her arms, then exited the hotel room unhindered. "We'll be in touch, Trooper. Now, you boys have a nice night. And stay safe."

Adrenaline kept Wakefield warm during the walk back to the Jeep. Halfway to the parking lot, Danny cast a sideways glance at his companion. "You okay, Constable?"

"I'm fine." She cast a bitter glance over her shoulder as they left. "Worthless inbred pig," she snorted. "Real cops are buff, not fluff."

"You sure you're okay?"

"I've been hit harder than that, Wakefield."

Danny thought back to the bar fight at Miss Kitty's and how easily Not-Wilson held her own. *I bet you have,* he mused. *I bet you have.* "That was good thinking back there, misdirecting the trooper so that you could get to the second camera."

"I told you putting them in the room was a good idea."

"Well, I didn't know you brought them with you until you mentioned it," he admitted. *Just one more thing I don't know about you.* "And even then, to be honest, I thought you were up to something kinky."

"Either way," the counterfeit constable teased, "they turned out to be useful."

"Maybe. If they give us something to go off of." The Jeep was still warm when they climbed back into it. "Now, let's see if we can make it back to the Johnson's cabin before Dietz and his goons try something even less subtle than a hotel room hit."

CHAPTER 18

WAKEFIELD HURRIED through the most abbreviated version of his bathroom routine he could imagine while the ersatz Mountie in the next room did God-knew-what. As he rushed through his business behind the only door he could close without raising questions, Danny quickly keyed his phone and transmitted his photo of the woman who claimed to be Anita Wilson to Derek back in D.C. *It's late,* Danny resigned, *and there's no way he's at work.* There was no telling how long it would take Little D to identify the mystery woman, but Danny knew that nobody would be able to get him answers faster than his friend.

I'm supposed to be on vacation, he fumed. *This is supposed to be* my *time. Why does this stuff always fall on me?* Danny flushed the toilet, washed his hands, and tried not to look rushed as he returned to the Johnson cabin's main room with his leather toiletry bag in hand and a fluffy towel draped over his shoulder.

There he saw her, stooped near the weather radio perched upon a bookshelf at knee height. For a moment he almost forgot she was a dirty deceiver. The sight of her bare legs and the black panties that peeked out from beneath her loose white night shirt - which was apparently made of the same type of jersey cotton as his sleeping shorts - temped him to forget that the woman was not the ally she claimed to be. For that barest of moments, he wished the brunette beauty really was someone he could trust.

But she was not.

She's trying to keep me distracted, he reminded himself. *Keep me off balance.* Sexpionage. That was what they called it. The use of sexuality to lull a target into a false sense of security or to illicit information from a mark was one of the older tools in spycraft. Westerners were particularly vulnerable to it. Modern history showed time and again that Americans, more than any other players on the global stage, were especially prone to being exploited by the technique. Wakefield was no stranger to the trade. For a moment his pride made him feel just a little insulted by the idea that his adversary - whoever she really was - assumed he would fall for such a cheap and amateurish ploy. *Then again,* he reminded himself, *I kinda did last night. Didn't I?* Just as soon as it appeared, he pushed the bruise to his ego aside.

The path to victory began by recognizing the battlefield one was on and the nature of the game being played. *Father told me to find out who she is,* he allowed his smile to spread across his face. *Let's play.*

"... issued a severe winter weather warning for western Montana," a recorded voice flatly announced through the static, "severe winter storm advisory until *whrrr-sssshhh*... storm is expected to produce *fzzz-rrr-wheee* inches of snow, with the possibility of *whrr* and hail."

"Your father was right about the weather." The counterfeit constable deactivated the radio. "Sounds like a rough one's moving in." She stepped over to the wood burning stove and stuffed another modest log into its glowing maw, then shut the iron door. "Does this place have a generator? We might lose power tonight."

The main room's western wall creaked as a fresh blast of wind hammered against that side of the cabin. Near the front door, the north window whistled as snowflakes and bits of ice blew past it. A flash of light outside drew Danny's attention. He left his dopp kit on the table as a slow rumble rolled across the sky and padded barefoot across the radiant heat floor. "Thundersnow," he mused as he ducked down to peek through the portal into the blustery night. *Hope the real Wilson's plane gets here before this sets in.* "That's different."

Thunderstorms, with all of their fury, were a common enough in the northern plains, but thundersnow was a meteorological event so rare as to be thought of as a myth by many people. The same forces which created severe rainy weather in the spring and summer could, when temperatures plummeted, also produce a spectacular show starring water's frozen forms - snow and ice. Wintry precipitation danced through the air and piled onto the cold ground below as lightning flashed and arced within the thick clouds overhead.

Danny willed his vision to penetrate the darkness so he could behold the storm's savagery. In his travels he had seen hurricanes in the mid-Atlantic, tornadoes in the Midwest, and *haboob* - epic sandstorms in the Middle East. But Wakefield had never witnessed fury of a thundersnow, and to miss so much of the phenomenon due to something so trivial as the time of day made him suspect that maybe some cosmic force in the universe was determined to rob him of any fun in life.

And it was not the first time in recent history where larger events seemed to conspire to make Danny feel unblessed.

"Generator's on the driveway," he answered, "between the Jeep and the house. Fuel tank is topped off and there's a fresh can of diesel right next to it. We should stay nice and cozy if the power lines snap."

A pair of small hands snaked around his bare torso from behind him. "Speaking of cozy," her voice purred softly as the warmth of her breath traced a line up Danny's back, "I think I know another way we can keep warm tonight."

Wakefield rose as he pulled himself from the window and turned toward her embrace. "Oh really?" he took her shoulders into his hands and grinned. "A heated round of Yahtzee, perhaps? Or a spirited cribbage match?"

The intimate stranger's eyes flashed. "I think you'll like my game better." Her right hand slid around from his back and she drew her fingertips up his torso until they painted an imaginary circle around the eagle, globe, and anchor tattooed on his left pectoral muscle. "Of course," she smiled, "to score in this one you'll have to 'be all that you can be.'"

"That's the Army's slogan," he corrected her, "I was a Marine."

"Oh. Well, what do they do?"

"Adapt." He scooped his hands under her arms and hoisted her up until her bare legs wrapped around his waist. "Improvise." Danny locked eyes with the woman who called herself Anita. "And overcome." He kissed her deeply, the way a man would as if he actually wanted her. He told himself that he only did so because he had to sell his performance and make her believe him. But the taste of her lips and her soft, nimble tongue labeled the sterile thought as a lie.

Keep it together, Wakefield, a voice in the back of Danny's head warned him. *Don't lose control.*

After a heated bout of lip judo, the beautiful brunette pushed herself up for air. "You know," her svelte chest heaved she breathed deeply, "if your government didn't keep jerking you around, you wouldn't have to 'adapt' and 'improvise' so much."

Wakefield flashed a proud grin. "But then I wouldn't be an overcomer."

"Oh," she adjusted her supple legs, still wrapped around his trunk, and ground her pelvis into his, "we both know that's not true." She unfurled her lower limbs with slow, gymnastic precision and returned to her feet. "But seriously, Wakefield. Why do you stay with them? Why don't you leave the service?"

"Gotta finish my twenty," he said matter-of-factly. "Still got a few years to go."

"And then what?"

"Retire with a full federal pension." Danny's reflexive answer was as pragmatic as it was rehearsed. He had given it a thousand times before, and would continue to do so until that magical date circled on a calendar he tried not to look at too often.

"There are other things you could be doing."

Ain't that the truth, Danny marveled. "You mean, like, get back to enjoying my vacation?"

"I mean," she slipped from his arms and sauntered back to the table and what remained of a bottle of Jameson, "you have skills. Marketable skills."

"Communication?" he baited her. "Emotional regulation? Problem solving and critical thinking? Soft skills like that?"

"Actually," Not-Anita poured a dollop of whiskey into one of the tumblers laid out for them, "I was thinking about your hard skills." She emptied the bottle into the second tumbler. "Weapons proficiency speaks for itself," she inspected both glasses, then sampled the fuller one. "You know how to fight, how to move on target." She offered the less full glass to him in her outstretched hand with a sly smile. "You're trained in intelligence collection and interrogation. Time at the Secret Service hasn't dulled you yet."

"What's that supposed to mean?"

The mystery woman jiggled the glass she prepared for him. "Your military skills are wasted on those fools in Washington, Wakefield. And it shows. Even so, I don't know what they have you doing at that desk, but clearly you haven't lost your edge."

Danny took the tumbler from her. "Thanks." *Where is she going with this?* he wondered.

Not-Anita took another hit from her glass. "Oh, c'mon, Wakefield. You're a field operative, not a desk jockey. Why waste your time in Washington when you could be making some real money?"

"Get tattoos up my arms and join those dirtbags at Blackwater? No thank you." Danny drank his whiskey as he walked back to his toiletry bag. "Those mercs ain't soldiers. Just thugs."

"Well-bankrolled thugs," she insisted. "But, there are other options." She drained her tumbler of its remaining contents. "With the right connections, you could do quite well for yourself."

Cops did not usually talk about these sorts of things. Generally, they did not even know enough about what went on in the shadows to form a meaningful opinion. Neither did most government employees - not from any government agency Danny had worked with in the past, anyway. *Well,* he considered, *maybe the CIA.*

"Who are you? Really?"

"Who do you want me to be?" Not-Wilson held the tumbler delicately in both hands. Her face softened just a bit. "I can be anybody, Wakefield. Anything I need to be. Whatever it takes to get the job done."

Red flags shot up in Danny's mind. Days of lies within lies, having his grief played upon so he could be manipulated, his personal time wasted on a fool's errand based on somebody else's problems, and now the woman who was not who she claimed to be and was altogether too comfortable with violence had just turned the crazy level up one notch too high to be safe. *I'm tired of playing games,* he seethed with clenched teeth.

Danny's .45 was in his hand before he was consciously aware he had drawn it from his hygiene bag. "Hands where I can see them," he ordered on instinct as the pistol's front sight post found its way to her center mass. "Do exactly as I say, or I'll burn you down."

"What the Hell, Wakefield?" The mysterious brunette was clearly caught flat footed by his move.

"Shut up." Danny's mind raced through a tactical analysis of a situation that he feared he did not fully control. *Big room,* he noted. *Inspires ideas. Makes someone think about possibilities. Increases the odds of a fight.* A memory flashed through his head in a microsecond - the sight of his companion as she easily held her own in a bar brawl. Her name might have been a mystery, but she was a fighter. Of that, Danny had no doubt. "Move to the back room," he ordered. "Slowly. And keep your hands where I can see them."

"Okay," Not-Wilson offered a confused, slow reply as she placed her glass on the table and obeyed his commands. "But, seriously, Wakefield. I figured we'd end up back there in a bit, anyway. There's no need to -"

"Shut up," he reiterated. When they entered the bedroom, Not-Wilson started to walk toward the right side of the room - where her bags sat covered by her puffy winter vest. "No," he stopped her. "Get on the bed. On your knees."

"Indeed," she coyly called back to him as she followed his instructions.

Danny ignored her flirtation. *Probably trying to distract me so that she can get the drop on me.* "Grab the headrail," he ordered.

Not-Wilson sang a musical shutter as she submitted to his command. "Oh, my, officer." She wiggled her tight rear in invitation. "Are you gonna frisk me?"

"Actually," Wakefield kept his Colt trained on her with a one-handed grip while he fetched a pair of handcuffs from the collection of pocket litter she laid out on the dresser. He quickly checked the stainless-steel bracelets' integrity - they seemed legitimate - and secured her left wrist tightly to the wrought iron frame. "Yeah." There was no trace of humor in his voice at all. "I am."

"What the -" she jerked and struggled against the stainless-steel manacles. Her eyebrows furrowed and her naughty smirk was replaced with a frown as frigid as the blustery air outside the cabin. "What's going on, Wakefield?"

Danny scanned the small room and found his rhino action revolver atop the dresser on the far side. It was well out of his handcuffed hostage's reach. "I know you're not Constable Wilson," he explained as he ran his left hand down her left flank. Her thin cotton night shirt and skimpy black panties did not provide many opportunities to conceal a weapon, but Wakefield was not in the mood to leave anything to chance. "The real Wilson is on her way here from Washington. She's been there all week with my boss," he continued as his hand brushed up her right side. "So who are you, really?"

Lighting flashed through the window's thin drapes. Something - a heel, based upon the feel of it

- slammed itself hard into Danny's pubic bone. It missed his more private parts, but the force of the precision blow to a tender area still doubled Danny over in half and drove the wind out of him. His captive's left leg snaked itself into his left armpit and her right leg collapsed his right elbow. Wakefield had not even recovered his lost breath before he was flipped head-over-heels.

Instincts and training took over his body. Danny's trigger finger transitioned to the pistol's frame while he was in midair. He tucked his chin in time to spread his impact with the bed safely below his shoulder blades. His right thumb blindly found the 1911's magazine release and ejected the handgun's ammunition source.

Not-Wilson's right leg slipped up from Danny's elbow and found purchase against his carotid artery. Her legs constricted like steel cables around his chest and neck. Under other circumstances, laying in bed with his face buried between a beautiful brunette's thighs would have been an absolute delight for both parties. But the way the unorthodox stranglehold cut off his air supply and restricted his blood flow diminished Danny's enjoyment of the situation somewhat.

Wakefield let his gun fall from his hand, balled up his right fist, and drove it mercilessly into Not-Wilson's midsection. Splayed out on his back, Danny could not put his weight behind the blow. But years of training and fitness provided him with quite a bit of useful muscle mass, and his fist still slammed into the woman's abdominal muscles like a sledgehammer. Tight as those abs were, her smaller body yielded to the laws of physics. The vice around

Danny slacked a bit. He hit her again, and this time was rewarded with a total release from his neck.

Danny cleared the thigh from across his face and returned to his feet, now on the opposite side of the bed from where he had started. Not-Wilson coughed and sputtered against a spasming solar plexus as Wakefield recovered his handgun. "If you think I won't shoot a woman," he retrieved his magazine from the floor and reloaded the pistol, then resumed a proper firing position from the foot of the bed, "you're wrong."

The raven-haired wolverine rolled onto her back and glared at him past his own sight posts. "Prove it," she dared him.

From a certain point of view, the path of his life was littered with bodies. From his time in the Marines, first as a sniper and then hunting terrorists as a TACHUMINT operator, to his last week in Washington, Wakefield spent much of his career - too much, some might argue - either laying bodies in the ground or helping others to do so. To say that he was not a killer would be disingenuous at best - and in all honesty, an outright lie. But Daniel Wakefield never killed anyone who did not pose a legitimate threat to himself or innocents. He was not a murderer.

Danny reset the 1911's safety lever and lowered it a bit. "Who are you?" He asked once more.

Suddenly, the fearsome beauty could not maintain eye contact with him. "You're better off not knowing."

"I'd say I'm better off having never met you," he stabbed. "But that ship's already sailed." He crossed his arms and leaned back against the wall next to the door. "We can stay here as long as it takes," he sarcastically offered. "The real Wilson's on the red-eye into Bozeman. You can tell me now, or you can tell her after I get back to my leave."

The wind howled outside as it drove heavy snowflakes against the cabin's wall, but the bedroom's gentle light was steady. Neither of them flexed a muscle or so much as blinked. Even the room's air remained motionless. But an invisible mask worn by each of them fell.

A very smart man once described time as less of a force and more like the wake left behind when objects within the universe interacted with each other. That description seemed to perfectly describe reality as the utter lack of any activity in the room stretch the space between each heartbeat into what felt like an eternity. Danny felt himself grow a year older with every breath as he waited for his captive to break.

Another flash of lighting outside gave birth to a peal of thunder. The slow rolling echo broke the stillness in the room. Finally, the brunette's brown eyes rolled. "My real name," she relented, "is Brenna." Her Canadian accent vanished. Her words suddenly carried extra phonemes, sounds that could only be explained if she was taught a version of English where the vocabulary was loaded with invisible letters which were somehow mixed into the normal lexicon. *Definitely not North American,* Wakefield noted.

"Brenna," he repeated. "That's nice. Brenna what?"

"Brenna Noneofyourbusiness, ya munter."

Danny pursed his lips and thought about all of the voices he had heard from all around the world. "That accent," he mused aloud, "Aussie? Kiwi?"

"Just let me go," she jerked against the manacle that held her to the headrail, "I'll head back."

"I'm betting on New Zealand," he resolved. "So why are you here, Brenna from the South Pacific?"

She rattled her handcuff again. "Had a job."

"Why do I get the feeling that job was *not* just to ruin my vacation?"

"Take off these bloody cuffs," she offered coldly, "and I'll disappear. You can get right back to it."

"Nah." Danny lowered his weapon to his side. Still wearing nothing but his pajama shorts, he casually turned and sauntered out the door. "But I *am* gonna get a drink." He made a point to let her see him take his time as he walked out of the room. *Let her think about how long, slow, and boring the night will be,* he plotted. *Boredom can make people want to talk about all sorts of stuff.* "I'm thirsty," he announced with a healthy dose of melodrama mixed with a splash of guilt. "Getting lied to always makes me thirsty." He made sure that he was plenty noisy as he reached the fridge and lazily plucked a bottle of water out of it. "I bet lying makes you thirsty," he offered over the sound of metal rattling against metal in the next room. "You want some water or something?"

Wakefield waited a moment with the door open, then shrugged at Anita's - no, *Brenna's* silence and let it swing shut. "Suit yourself." He opened the cool bottle and took a long, refreshing pull from it as he dragged his feet lazily along the hardwood floor. "Let me know if you change your mind."

Two steps shy of the bedroom, Danny saw the bed through the door frame. It was empty. "What the...?" Danny dropped his water, raised his .45, and rushed toward the dented pillows, ruffled sheets, and a pair of stainless-steel handcuffs that dangled from a wrought iron headrail. "Where did you -"

Barely a full step inside the room, something thrust Wakefield's gun upward as he swept his aim toward the blind corner to his right. He felt, more than heard, the *click* as something connected with the point of his jaw. His head snapped backward and his vision tunneled. Then something rammed into his groin like a charging bull. Danny doubled over as the urge to vomit fought against the need to scream. Finally, something hard hit the back of his head and he fell unconscious on the way to the floor.

CHAPTER 19

BRIGHT LIGHTS BLAZED inside the Gray Wolf Peak Casino. The lights on the walls shone solid.

The bulbs which floated amidst a sea of slot machines pulsed in waves, flashed, and whirled about in a visual vortex designed to draw the patron's eye - and their money - inexorably toward them like Charybdis itself. Warm whites, piercing pinks, beaconing blues, and glowing greens assaulted the eyes with a pallet which was preferred by the gaming industry and fast-food industry alike because some psychologists published a report years ago which indicated these particular colors excited people and made them want to *spend*.

Outside, the sum total of winter seemed to fall upon Montana all at once. But none of Wolf Peak's patrons noticed. There were no windows to offer a view of the Hellish weather or to remind a visitor of what time it was. There were no clocks, either, or any other visible indicator that some external variable might compel a person to leave. Exits were few and well hidden, and the air was thick with smoke so there was no need for addicts to even step outside for a quick nicotine fix. Like every other casino, Wolf Peak was designed to invite the weak willed and keep them there until they exhausted all of their hard-earned money on one vice or another. And if legalized gambling at machines and games rigged to favor the house did not do the job all by itself then there was always a buffet fully loaded for the gluttonous and morally flexible staff willing to provide bodies, drugs, or anything else to paying customers while their employer turned a willingly blind eye to their poor life choices.

"Y'all need to be hanging low," the beefy black man in the designer knock-off suit jacket and turtleneck sweater warned. Years working in a smoke-filled environment added gravel to the bouncer's naturally baritone voice.

"What we need," the younger Gage brother insisted, "is to find the dirty little wetbacks that're dogging us and put 'em in the ground."

"What Jimmy means," Justin interjected, "is that if you know where we could find your Sinaloa buddies," he unconsciously rubbed the potbelly protruding from his jacket, "we'd like to have a word with 'em."

Though he lacked much of a visible neck, D'Licious still shook his head slowly. "Look, man. You drop here. They drop here. The house plays to the customers' needs and everybody wins. I ain't paid to play favorites and my boss don't choose sides. I help mine. An' that helps everyone's business around here. I sure as Hell ain't gonna mess up my thing by rattin' on nobody."

"C'mon, my man," Justin slapped the oversized man on a shoulder that was as solid as a side of beef. "There's no way this comes back to you."

"There's a thousand cameras up in here," Dee-Licious reminded him. "You talkin' to me'll be on YouTube, anything happens. Or worse."

"And all those cameras," James spread his hands wide to either side in a gesture which universally signaled frustration, "just saw you tell us 'no.'" He withdrew one hand from his jacket pocket and tussled his teased and frosted hair. "So now nobody'll suspect you told us."

Justin scratched an itch somewhere within his scruffy face muff. "We just wanna talk to 'em, Dee. That's all."

"I ain't their momma," D'Licious insisted, "an' they ain't my people. I don't know where they hole up. an' I don't care where they bed down. They come here to drop product. Same as you. I got no reason to go to them."

James withdrew the second hand from his pocket. As he did so, a small green-white wad of paper fell to the floor near his foot. Neither of the Gage brothers acted like they noticed. But Dee-Licious caught sight of a familiar textured pattern on the litter as it fell and instantly recognized that it was not the wadded-up wrapper from a stick of gum. "People talk, Dee." His eyes flashed for the merest fraction of a second. "You never heard anyone talk about a place where a fella might hook up with the Sinaloas?"

The oversized black man's jacket sleeves threatened to split at the seams as D'Licious folded his beefcake arms across his barreled chest. His eyes flashed down to the paper wad barely a foot from James' shoe. Then he reached up with his right hand and scratched his bulbous nose with his thumb. The movement completely obscured any view of his mouth.

"Fox," D'Licious sniffed. He tucked his hand back into the crook of his left elbow. "You can play, or you can leave. I don't owe you guys nothin' either way."

"C'mon, Jimmy." Justin twirled his finger in the air. At his signal, James followed him to the nearest exit.

D'Licious stood in his place near the door like a small, blackened brick house and watched the Gage brothers for a half-dozen steps. Once the two little white boys were far enough away, the heavyweight bouncer stooped down to pick up James' litter. He tucked the paper wad, which had the unmistakable texture of American currency, into his suit jacket pocket. As soon as the drug delivery duet was out of sight, D'Licious ducked into a nearby bathroom and angled for the deepest corner. In the back stall, he unfolded the newly acquired paper wad and regarded an easily earned hundred-dollar bill. He smiled, folded the c-note, and tucked it into his pants pocket. He flushed the toilet - just to cover his tracks - then moved to the bathroom sink.

"Crackers gonna get themselves killed," he shook his head as he washed his hands.

*   *   *

Danny swam from the wrecked ship as quickly as his arms could pull him across the ocean's surface. Behind him, water flooded into the wooden vessel through a cavernous hole ripped amidships. The main mast and its sails laid out across the rolling sea. Wakefield spared a glance behind his shoulder as the mizzen and foremast bent impossibly inward and crossed as the once-mighty tall ship's bow and stern both rose into the air, and then each of the giant wooden daggers stabbed angrily into their opposite's deck. The self-impaled segments tumbled in death's embrace and slipped into the depths.

A few hundred yards ahead, a cliff face rose out of the sea. With renewed vigor, Danny kicked and pulled his way through the swells and toward *terra firma*. The tide's ebb and flow bobbed him up and down, back and forth, as he fought to reach safety.

The shore was impossibly far away, and the sea fought him with each stroke, but Danny paddled onward. In the face of long odds and impossible circumstances, he knew that he would either reach dry land or die trying. Those were his only options. Because it was neither the pounding waves nor a reef strike that cracked his ship's keel.

An angry mouth filled with a thousand teeth leapt out of the foaming surf where his vessel had just disappeared. A mask the color of pale death covered an otherwise cold, gray face whose jet-black eyes were orbs of the most vicious and hateful death in the sea. Even as surely as Wakefield knew sharks did not really roar, he swore he heard a murderous call from the thirty-foot-wide maw as the massive creature seemed to hang impossibly in midair, fix its stare upon the lone swimmer, then crash back into the sea.

Danny crawled across the sea with such fervor that it was little wonder he did not rise out of the water and run across its top. As he poured all his strength into the effort, a voice echoed in the back of his head. *A quick human can swim about three feet per second,* the unseen drill sergeant sneered in grim humor. *A shark is more than ten times as fast.* Wakefield did not know where his drill instructor got that information, but the monstrous fin that rose out of the water behind him belonged to a creature whose speed was scaled to its size. Danny might as well have been a gerbil trying to outrun a Ferrari as try to out swim the beast that pursued him.

Mid stroke, Wakefield *felt* the behemoth's jaws come out of the water as much as he *saw* them. Row after row of super-sized, razor-sharp, jagged teeth rose to either side of him as the carcharodon breeched the surface on its side. The world around him shrunk into blackness as the creature snapped its cavernous mouth shut. Danny's final image was that of countless giant teeth as they converged on his chest cavity -

Wakefield woke with a heavily drawn breath. His brain fought through a cottony fog that clung to his mind. *Sharks,* he groaned. Experience taught Danny that he only had shark nightmares when he slept in the cold. He forced his eyes open and stretched under the heavy blanket draped over his body. *If it's that cold in the cabin,* he sniffed, *somebody let the fire die out.*

Unconsciousness rolled off of him like a wave that receded back into the sea after it cast back to the shores of reality. But instead of a sandy beach, Danny found himself sprawled across a hardwood floor. He pried his eyes open to a vision of the cabin's bedroom swimming into and out of focus.

Sunlight filtered through the curtains and told the agent that it was well past his habitual waking hour. Danny pushed himself up to all fours and willed his vision to clear.

Oh, no...

A week ago, Danny would have been perfectly happy to wake up alone to an empty, silent cabin. This morning, though, his previously precious solitude meant only one thing: his target - Brenna, she called herself - was gone. *If that is, indeed, her real name,* Danny grumbled inwardly and blinked repeatedly until his vision cleared.

Wakefield rose to his feet and surveyed the bedroom from the open doorway. *Nothing.* Aside from the disheveled linens on the bed - from which, he noticed, the blanket on the floor where he laid had come - there was no trace of the woman who had spent the last few nights with him.

The cabin's brisk air helped sober him. Danny rubbed his sore face, then gingerly traced his fingers to a throbbing welt on the back of his skull as he bumbled to the living room. His own backpack and clothes still sat exactly where he left them. A quick check of his laundry produced his wallet, still in the pocket from yesterday's pants.

Danny sniffed and headed to the kitchen and dining area. His phone sat on the table along with a pair of tumblers and last night's whiskey bottle. His bronze and black 1911 was placed near the phone in Weapon Condition Four - its magazine was ejected and the slide locked back to reveal an empty chamber.

But there was no sign of his White Rhino.

Danny shook his aching head. *Bitch still has my gun.*

A knot appeared in the pit of his stomach. Regret at having ever trusted the strange woman grew into insult at having his gun stolen from him. It multiplied into dread of what she might do with the firearm and became a cloud of impending blame that would fall squarely on Danny's shoulders in the aftermath.

Wakefield scooped up his phone and shuffled to the door. He punched up his father's phone number, then opened the portal to behold a vast sea of snow which was at least waist deep, but shallow enough to show him that the driveway was empty.

My Jeep! Danny stood wide eyed. Bracing air blew past him and rushed into the cabin, but the wind was not what froze his hand halfway to his ear. *That. Dirty. Bitch!* Pain behind Danny's eyes throbbed and pulsed once more.

Snowflakes the size of postage stamps floated lazily through the air as they fell to the ground. Last night's thundersnow had expended the worst of its energy, but today's clouds still held a full wintery payload. Any other day the sight of such weather would have been beautiful. But now every falling flake felt like a boulder dropped between Danny and any solutions to his problems.

A distant voice sounded from the phone clenched in Danny's outstretched hand. His mind snapped back to reality. He blew the breath out of his lungs and shivered as he closed the door and moved toward the fireplace.

"Hey, Dad," Danny lost the fight against a shiver. He switched to speakerphone mode and busied his hands with kindling. "Everything okay there?"

"I'm fine," the elder Wakefield lazily replied. "Tyler's late gettin' in this morning. Says he can't be out here to work until the plows make it out to his neck of the woods. I told him to trade that little coupe of his for a four-wheel drive," David grumbled. "Oh, well. Live and learn. I'm just keepin' warm in the house 'til he gets here. No point breakin' my back doing a young man's work out there."

"How's the livestock?"

"Cows'll take care of themselves," David assured him. "At least, for a while. If they couldn't, they'd've gone extinct a long time ago. You okay, son?"

Danny stuffed a fire starter under the kindling, then plopped a small log atop the nest. "No," he admitted, "I'm not."

"This got anything to do with the Troopers who've been in and outta here askin' about you?"

"Actually, Dad… I could use a hand with that."

"What's the problem?"

Shame joined the regret and worry in Danny's gut. It felt like the time back when he was a teenager when he had to tell his dad that he wrecked his car. He recounted the last thirty-six hours' events in the briefest terms possible.

"Well," David's voice was slow. Cautious. "I was plannin'' on headin' up to the Wilkers' ranch later today. But that can wait, under the circumstances. What do you need?"

Danny breathed a sigh of relief. "I'll need my winter kit bag," he extended his first finger. "It's the black duffle in my closet." He counted on a second finger, as unseen by his father from the other side of the phone as the first one was. "And my gray AR-pistol kit," he threw a third out, "and my four-wheeler."

"I'll grab your gear," David acknowledged, "but your four-wheeler ain't here anymore."

"What?"

"You gave it to Miss Kitty to cover your part of the damage to her place the other night."

"Oh, I did, did I?" Danny's eyes went wide in disbelief. "And when, precisely, did I do that?"

"About an hour after you left here with your treacherous new lady partner," the elder Wakefield answered rather matter-of-factly.

Danny's head spun as he became more sanguine about his utility vehicle's fate. *Dad must've given it to her*, he realized. *His way of apologizing. And paying for the damages.* "Well," he huffed, "I hope she gets good use out of it."

"I'm sure she will." The phone did little to hide the smirk in David's voice. "Well, it'll take me a while to get up there in this crap. Interstates're mostly clear, but it'll take a while for crews to clear all the streets and get into the back roads. Probably best I grab your stuff and burn pavement. You need anything else?"

Like another kick in my balls? "No, Dad. I'm good." Danny plucked a wand lighter from its perch next to the fireplace. He flicked it on and set to ignite the fire starter when inspiration struck him. "Actually, Dad, can you bring my winter bow and quiver, too?"

"They're still in my truck from last week," David reminded him.

Small points of flame glowed on the starter block. "Great." In a moment, the starter would ignite the kindling, which in turn would light the main log and, in turn, put some heat back into the chilled cabin. "Thanks, Dad."

"I'll see you when I get there, Son."

CHAPTER 20

BRENNA'S EYES FLICKED back and forth between the screen built into the Jeep's dashboard and the building before her. The building's frontside was adorned with wide overhead doors, and the back apparently opened into the gated area that doubled as both salvage yard and parking for finished vehicles. And according to the history on Special Agent Wakefield's helpful tracking program, a certain highway patrol cruiser visited the establishment well after business hours last night, lingered for a bit, then hit the open road.

Brenna knew a chop shop when she saw one. The innocuous looking building in the middle of nowhere was just a little out of synch with the local area. *Salvadore's Auto Repair,* the sign read. Not Bob's, or Jake's. *How many Salvadores could there be in Big Sky Country?* she wondered. *And how many gringos would rather take their car to Salvadore than to Joey? Or their Uncle Mike?*

Salvadore's was a little too big, Brenna decided, a little too far removed for casual traffic to just wander by and see shop's daily activities. The fences, metalwork, and fixtures on the doors were just a little too new. They showed no evidence that the business suffered from typical struggles such an establishment might be forced to manage.

Brenna shut off the borrowed Jeep's motor and took a deep breath. She jumped out of the truck and tried not to slip in the snow as it crunched under her boots. The parking lot had obviously been cleared once this morning or she would've been forced to wade through powder up to her chest, but fat flakes continued to fall from the gray sky with no end in sight. She kept her hands in her puffy vest's pockets as she rushed through the freezing wintery air and into the building's customer entrance. A cowbell rattled against the door's interior and signaled her arrival.

The building's interior was home to a miasma of motor oil mixed with a tinge of sweat and cigarette smoke. The odor hung in the air, assaulted the nose and eyes, and penetrated the pores. Brenna wrinkled her nose and kept her breathing shallow. *I'm definitely gonna need a bath when I leave this place.*

Loud music from the maintenance bay flared and then returned once more to a dull roar as the door that separated the main workspace from the customer service area opened to admit a resident grease monkey, then closed once more. The mechanic wore a ragged red ball cap with the local high school's mascot stitched onto its face. The lad looked to be just a few years younger than Brenna and could have been cute enough in his own way if the same variety of fluids that stained his coveralls had not seemed to have found their way into every pore, crack, and crevice on his face.

"Hey there," the mechanic smiled from the far side of the littered countertop that which obviously did double duty as a customer service space and - based upon the dusty ashtray and stray particles strewn about - smoke pit and wiped his oil encrusted hands on an old towel. "What can I do you for?"

Brenna stayed near the door and pointed out the window. "My Jeep's actin' kinda funny," she answered in a Southern drawl and a shrug. *A good country accent,* she reminded herself, *makes guys think you're dumb. And easy. Just don't lay it on too thick.* "Once it warmed up it ran oh-kay, but when I first started it this mornin' it was a li'l rough."

"Might just be the cold," the grease monkey opined. "You got a block heater on it?"

"I," she toed the floor sheepishly. *Tennessee,* she told herself inwardly, *not Alabama. You're from Memphis, Tennessee.* "Uh, I don' know what that is."

The mechanic looked at her dubiously. "How long you lived up here that you don't know to have a heater on your engine?"

"Well," she let out slowly, "it's really my boyfriend's Jeep. And he usually takes care of that kind of stuff. But he's outta town for a few days. He's a driver, and they've got him hauling a tanker from the oil patch."

"Ah," the dirty dude smiled. "I see."

"I really hope I didn't do somethin' to it," she mewled. "He'd be so pissed if he came back and thought I broke his Jeep."

"Well," the mechanic came around the counter and peered out the dirty front window, "I can take a quick look at it and see what's what."

"Oh, thank you!" Brenna brightened.

"Billy," he extended his right hand, which Brenna figured was as clean as it was likely to ever get.

"Jesse," she smiled as she shook his hand. "Thanks, Billy. You're a life saver." His hand held onto hers for far more shakes than it normally should have before he finally released it.

"So, how long until your boyfriend gets back?"

Brenna looked out the window nervously to hide her covert scan of the room. "Should be back tomorrow. He's been gone a while." Her sweet faced suddenly soured. "I hope this won't cost too much." She dug her hands deeply into her puffy vest's pockets and adopted a shy, helpless posture. "Things've been kinda tight lately. Honestly, we need the money from this run just to get through Christmas."

The rancid mechanic drifted just a little closer to her. "Well," Billy looked back and forth between the red Jeep in the window and the raven haired beauty before him. "We might be able to work something out." His eyes flashed. "If you catch my meaning."

"What do you -" The most genuine expression of shock exploded across Brenna's face, timed perfectly to mimic comprehension of the scandalous behavior implied by his offer and painted with a sense of surprise that she did not feel in the least. It was a well-practiced look. "Oh. I mean, won't you get in trouble?"

The greasy mechanic shook his head with a smirk. "Nobody back there'll notice anything," he assured her.

Brenna bit her lower lip and pointed above the door. "Well, what about that camera? I don' want this turnin' up on the internet for everyone to see."

"It don't work," he scoffed. "Cameras here are just for show. They're all dummies. Keeps folks from pinching parts off the shelves, them thinkin' we're watching out for thieves and all." The twenty-something's face transformed into a visage that Brenna had seen many times before - that of a man whose mind had become fixated on his own genitals and where, precisely, on her body he could get away with putting them within the next few minutes. His lecherous gaze drifted down the length of her torso. His lip curved and his eyes flashed as they lingered on the curve of her hip, so visible thanks to her skintight leggings...

... which left him completely unprepared for her right hand as it slammed into his trachea. Stunned, the grease monkey choked as the sensitive tissues in and around his windpipe flared and swelled shut. Instinctively, he clutched his throat with both hands and coughed for air. Brenna quickly snaked both hands around the idiot's neck. Her left hand cupped the base of Billy's skull and the right cramped down on his jaw. Then she twisted his head hard in a spiral. The leacher's neck *popped* and his eyes, already half closed, rolled backward as he fell to the floor like a sack of potatoes.

Brenna dropped low and dragged Billy's body across the floor. She tucked him in tightly behind the ashy customer service counter, then crept over to the door into the service bay. The normal chorus of tools, music, and voices sounded from the cavernous space, but there was no indication of alarm or concern from its occupants.

She stayed low to the floor as she withdrew the aluminum spike concealed within her vest and slinked through the door and slipped along the garage's interior wall. Brenna's every movement was silent, purposed, like a lioness which circled a herd of gazelles in the savanna. Right before her, like a gift from the universe, stood her prize: a blue Peterbilt tractor truck with freshly filled patches in the body. The primer over the repaired panels looked like it had not quite dried yet and there was an unmistakable tinge of paint fumes in the air. *Bingo,* she smiled. *Now, where are you cheeky little bastards?* Her eyes scanned the room, peeked around obstacles as new sight lines opened up to reveal potential targets.

Brenna spied a pair of beat-up boots from under the Peterbilt as they rounded the truck's far corner and angled toward her. She dove under the big truck's chassis and slid headfirst across the smooth concrete pad. Brenna barely caught the metal lip of a cavernous pit beneath the big vehicle with her free left hand and turned a potentially painful fall into a soft, graceful landing. An attendant, startled by her unannounced appearance as he worked on some random issue with the truck's undercarriage, jumped. Brenna thrust her dagger into his voice box and silenced him before he could make a sound. The mute mechanic fumbled at his throat in vain as he choked on his own fluids. Brenna kept her brown eyes up and her ears perked for any indication of alarm as she lowered the dying man to the floor in a rumpled heap.

One less, she told herself. *How many more to go?*

An impact wrench sounded in bursts from the far side of the bay. Brenna counted the torque gun's whines as she caught sight of the ratty boots which had circled the truck to the side from which she came. The boots continued for one, two, three rattles. Then two more bursts from the pneumatic tool. The walker was near the Peterbilt's front driver side wheel when another whine sounded and Brenna lashed out. She seized the boot's ankle and yanked hard. The sound of the pedestrian mechanic's impact with the ground was masked by the windy gun's wail. Brenna pulled him into the pit like an unseen demon and sent the shop worker to Hell with a thrust of her weapon to the base of his skull before he regained enough breath to scream.

The petite brunette stood in the pit and peered around the rest of the bay in search for more targets. A dozen paces away or so, a tool jockey dropped his pneumatic driver onto the concrete slab, scooped up a mallet, and started banging on something Brenna could not quite see. That far again past the garage monkey, a closed door led to what she assumed was the manager's office. The view under the other vehicles in the bay did not reveal anyone else.

Brenna breathed deeply through her mouth to oxygenate her blood. She crouched down, wiped traces of gore from the Deathridge Toothpick on one of the bodies at her feet, and tucked the spike back into her vest. The adrenal singing in her ears quieted as her heart rate approached normal.

With her mind clear and her senses perked, she drew the suppressed Walther from its place of concealment and climbed out of the oil pit. The mechanic's grunts overshadowed the faint *click* of the pistol's safety as Brenna thumbed it blindly. She kept her head on a swivel and checked the office door every few seconds as she silently padded up behind the oblivious worker. Barely two paces from the stooge, she raised the pistol from the low-ready, took aim at the back of the greasy guy's head…

… and swore under her breath the rear bay door opened unannounced. The mechanic turned his head toward the rising bay door, which allowed him to see Brenna in his peripheral vision. His startled jump caused her shot to enter his shoulder instead of his skull. A quick clean-up shot finished the doofus, but Brenna had to leave the body and scramble for cover behind the Subaru Outback the attendant was repairing.

Sunlight, amplified by the reflective blanket of snow on the ground, washed into the garage through the yawning maw. A wave of cool air blew into the bay. Brenna crouched down, held her pistol near her ear, and bit back a curse through clenched teeth.

"Julio?" a guy's voice called, "you about finished with that break job?" Brenna lowered her head and peeked under the car's green bumper to spy a pair of rich, chocolate, alligator skin boots stomp white powder onto the gray floor. The boots started clockwise around the car and headed toward the office door. "We're gettin' backed up in here, guys. Hey -" the boots paused after a few steps, "where's Trevor?" The boots altered their course a few degrees and continued to circle the Outback more quickly. "Hey, Julio? You hear me?"

The fancy footwear's equally slick-looking owner rounded the car's hatchback and turned to see Brenna on one knee with her pistol aimed at him. Normal people froze flatfooted at such a sight, but Salvadore's startled yelp was accompanied by a jump and desperate dodge at the precise second Brenna loosed a double-tap at her target. A pair of chalky clouds erupted from the painted cinder block wall above and behind where Salvadore had been just a split-second prior.

Brenna rose and tracked Salvadore's dive around the blind side of a red Honda Civic parked behind the Subaru. She rounded the little coupe with her pistol ready and just in time to see Salvadore scramble around behind the car. Brenna reversed her direction and shuffled between the Subaru and the Honda to cut him off, but when she cleared the smaller car there was no sight of Salvadore on the other side.

Brenna stared past her Walther's sights as she slowly walked around the little red obstacle. "Seriously?" she taunted. "Are we really gonna play this game, Salvadore?" She arrived at the back of the car, but was met once more by bare concrete. "You gonna make me chase you like a kid around the couch?" She crossed behind the coupe, came around the rear quarter panel -

Salvadore sprang like a snake from concealment behind the rear wheel. The Walther spat once more as he drove the pistol up above his head. Momentum carried him bodily into her and drove Brenna backward into the big bay door, which rattled with the impact.

A crippling strike from Brenna's left knee collapsed Salvadore's right leg, and a double hammer blow to his chest dropped him to the pavement. But Salvadore maintained a death grip on the Walther all the way down to the ground. As he fought to keep the gun pointed away from himself, Salvadore slammed the point of his left boot into the side of Brenna's face. Blinding pain erupted from where the kick connected with her cheek. She tripped on Salvadore's pronate form, stumbled, and her grip on the gun slacked as she fought to remain conscious.

When Brenna's eyes opened again, she found herself staring down the business end of her own suppressed pistol. Formless yellow and red ghosts clouded her vision and painted paisley patterns before her eyes. She blinked hard against the sight of Salvadore holding her handgun and scooting backward along the ground.

"Hands on your head, *puta*," the chop shop owner ordered. With no alternative other than a bullet, Brenna obeyed. "I don't know who you are," he growled as he pushed himself back up to his feet, "but you messed with the wrong *hombre*." Salvadore sneered and kept the pistol trained on her. "Now, get on your knees."

Buy time, Brenna silently told herself as she sighed and lowered herself to the cold pavement. *Wait for your opportunity.*

"Now, put your hands on the ground," Salvadore ordered.

Brenna slowly complied. "You know," she heckled from her hands and knees, "you really ought'a -"

Salvadore cut off her smart remark with a kick to her head that would have scored the winning goal in the World Cup.

CHAPTER 21

"THAT SONOFABITCH." James held up two steps inside the diner so he could digest the sight before him. The diner was filled with plow drivers and long-haul truckers who stuffed themselves into booths and surrounded tables as they warmed themselves up with hot meals and bottomless cups of coffee in between runs. And at the main counter, with their backs to the entrance, a trio of Mexicans marked with Sinaloa tattoos on their hands and necks sat laughing and joking with Russel Gage.

"Play it cool, Jimmy."

"Can you believe this shit, Jay?"

"I said," Justin patted his younger brother on the shoulder in caution, "cool." The elder Gage brother's eyes moved behind a set of reflective sunglasses, the kind favored by commercial drivers. He rubbed his rotund belly unconsciously as he took in the quartet's layout. His father's attention was split between a single Sinaloa on his left and two who sat to his right. Justin weighed his options. "Follow my lead," he purred. "But go right, just in case."

The Sinaloas chuckled as Russel turned back and forth with wide-eyed amusement. "So then I says to the guy, 'Wrecker? I don't even *know* her!'" His rasping cackle was joined by a slap to table and elicited laughter from his lunch companions.

"Hey there," Justin leaned against the counter next to the gang banger on the far left and stared past the cartel member and into his father's eyes. "How's it going?"

James appeared uncomfortably close behind the *chollo* on the far right. "*Hola!*" he offered with a sarcastic smile.

The quartet suddenly grew silent. Patrons who sat to either side of them at the counter wordlessly cleared the vicinity and found reasons to be in other areas of the diner. A few customers dropped bills on the counter and walked out the front door to continue their day with far fewer troubles than what looked to be brewing behind them.

"N-n-now, boys," Russel stammered.

"Pick a side," Justin warned his progenitor in a low, slow voice. "Right now. *Dad.*"

The Sinaloa closest to James started to rise, but the youngest Gage clapped a hand on his shoulder hard enough to push him back down to his stool. "We don't wanna do this here," James mewed into the younger guy's ear as his right hand, unseen between them, traced a line over the Sinaloa's kidney with his karambit. "But we will. If you make us."

Sweat beaded on Russel's forehead as he pushed down on the air over the bar with both hands in a soothing gesture. "Now boys," he said more softly than before, "let's just take a step back and calm down here."

Justin placed both hands on the shoulders of the Sinaloa in front of him, but his eyes remained locked on Russel. "We're all goin' for a ride," he sneered. "So, you wanna ride up front with us? Or in the back... with them?"

"N-n-now, boys," Russel explained for the umpteenth time, "I had no idea they was after you."

There was no shortage of wide-open spaces in Montana. That was part of the appeal the state had for a lot of people. What a man did in such vast, ungoverned territory was largely between himself and God. And God rarely filed a police report.

The white Ford F-150 King Ranch sat parked in just such a private expanse with nary a soul in sight but for the Gages save the three Sinaloa members, each of whom was zip-tied to one of the pickup's aluminum wheels. The truck's fourth wheel remained free - for the moment. But everyone there knew whether it stayed that way or not depended entirely upon how Russel Gage handled himself over the next minute or two.

The cold did not make Russ shiver as much as the revolver his firstborn pointed at him while they talked. And the two-pound engineer's hammer which bounced in the youngest Gage's hands chilled Russel straight through to the bone.

"If that's true," Justin wagged the .38's muzzle like a finger in a *naughty, naughty* gesture, "then yer brain's fried from all that dope you been smokin'."

"And if it ain't," James opined, "it means you were about to sell us out." He slapped the engineer's hammer against his palm again. "Probably for more drugs."

"I n-n-never... They came to me, okay? They was askin' questions. But I di'n' tell 'em nutin'. Just like them cops."

James cocked his head. "What cops?"

"Them cops 'at came out lookin' fer you the other day. I told you 'bout 'em, di'n' I?"

Justin scanned the horizon for the hundredth time since they stopped the truck in the middle of nowhere, but the only sight to be seen in the gray afternoon was more falling snow. "What'd you tell 'em, Pop?"

"N-n-n-nutin," Russ insisted. "An' there was, like a dozen of 'em at least. One as big as a bear! Must'a called in ev'ry SWAT guy this side a' Helena." Whether born from pride, brain damage, or drug-induced hallucinations, Russel's interpretation of his encounter grew even more epic than a strictly literal version. "They laid inta me good. But I d-d-di'n say a word 'bout you boys."

James shook his head in disgust and grabbed Russel roughly by the back of his neck. "You're sure about that, old man?"

"Don' you lay hands on me, boy," Russ slapped his youngest son's hand away from himself. Suddenly and inexplicably, he found his backbone. "I'm yer father! I'll lay a whoopin' on you so fierce -"

An upper cut to Russel's gut ended his paternal threat before he could finish. James stepped aside before the oldest Gage puked, then grabbed him once more by the scruff of his neck. "We ain't kids no more, ya' little old bastard." He hoisted Russ and growled into his sire's face, which trembled with indignation mixed with pain. "You ain't got the horns to tussle up with a real man." Mercilessly, he threw the stringy old man face-first down to the snowy ground.

"Throttle it back just a bit, Jimmy," Justin cooly ordered. "It seems," he called out to his captive audience, "that there's no shortage of folks lookin' to cause problems fer me an' my brother here." He paced through the snow with his eyes on the horizon and his empty left hand on his belly. Up on this raised knoll the found in the middle of nowhere, the powder was only a little more than knee deep. "So here's what we're gonna do. The first one of you that starts tellin' me what I wanna hear gets to walk away. If yer lucky, you'll live long enough to make it back to the highway. Might even manage to hitch a ride before frostbite takes all yer toes."

"I swear," Russel shivered and wept on all fours, "I di'n' say -"

James booted Russel in the face like a field goal kicker trying to win the Super Bowl from the wrong side of the field. The force of the blow knocked the old man onto his back. His unconscious body punched a fresh hole in the thick snow the shape of a fallen angel. The older man stopped shivering and laid in the deep powder. More flakes fell from the sky into the hole and buried him in a frozen grave.

"Anyone else got anything to say?" Justin demanded. "Anything worth hearing?" The only sounds uttered by the Sinaloas were the panting grunts of desperate men as they tried to escape their bonds. Even fueled by adrenaline and fear, though, the supine thugs were no match for the industrial strength polymer fasteners which secured them to the pickup's thick aluminum wheels. "No?"

James slapped his arms in a bid to warm himself, but to no avail. "C'mon, Jay. We're gettin' nothin' but cold out here." He walked over to the Ford's unoccupied tire and kicked the powder from his boots.

Justin stepped over one of the Sinaloas - who tried to trip him on the way to his door - then climbed up into the driver's seat and brushed the snow from his legs. He started the engine and listened to the gangbangers' renewed efforts as he kicked his own boots against the truck's step rails once more to clear any remaining powder from his footwear. As soon as he heard his brother's door open and close, he shrugged and slipped his legs the rest of the way into the vehicle.

Screams of protest sounded from three of the Ford's corners, but Justin heard nothing that helped him. "You know," he slipped the big truck into low gear, "given enough time, I think they'd be able to find an edge an' saw through those ties." He waited patiently as James adjusted the cabin heat, then released the brake and drove lazily across the open terrain. The big 4x4 truck plowed a fresh path through the virgin snow. They bounced every now and again - whenever they drove over a particularly large rock or an especially thick patch of frozen grass hidden by the deep powder.

*   *   *

"It's not funny, Dad."

David Wakefield made no effort to stifle the chuckle that bubbled up as he examined the Johnson cabin's bedroom. "Ho, but it actually is." Danny's frown made it clear to David that his son had still comically missed his point. "You still don't see the error, do you?"

"Never trust a woman?"

David shook his head. "You're not a cop. *That's* the point." He rubbed his eyes and sobered his mind. "You were a helluva Marine, son. And you're great at being an investigator. But you're not a cop. You're not trained as a cop. You don't have cop experience. And as a result, you made a rookie mistake."

"I let my prisoner out of my sight," Danny nodded.

"Nope. You didn't properly frisk her."

Danny thought about his brief scrape with the woman he now knew to be named Brenna. "She wasn't wearing much, Dad. There weren't a lot of places for her to hide anything. And I didn't feel anything when we grappled up."

"Look at the facts, Son," David insisted. "Follow the evidence where it leads you." The retired cop pointed at the top of the bed frame. "The headboard's undamaged. That means she didn't break loose. She unlocked her cuffs. Probably had a handcuff key tucked into her panties or clipped inside her headband. Was she wearing a headband? Or a bandaid somewhere? Bah, it doesn't matter. Point is, you're not used to dealing with detained folks. So you're not used to thinking like a cop - or like a desperate inmate. Or a career criminal. So you don't have cop habits - like thoroughly frisking your detainee and sweeping the insides of their clothes - socks, skivvies, everything - for surprises. And checking their mouths. And any other body cavities where they might've tucked something." For the first time all day, David's eyes grew deadly serious. "You're lucky, son. You know that?"

Danny did not want to admit that his father had a point. But at this juncture, his pride would only get in the way of any chance he had at success. "How do you figure, Dad?"

"Gal's got skills," David reminded him. "And she slipped right out from under your nose... *without* hurting you."

Danny pointed to the shrinking welt on the back of his head. "Not *totally*, Dad."

"It'll heal," the elder Wakefield waived off the minor injury. "Sure, she took your Jeep. Your pride's the only thing she really injured. But she could'a killed you, son."

"I suppose."

"No question," David affirmed. "Except, of course, as to why she didn't." He looked his son meaningfully in the eye. "Now, maybe your bruised ego isn't letting you think straight at the moment, but a cop would ask that question."

Danny scratched the back of his head. The welt felt better - as long as he left it alone. "Alright, fine. Why didn't she kill me, Dad?"

"Normally," the elder Wakefield stroked his whiskered chin thoughtfully, "the most likely explanation would be that she didn't see you as a threat." He looked at his son. "Now, anyone with half a brain knows you're a fighter, son. And she's seen you in action. So that's probably not it. Not this time." David tapped his chin. "After all the cloak and dagger you said she's been pulling the last few days, makes sense to me if she left a witness that can identify her then it wasn't by accident."

"Maybe she doesn't think I'll figure out who she is. With that thick of a Kiwi accent, I bet money she's not living in America full time. There's a good chance she's not in the system."

"Nah," David waived the idea away like an annoying insect. "No matter how careful you were up to now, she's gotta figure she's on borrowed time now."

"Unless," an epiphany struck the younger Wakefield, "she assumes the opposite."

David's skeptical eyes scrutinized his son. "You think she stole you Jeep and assumes you're not gonna call it in? Why? Out of embarrassment?"

"Maybe she assumes I'll come after her." Danny looked out the window to Montana's thick wintry blanket. "Maybe that's what she wants me to do. Maybe she's not escaping. Maybe she just wants a head start."

"That's a lot of 'maybes,' Son."

"She wants me to follow her," Danny decided. "You said it yourself, Dad. She's got skills. But she's also not all that bad - in the evil sense, I mean. You're right: a stone-cold killer would've done me in last night while I was out."

"Maybe she's sentimental." David spared a meaningful glance at the bed. "You've been up here a couple of days. Alone with a pretty little thing like that." Pride mixed with a jocular grin on his face. "Maybe you made an impression?"

"It's not like that, Dad."

David's eyes cut back to his son. "You're telling me you two didn't go to the mattress rodeo while you were here?"

"No," Danny blushed, "I'm saying that she acted like she was recruiting me for something. She was testing me, Dad."

"And?"

"I think she wanted to see if I'd go off the reservation. Whatever she's up to, it's something she doesn't think a strait-laced federal agent would be down with. And since I couldn't do it with her, this is the perfect way for her to get it done."

David shook his head. "I think you're reaching, son."

Danny's phone erupted. "That'll be Little D," he smiled. *That was quick. Finally, I catch a break.* But as he activated his phone, the agent did not recognize the inbound number. "Go for Wakefield."

"You're ruining my Christmas, Chumly," a voice equally familiar and unfriendly growled through the handset.

"Oscar." Danny furrowed his brow and double-checked the incoming number displayed on his phone. "This isn't your work number."

"I'm not at work," the diminutive man explained.

Danny heard a soft slurping sound from the other end of the phone. *Is he drinking?* "Where are you?"

"Atlantic City," Oscar replied. "I'm on vacation, Stretch."

Danny's face wrinkled in confusion. Of course, this close to the holidays most people took some time off from work. But Wakefield knew his buddy from the National Security Agency well enough to know that the homunculus was a native of the D.C. metropolitan area. "Doesn't your family live in Fairfax County?"

"Yep," Oscar sighed, "and if I wanted to spend the holidays with those turds, I'd be in Virginia." Oscar took another long, audible pull from his drink. "Look, Chumly, the office isn't supposed to bother me unless it's an emergency. Hence the clean phone. But when they buzzed and told me your buddy Martin was calling on your behalf, well…" He paused, then lowered his voice in the closest approximation of sympathy he was capable of delivering. "I know the last few weeks've been hard for you, Stretch. If this was for anyone else, I'd still be at the table."

Danny's mind flashed to Oscar's involvement in the incident that ultimately claimed his lover's life. Wakefield didn't blame the NSA analyst for that night's events. He was just there to help Danny take down a serial killer. But even someone as openly misanthropic as Oscar was capable of feeling a certain level of guilt for a comrade's loss. "Thanks, Oscar. I appreciate that."

"Well, let's not spend all day at the condolence parade. I've got to get back to work."

"I thought you said you're on vacation," Danny countered.

"Working vacation," Oscar expanded. His voice changed. It took on a strange buzz, like he was talking with his teeth clenched. "I put a hundred bucks a paycheck aside all year long. Each December, I take the cash and hit the casinos."

"You gamble?" Danny's eyes went wide in disbelief. "The guy who's always poo-pooing on the lottery?"

"The lottery's not a game of chance," Oscar hissed and buzzed. "It's a surtax on stupidity."

"And what're you doing?"

"Blackjack. Which, when you think about it abstractly, is just applied mathematics and probabilities."

"Maybe. Until the money runs out."

"Losers run out of money, Chumly" Oscar corrected him. "I'm up two gee's so far today. I don't gamble. 'Gambling' means there's a chance you might win or lose. I do math. Blackjack's all about counting cards, calculating probabilities, and reading the other players. I've got a system."

"If you're in a casino right now, Oscar, you *have* to know that you're on camera. And they employ lip readers to work in the security booths, watching the feeds."

"Of course they do, Stretch." Oscar sounded just a little offended. "That's why I'm talking to you without moving my lips. While standing with my face less than a foot from a blank wall."

Danny snickered and shook his head. "You truly are the most paranoid person I know, Oscar."

"Thank you. What you call 'paranoia' I call 'tradecraft.' Besides," the NSA analysts' already-hushed voice dropped even lower, "if they figure out my system, they'll blacklist me."

Wakefield let loose a melodramatic gasp. "So then you'll have to vacation like normal people?"

"I usually bring home ten to twenty grand after a week in places like this," Oscar grumbled. "Two years ago, I took a couple of joints in Vegas for close to fifty large. Saying goodbye to that kind of money has effects on my lifestyle. And my portfolio."

Realization dawned upon Danny. *I always thought you lived pretty nicely for a GS-12.* Previously, Wakefield assumed that Oscar's comfortable lifestyle - his underground home beneath a Maryland winery, his posh dining habits, his cozy car, and so forth - was the product of yet another a government employee who spent half their time day trading penny stocks at work. With no dependents, almost zero supervision, and access to high-speed internet, Oscar would be far from the first federal employee to earn a recreational income on the taxpayer's time. But it turned out that the diminutive cryptologist had a very different alternative revenue stream from what Danny ever would have guessed.

"So, Chumly," Oscar's voice returned to normal, "let's cut straight to it. You're in over your head. Go home."

"I was home," Danny countered. "That's how this whole mess started."

"Well, then drop it and go back."

Confused and annoyed, Danny shook his head. "Why? What do you know? What's going on?" He switched on the phone's speaker function and silently pantomimed a *shush* to his father so both Wakefields could hear Oscar's explanation.

Static drifted across the line, which Danny assumed was caused by a sigh from Oscar. "Fine. Agent Martin forwarded the pic you sent him to me for facial recognition. Nothing special about the cop. I mean, he's got a couple of suspects in his past who wound up as corpses and a funny pattern of mucking up cases involving druggies tied to the Sinaloa cartel just enough for the perps to walk. It's all low-level stuff, easily explained away and spread over the years. But it's too many sigmas from the norm to be nothing. Still, even your little brain was probably tracking some of that."

"Pretty much."

"Well, Chumly, what you don't know is that the cute little piece of trim next to the window is one Brenna Jacobs."

"And now I have her last name," Danny nodded. "You say that like I should know who she is."

"You're lucky you don't have a grave," Oscar's disembodied voice countered. "Jacobs is a gun for hire. High dollar, too."

Danny's eyes went wide. "She's a hitwoman?"

"She's a top shelf international wetworker," Oscar re-iterated. "She makes Delta guys look like Special Olympians on Valium. We don't even have an intelligent estimate as to how many bodies she's put in the ground. Sometimes she shwacks a mark herself. But her stock and trade is getting others to do her dirty work for her. That's why we can't get a firm body count for her. Remember the guy from the Kenyan parliament a few years back?"

"Honestly, no."

Another burst of static sounded from the speaker. "You Muggles are so cute, what with your tiny world view and short memories. Anyway, we have reason to believe she was recently hired by a Dutch ecstasy syndicate to neutralize the Jalisco cartel. They're an outfit outta Mexico that's been flooding the drug market here with their own cheap product. They call it MeX. It's a portmanteau of Mexican Ecstasy."

"Yes. Thank you, Oscar. I got that."

"Well, Chumly, it's cutting in on the Euro-trash's profits."

Danny nodded. "That would explain why she's looking for a pair of Jalisco drug runners."

"Honestly, Stretch," Oscar's laughter was anything but joyful, "sometimes it's painful to watch you neurotypicals all swing and miss at the easy pitches. You don't hire someone like Jacobs to snuff out a few piss ant mules, Chumly" the little man condescended. "You hire her to start a war."

"Wait," Danny started grappling with an idea. "You said the dirty trooper is tied to Sinaloas. But Brenna's after Jaliscos." *What was it she mentioned?* he fought to remember from an earlier conversation. "Was there a hit along the Canadian border recently?"

"Just north of you," Oscar confirmed. "Couple of Border Patrol guys ate it. Surveillance video shows a couple of truckers, too. One of 'em dropped a few of the hitters. Mostly with a knife."

"James Gage," Danny confirmed.

Oscar continued. "Dead bad guys came back as Mexican Army vets with checkered pasts. Exactly the kinds of guys cartels court as enforcers. None of these idiots were choir boys, but there's nothing solid tying any of them to anyone in particular. Looks like budget muscle. None of them in Jacobs' league."

"That's it!" Danny hissed. "She's trying to start a war between the cartels. Get them to wipe each other out. So she hired a disposable crew to do some of the heavy lifting and then let the chips fall naturally."

"I knew you'd catch up eventually, Chumly."

"Now you see," Oscar's voice took on a new level of humorlessness. "This is none of your concern."

"Look, Oscar, I've got orders to -"

"Not your monkeys," Oscar cut him off, "not your circus. Do yourself a favor, Stretch. Take a dive. You don't always have to win every fight."

"How would you -" A dark sensation in the pit of his stomach made Danny stop himself mid-sentence. *She's a bad person who leaves no trace of her involvement in bad things,* he blinked again. *And the NSA is knows her well enough that Oscar called to warn me away from her.* "Dude. Tell me she isn't one of your assets."

"Not mine," he insisted. "But I'm not the only person who works in the Puzzle Palace, am I?"

"Dude."

"All I'm saying is that I owe you one for that screw up at the White House, Chumly. And I'm settling that debt right now by telling you this: this road only ends in pain for you. And that's the best-case scenario. You don't want anything to do with this bitch or anything she's involved with."

"She's got my Jeep," Danny insisted.

"Then call LoJack. File a police report. Let the insurance company buy you a new one. Walk away from this one, Stretch. While you still can."

"Anything else?"

Wakefield's question was answered with a *click* and a dead line.

CHAPTER 22

"WELL," DAVID SNIFFED, "ain't he just a beam of sunshine?"

"Oscar's an acquired taste," Danny scratched his beard as his mind raced through options. "Thanks for bringing my gear, Dad. I'll see you back at the house in a day or two."

"Oh, no. No, no, nononono. You aren't seriously going after this chick. Are you, son?"

"You've got things to do, Dad."

"Son, think this through."

"I am, Dad."

"Are you?" David challenged his son. "Are you really? 'Cause right now, it doesn't look to me like you're thinking with your brain."

"What's that supposed to mean?"

"Son, I love you to the end of the Earth. But right now, you're gettin' led around by your pride."

Danny thought back to the phone call with his boss. "I've got a job to do, Dad." After he heard the words as they came out of his own mouth, the younger Wakefield thought that with just a little more conviction he could almost convince himself that he meant them. "Wiley wants to me to crack her. Find out where it leads."

"Sounds to me like everyone else knows more than you," David snickered. "What else could your boss hope to learn?"

"Clients?" Danny guessed with a shrug. "Contacts? Who knows? Maybe he thinks she's behind something he's chasing. I don't know."

"Think, Son," David insisted. "How are you supposed to investigate something when you don't know what it is? You just gonna go fishing around in this gal's world until something your boss likes bites? I thought I raised you to be smarter than that, boy. How are you supposed to hunt something when you don't know what it is you're after?"

"But I *do* know what I'm after," Danny hummed as he fished a pair of winter camouflage bibbed pants from the big black duffle bag his dad brought him. "I'm after Jacobs." He slipped the camo layer over his trousers. "And the key to finding her is finding my Jeep." He stepped into his thick boots, then withdrew a pair of camouflaged gators from the bag. "And thanks to Little D," he switched his phone to display a map with a waypoint highlighted on it, "I know exactly where that is." The former Marine dropped his phone on the table and pulled his boot laces tight. "Phone's synched to the Jeep. Updates the location for me every time it parks." He fastened the gators over his boots, then pulled a matched jacket from the bag. "Like I said, Dad. She wants me to follow."

David looked at the location highlighted on the phone's screen. "I know that place," he scratched the scruff on his chin. "Night like tonight, they'll see headlights comin' miles away. And even with that heated gear, you'll freeze in this weather tryin' to go on foot."

"Drop me off a couple miles out," Danny instructed as he checked the batteries that powered his jacket's built-in heating coils. "I'll hump it in from there."

"Better yet," David pulled his own Colt 1911 - a plainer version of the same .45 Danny carried - and checked to make sure there was a round in the chamber, "we can go in on horseback. Dismount a couple hundred yards out at a spot I know."

"What'd'ya mean, 'we,' Dad?"

"This ain't you flyin' off to Afghanistan, Son. You think I'm gonna go home and sit in a rockin' chair like some geezer while my boy goes into harm's way? Out here? In my own backyard?"

"Dad," Danny warded him off, "this isn't cop work. This is either gonna go real easy, or it's gonna get real ugly."

"Lucky you I ain't a cop anymore," David smiled as he re-holstered his pistol. "There's a tree line just East of the main road," he traced an imaginary line along the map on phone's screen. "I'll cover you from there. You go in soft, slow, and quiet like."

"Cover me with what, Dad?"

"Son," David offered a wizened smile, "you don't think I only brought *your* bag, do you?"

*   *   *

"Dirty *puta* killed four of my guys!" Salvadore spat. "That's more than half my regular crew!"

In the chop shop's rear storage room, cleared of its normal contents by his remaining minions, Salvadore paced back and forth in a rage. At the center of the room, where there used to be a collection of auto parts on neatly organized shelves, his would-be assassin stood with her hands bound and raised by an engine hoist. The skin around her right eye darkened by the minute in an expanding patch of pink-turned-green-turned-violet.

"Easy there, *chefe*," Justin held out his hands as he tried to placate the angry shop head. "That ain't our fault."

"Seriously?" Salvadore's eyes went wide in disbelief. "You two roll in here with a truck fulla bullet holes, and the very next day this crazy chick comes in and whacks my guys, and you don't think that's related?" He pointed through the closed door and out toward the main bay. "I've got Trevor painting over bullet holes in my own wall where she nearly shot me! You know my rules, *mayn*! You don't bring trouble into my house!"

James leaned against one of the walls with his feet crossed and his hand on his chin. It was a rare moment to see him in such a contemplative mood. "Hate to admit it, Jay, but he may be right." The younger Gage looked at the metal surplus desk which remained in the room and the collection of hardware laid out upon it after their prisoner had been searched. "Judgin' by that knife an' the work she did with it, I'd say this ain't her first rodeo.

And," he pointed, "that ain't the first pistol with a homemade can on it we've seen lately."

"What'er you?" Justin sneered at his little brother, "Colombo? Alluva sudden, you're on his side?"

"No, Jay. All I'm sayin' is it looks like whoever's got a hard on for us is willin' to come after us on neutral ground. That ain't good for anyone."

Salvadore's phone instantly appeared in his hand. "Now I gotta call in extra guns to watch the place while I scrounge up a new crew. *Hijo de las mil putas!* I ain't playin' with this bullshit." He stopped mid-dial. "I don't know who you pissed off and I don't care who it is. The next *mamahuevo* who come out here lookin' for trouble is leavin' inna body bag." He glared at the Gage brothers. "Your truck will be ready in the morning. Take it and get out."

"As you wish," Justin nodded.

"And don't come back," Salvadore barked. He punched two more digits into his phone, then his eyes came back up again. "Oh, and you owe me extra for the cleanup on that Ford. It looks like you took it off-roading in a field of hamburger." With his piece evidently said, Salvadore raised the phone and stormed out of the storeroom.

With their host's attention temporarily focused on other matters, the Gages were left to entertain themselves. Justin looked at Brenna, strung up by the engine hoist. "Now," he slowly traced a circle around his bulbous midsection's perimeter, "what did we ever do to draw the ire of a gal such as yerself? Eh?"

"Sod off," Brenna growled, "ya wainkstain."

Justin snickered at the barb and responded with a surprisingly powerful punch to her gut. "Now, I done asked ya once who sent ya." He brushed the hair from her face. "If I gotta ask you again, you'll have *two* black eyes."

"That ain't gonna work, Jay," the younger Gage clucked as he watched his brother's efforts from beside the desk. "Just look at her. Some bitches like to get hit. They're fighters. They don't break like that. They get off on it. She's one of those."

"And you've got a better idea?" Justin challenged.

The younger Gage measured their captive with his gaze. His eyes traced a path up one side of Brenna's figure and down the other. "Gimme a few minutes," James tossed his thumb toward the door. "If I can't crack her, she's all yours."

Justin spent a long moment considering the request as he tossed his fist into his own hand as if he was warming up a baseball mitt. "Fine, Jimmy," he relented. "But I'll be back in ten minutes with a wrench to do it old school." He glared at the petite brunette. "We'll see if takin' her kneecaps out takes the fight out'a her."

James watched his older brother close the storeroom door behind himself, then pushed off the desk and walked slowly toward Brenna with his wickedly curved knife in hand.

"Tough guy when you've got me all tied up," Brenna sneered. "Let me loose and we'll see how tough you really are, tosser."

James ignored the taunt. "I heard this guy on the radio," he picked some unseen debris from the *karambit's* curved tip, "talkin' about when they're about to abort a baby, the first thing they do is slice the vocal chords." He pressed the blade's unsharpened trailing edge hard against Brenna's throat just to get her attention. "That way, they don't have to hear the baby's screams." His breath came wet against the nape of her neck. His whispered voice was heavy in her ear.

Brenna closed her eyes and bit back a scream as the *karambit's* unsharpened side descended over and past her clavicle. She felt cold steel upon her breastbone, then heard the *rip* of fabric as the blade caught her zippered top and tore a long line down its front until it cleared the bottom seam. Her jaw set itself firmly closed as James' rough hand seized her exposed chest and pulled her backward into his aroused body.

"I like to play games," he purred into her ear as he pulled on her waistband. "My favorite is the rape game." He slipped the knife between her leggings and her butt cheek. "Have you ever played the rape game?"

"No," Brenna shuddered. She tensed as the cold steel blade ripped a line through her leggings' thin fabric. James dragged the weapon slowly from the top of her hip, over her tight muscles and down the back of her thigh.

"Oh, good," James said slowly, "you know this one."

CHAPTER 23

DARK PATCHES BROKEN up by rivers of white in her coat made Cinnamon disappear against the nighttime wintery landscape. The snow had finally stopped, but the thick blanket of powder muffled hoofs as they struck the frozen ground. A camouflaged poncho broke up his visual outline and made it hard to distinguish Danny as a human form. Under the poncho, battery powered hunting pants and a matched jacket kept him warm as he bounced on his broken in saddle. A step to Cinnamon's left and a half step ahead, David Wakefield's mount pushed through the snow and led the way.

Danny felt a tingle in his breast. He reached inside his thermal layers and found his phone as it vibrated in silent mode. Embarrassed, Danny halted his horse. *We're far enough out I better take this,* he decided when he saw the Washington area code on the screen. "Go for Wakefield," he answered quietly.

"Danny Boy," Jonas Wiley's bright voice greeted him from a thousand miles away. "What's going on?"

"Living the dream," Danny dodged. "Where's Wilson? I saw online that her flight last night never made it."

"Yeah. It got re-routed to Regina. Up in Saskachewan."

"But she got another flight, right?" Danny fished. *Please, tell me she didn't get another flight.*

"That close to home, the Mounties called it all off," Wiley explained. "Gave me a line about budget and whatnot, but if you ask me, nobody wants to work tomorrow."

Danny nodded as he considered the date. "Christmas Eve is usually dead for most offices." Officially, government offices were only closed for weekends and declared holidays. Even then, policy was to keep essential services running to ensure agencies provided critical functions like law enforcement and fully operational military capabilities. In practice, though, non-essential personnel who worked for the federal government tended to find creative ways to transform a federal holiday from one official paid day off into three, four, or a week. In the case of Christmas, that typically snowballed into the entire month of December getting transformed into a period of non-productive time in just about any federal agency or office. And even essential services tended to run on skeleton crews for Christmas and the surrounding days.

"Ain't it funny how many people who hate Jesus the rest of the year insist on milking His birthday for all it's worth?" the old Jesuit quipped. "Anyway, the Mouties still want your suspect, even if they're not willing to do any of the work themselves. So they asked me to have you just bring her in. Just drop her off wherever's convenient. We'll arrange transfer of custody from there from this end. You're back on vacation."

Danny blew a cloud of smoke into the frozen night air. "Well, boss, that's gonna be a bit of a challenge."

"Oh, Hell." Jonas suddenly sounded like he had not slept in a week.

"You see, I tried calling you, but cell service has been spotty since the storm, and I just got into an area where I could get a signal."

"I'm not gonna like this at all, am I?"

"She gave me the slip, sir. At dinner," Danny wove, "just a couple of hours ago. Went to the ladies' room at a restaurant and slipped out the window."

"You spooked her," Wiley resolved.

"No, sir. You know me. I'm better than that."

"Then why'd she ghost on you?"

"My best guess? Whatever she's really up to, it's going down tonight. And she didn't want me to see it."

Dr. Wiley grumbled unintelligibly on the other end of the phone line. "Do you have any idea where she might be?"

"Little D got me her real name." Danny's bluff was close enough to the truth that he hoped his seasoned boss did not detect any deception in his voice - or if he did then he dismissed it as simple stress. "I'm working a short list of associated locations right now."

"Look, Danny Boy, this has rather quickly become Not Your Problem."

"I've got this, sir."

"No," Wiley grew insistent, "listen up. You were on personal leave when this fell in your lap. And now the justification for using you is pretty much evaporated. This isn't a cooperative case anymore. We're getting played. And I'm not gonna ask you to put up with it. Especially not over the holidays. I'm putting an end to this."

"Sir?"

"This is no longer a matter of expedience or convenience. Not for you and not for the Secret Service. The Bureau's field office in Seattle has jurisdiction. I'm handing this off to them. You're back on vacation, son."

"I've never failed you before, sir -"

"And you still haven't, son," Wiley cut him off mid-sentence. "Martin gave me the biography on this bitch. Under the circumstances, there's no shame in getting out maneuvered every once in a while."

"Sir," now it was Danny's turn to insist, "I've got this."

"Those are the most dangerous words in the English language, Wakefield," Jonas warned. "At this point, son, the juice just isn't worth the squeeze. You've got a few more days on your vacation. Take them, then head back to D.C."

Danny sat upon his horse as unmoving as an island in a sea of snow. "Yes, sir," he relented. "It's a two-day drive, but I'll leave on the twenty-sixth and be back by New Year's Eve."

"See that you do, Danny Boy," Jonas directed. "There's work for you to do here."

"Roger that, sir. Out." Danny powered his phone off and stuffed it back inside his electrically heated jacket. He blew a stream of air out of his nostrils as if his nose was a pressure valve. Barely three yards away, his father stared at him through the darkened night from atop his own saddle.

"I hope you're more honest with me than you are with your boss," David scowled.

"It's more or less true," Danny hedged. "Close enough for government work, at least."

"Sounds like your reason for caring about this whole Brenna nonsense just disappeared." David's mount kicked at the frozen ground. "What'chu gonna do?"

What's the use? Danny wondered. *She's not my problem. I'm officially free again.* Oscar's warning, fresh in his memory, echoed between his ears.

"Your buddy had a good point," David opined as though he read his son's mind. "Smart move would be to head back to the ranch, report the stolen vehicle, and let the insurance agency and the authorities sort it out."

"Yeah," Danny allowed. Still, he did not steer his horse one way or the other. Something inside his gut ate at him. At first, he dismissed the discomfort as being born from the way he had been manipulated for the last few days. But the more he thought about it, here and now, the more he realized that he was disgusted with himself.

I've been selfish, he realized. *Wallowing in self-pity. Hiding from life. Refusing to carry on since* - he swallowed a lump that formed in his throat - *since Sandra.* "Dad," he managed aloud, "how'd you move on after Mom died?"

David sniffed a snoot full of cold air. "Well, Son, it wasn't easy." He maneuvered his horse so that he was once more alongside Cinnamon but faced in the opposite direction. "You wake up each morning," the elder Wakefield shrugged, "even though you don't want to. And you decide to just try to do your best each day not to fail the people who're counting on you." David patted Danny's shoulder with a heavily gloved hand.

Danny let his father's words sink deeply into his normally protected heart. They touched a previously unstruck nerve.

Special Agent Wakefield never really thought of himself before as anyone else's reason for living. He was sure his ex-wife never felt that way about him. He was confident none of his previous lovers did, either. And if he was totally honest with himself, he had to admit that his romance with Sandra had never really reached that depth.

"Your mom and I spent a lot of years together," David continued. "We lived for each other. When someone who means that much to you goes away, it hurts." He looked up into the cloudy sky. "But eventually, you find other reasons to live. And you do the best you can to make sure they're good reasons."

"Thanks, Dad. That really means a lot to me." Danny thought about his own situation. *I'm being selfish with my time,* he realized. *Sandra wouldn't want me to spend my days wallowing in self-pity. She'd want me to live.* His fallen partner was dear to him, but she was not his life. She never became his sole reason to live. Or to work. He did not have what his parents had with each other - not with her; not with anyone. But maybe that was okay. He could still feel the pain of her loss without being devastated for the rest of his life. He could honor her the same way he honored any fallen comrade: by trying to do the right thing in life.

An emotional fog thicker and darker than Montana's winter night seemed to lift from Danny's soul. The younger Wakefield drew a deep breath, then kicked his horse back into motion. Cinnamon snapped out of whatever daydream danced in her simple equine brain and pushed forward once more.

"Where're you going?" David asked, now a few steps behind his son.

"I'm done with the pity party, Dad."

"The truck's back this way," David reminded him.

"I know," Danny acknowledged. "But I'm gonna get my Jeep back."

CHAPTER 24

BITS OF MOONLIGHT filtered between cloudy patches which dotted night sky. Light and shadow danced with each other, traded places, and transformed the snow-covered ground into a silvery quagmire. Winds came and went sporadically in the aftermath of the storm. They reshaped the snow, creating gullies and snowdrifts which sculpted the previously flat landscape into a terrain littered with white hillocks and powdery knolls.

Something that was neither shadow nor shimmer moved like a ghost from one tree to the next. Formless, it merged with the tree. It became the tree. After a moment, it emerged again and moved to its next host. If it left any tracks - and everyone knew ghosts most assuredly *did not* - that trail was lost among the shadows and shifting silvery powder.

The phantom stopped on the edge of the tree line a few dozen yards from Salvadore's shop. Its shadowy, hooded head surveyed the front parking lot. A prized red Jeep sat under a light dusting of snow near the customer service door. A Montana Highway Patrol cruiser occupied the parking space nearest to the Jeep. A smorgasbord of cars and trucks littered the streetside parking apron - not as many as were in the secured rear parking lot, but enough to account for a significant number of warm bodies on the grounds this evening. The ghost moved onward along the treeline to continue its tour.

One of Salvadore's mechanics huddled in the pool of light cast by the security lamp above the chop shop's side entrance. With an AR-15 slung across his chest, he shivered as he mumbled sweet words into his cell phone to someone who was disappointed that he was not home tonight as expected. He never heard the inaudible *thong* of a taught string's release. He never saw the 700-grain smokey gray shaft as it sailed through the air. He never felt the broadhead enter his skull and perform a spontaneous lobotomy on him. He simply fell face first into the snow and let his girlfriend continue her side of their conversation.

The gray and white ghost rounded the building's corner and drifted along the chop shop's rear exterior wall. It paused beside the office window and carefully peeked into the room to see a handful of people engaged in a heated conversation. Then the wintry specter continued onward once more. Another window gave the ghost reason to pause again, but this time its unseen eyes spied their objective. The ghost produced a heavy black blade, forced the metal instrument into the window's seams, and pried itself an unguarded entrance into the building.

Brenna was on her bare knees in the middle of the room. She hung slack from a pair of restraints fastened securely around her wrists and suspended from an engine hoist's cold chain. Tattered remnants of her sleeves remained on her arms. Strips of black fabric clung to parts of her legs. What was left of the rest of her clothing was cast aside in a heap in one of the room's corners.

Bathed in the room's harsh florescent light, the white and gray figure pulled off the poncho that obscured its form as it moved silently to the closed door. Covered by a white camouflaged mask, a much more man-shaped head pressed up to the hatch and listened hard at the sounds beyond it. Momentarily satisfied, he rushed to Brenna's side and set to work on her bonds.

Brenna shook reflexively and tried to squirm away from the camouflaged intruder. The ghost *shushed* as a gloved hand pulled his mask away and revealed Danny's face, painted with a mixture of sympathy and anger. "Can you walk?"

Brenna's eyes were a mixture of torment and rage. "I'll bloody well walk outta here." She was a mess. Wakefield's newfound pity was written all over his face. "Gage," she croaked in answer his unasked questions. Brenna jerked her bruised face toward the door. "Coming back," she warned.

One last tug on the knife freed Brenna's wrists. Danny helped her gently lower her arms. Stretched as they were and starved of blood, he knew the muscles had to reinvigorate before she could use them again. Once her hands reached her lap,

Wakefield stripped his heated white and gray jacket off of his body and draped it around her shoulders. He pulled the cozy garment tighter around her torso. "Less than thirty meters to the tree line," he outlined the egress route. "Horses are a bit northeast from there."

Before Danny could explain his plan any further, the storeroom door opened. A portly truck driver in blue coveralls stood with an oversized monkey wrench in his hands and a look of utter shock on his face.

Knife still in hand, Danny leapt across the room without thinking. The former Marine acted on pure instinct and conditioned reflex. He caught the wrench wielder's backhanded blow mid-swing with his left hand and drove his Kabar's thick blade straight into the other man's throat.

Wordlessly, the potbellied redneck's mouth opened and closed. His eyes defocused and the wrench fell to the floor with a *clang*. Danny lowered the sputtering, gurgling man to the ground, dragged the dying body away from the doorway, then quickly closed the hatch.

"One down," Brenna's gravelly voice confirmed as she rubbed her arms back awake. "That's Justin Gage."

Danny extracted his knife from the gristly wound and wiped it clean on the corpse's clothes. "How many others here?"

Brenna fed her arms into the jacket's sleeves, then pushed herself up to her feet. "Slotted four earlier. Heard them call in reserves." She fetched her weapons from the desk along the far wall.

"I dropped one on the way in." Danny strode over to the window and pushed it open wider. "Way back out should still be clear for a few minutes," he declared as he re-sheathed his combat knife.

Brenna pressed the magazine into her pistol, then checked the chamber. "Good luck," she coldly offered.

"Exit's that way."

Brenna crept toward the door. "And the knob head who did this to me is *this* way."

Even if Danny had not known she was an assassin, there was no mistaking the murderous intent in Brenna's eyes. He caught sight again of the ripped remnants of her leggings, which barely hung onto her calves.

Wakefield did not need an explanation for what happened to her. Nor did he want one. Without asking, his mind told him of the indignities this woman must have suffered. The memory of another raven-haired girl - Jenny, Carlos' girlfriend - painted a gruesome enough picture of what they did to Brenna before Daniel arrived.

Suddenly, it no longer mattered what her name was. The injustice of her treatment made Wakefield's blood boil. He did not care why she was there. The memory of is own reason for being there evaporated. His vision tunneled into a small field painted with crimson rage at what these animals had done to his companion - and his own failure to prevent it from happening.

Hell with it. Basic instincts ran hot through Danny's veins: the innate desire to protect someone against an overwhelming threat; his natural - and nearly pathological - need to see justice for the oppressed; a compulsion to hunt those who would prey upon others. *They're animals,* his instincts told him, *and they should be put down like animals.*

Danny drew his .45 and produced its suppressor from pouch on his left hip. He threaded the can onto its host and, out of unconscious habit, pulled the slide back a fraction of an inch. The sight of brass confirmed that a 230-grain hollow point bullet was in the chamber and ready to fulfill its created purpose. He joined Brenna at the door. "On three," he whispered.

Brenna swung the door open before Danny made it to '*one.*'

Still recovering from her injuries, the assassin ducked her already short frame and advanced quickly to the left with the graceful fluidity that only came from years of experience. Danny crouched low followed her through the door, but checked the right side of the room to cover her rear firing arc. His immediate firing arc looked clear, but he heard a pair of voices on the far side of the maintenance bay talking as he walked backwards and followed Brenna's lead.

Danny walked backwards as Brenna advanced, then took position on the opposite side of the closed door along the shop's rear wall and remembered his view into the room. Wakefield waved at Jacobs to get her attention before she burst into the room blindly. He held four fingers from his left hand aloft where she could clearly see them, then wiggled the thumb a few times and quickly dropped his first two fingers in an inverted 'V' shape. *Four or five people,* the universal hand signal silently said. He pointed at her, then gestured to the wall closest to himself. *You go right...* He pointed to himself, then bladed his hand to the opposite wall... *I'll cover left.*

Brenna burst through the door and drove her pistol into the office. A yelp sounded, but was quickly drowned out by a double tap from her gun. Danny was cleared the doorway a quarter second behind her and swept from left to right.

His suppressed 1911 barked at the first person along his line of movement. Then the second. Among the *thoom-thoom* of his .45, Wakefield heard the *pap-pap... pap-pap* of his partner's pistol. By the time he swept halfway across the room, there were no more targets to drop. Danny spared the barest of glances to survey the bodies on the floor.

Brenna nodded her head toward the corpse seated behind a cheap metal desk. He was dressed much more stylishly than the departed souls on the floor around him. *Not that those designer clothes could stop a .22,* Danny mentally noted.

"That one's the owner," Brenna narrated before she turned to leave the room. More voices sounded from the maintenance bay. They shouted nonsensically amongst each other. The petite brunette swapped her spent magazine for a fresh one and poised herself at the doorway. "One more to go."

A shotgun wielding thug burst through the door. Danny snap fired his .45 and dropped the tango before he could bring the shotgun into play. A silhouette just outside the open portal elicited two more quick rounds from the 1911 and fell to the concrete as well.

"Just one?" Danny mocked.

"Gage is the only one who matters," Brenna grumbled. "The rest of these mooks don't count."

"Their bullets do," Danny countered. "Just wait a second, okay?"

Brenna gritted her teeth in obvious protest, but she stayed in place. Her pistol was trained on the door, ready to burn down anyone who came through it.

Danny keyed the radio on his hip. "Dad," he called, "we need Aunt Brenda."

Back at the tree line, a little *pop* sounded from a nondescript shadow with a clear line of sight to the chop shop's rear parking apron. A faint trail of sparks - easily unnoticed, given the firefight inside the building - leapt from the shadow and arced gracefully over the parking lot's fence. The subtle, glowing ember at the trail's head bounced off the hood of a garish orange hotrod and came to rest under a 2000-gallon fuel tank.

The beauty of the 37mm firework's colorful burst was, sadly, lost by the secondary fuel explosion which illuminated the parking lot with a huge orange fireball. As the only individual who was prepared for the blast, Danny was also the only person in the building who did not duck for cover at the thunderous *boom* - save for Jacobs, who flinched slightly then seized upon the distraction as her opportunity to bolt out of the office. Either the explosion engulfed a power relay or David shot out the transformer - from inside the chop shop, the younger Wakefield had no way of knowing for sure. Either way, the main overhead lights all blinked and died. As the emergency wall lights kicked on, Brenna caught the first thug with a single shot through the crown. Danny raced out the door and swept the dimly lit maintenance bay right in mirror to her leftward advance through the cavernous chamber. A double tap from Wakefield splattered the rear bay door with red confetti. The thug from whom the ichor originated fell backwards and slid down the metal panels - one of which was adorned with a pair of half-inch holes which were not created by the original manufacturer.

A quick exchange of gunfire behind him spun Danny's attention backward, where he saw Brenna stride past two crumpled bodies on the concrete floor. Jacobs headed toward the shop's front showroom slowly, with measured steps. She stared down the sights of her suppressed pistol and scanned the blind side of every vehicle and piece of equipment she passed in search of new targets. Her eyes were wide with fury beyond any which Wakefield had ever seen before.

She isn't fighting these guys, Daniel's own sympathetic rage subsided just a bit with the realization, *she's slaughtering them.* Brenna spared neither a word nor a glance at her hands as she stripped the suppressor from her pistol and stowed both parts in the field coat's deep pockets. When her hands came up again, she gripped a wicked looking aluminum spike in her right hand like an ice pick.

Gunfire sounded from the front of the shop as Brenna and Danny angled around the blue semi cab and speed-walked toward the door to the customer service area. Wakefield blinked and looked at his partner a dozen feet away. None of the shots seemed to be directed toward them.

Brenna threw the door open in the blink of an eye. Just as quickly, she cupped the forehead of the thug who stood immediately inside the darkened room and drove her spike into the space between his first cervical vertebra and the base of his skull. The thug was dead and on the floor before anyone else in the room even had a chance to turn toward the door.

As coincidence had it, that fraction of a second was also the exact amount of time it took Danny's brain to realize that everyone in the other room had been staring out what was left of the front window.

Furthest from the window and flanked by a handful of thugs on either side, Trooper Dietz locked eyes with Special Agent Wakefield. "There!" he pointed through the door. "Take em -"

Even with the lights off, Danny saw the crimson fountain burst from the chest of the thug nearest to the shop's main entrance. Caught flat footed and with his attention split between the dark winter night and the federal agent, the crook fell to the ground and became little more than a heap of cheap laundry piled on the commercial grade carpet. The remaining members of Dietz's felonious posse shot their guns blindly out the gaping viewport and into the dark night. They sought cover from their unseen assailant among the store's displays and behind the service counter.

Reflexively, Danny ducked away from the doorway to avoid incoming fire. Then his brain kicked in. *Sniper's got them hemmed in,* he smiled.

Thanks Dad.

Jacobs moved like liquid death. Her athletic form flowed around the doorframe without seeming to take up any space of its own. She struck like mercury as her knife drove into the thug behind the counter twice, thrice, into this rib cage, then a fourth thrust into the side of his neck for the *coups de grace.*

Danny crept back toward the doorway with his 1911 at the low ready. As if in answer to an unspoken prayer, a flaming red flare flew into the room and lit its interior with a bloody glow. His view into the front room improved, he saw Dietz creep up to the far side of the counter Brenna was hidden behind with his pistol held high next to his ear.

Danny took aim and adjusted his sight picture to make sure he missed Jacobs. He fired the last round from his magazine. The 1911's slide locked to the rear. The shot went wide and struck the wall harmlessly past Dietz, who ducked further into the blind side the counter anyway out of habit.

More shots rang out while Wakefield loaded his final magazine into his pistol. A rapid series of holes traced a perforated line through the cheap wooden counter about a foot and a half up from the floor.

Dietz. Apparently fed up with all pretext, the crooked trooper fired blindly through the cheap cabinetry, which did nothing to slow the bullets headed toward Brenna's crouched form. Before Danny's slide returned to battery, though, Brenna pulled the lifeless form of her perforated felon up and used the dead man to catch the few projectiles that happened to sail her way. She fell to the floor under her human shield. Danny sent two rounds of his own through the furniture. Dietz, ever determined, sprang up like a Jack-in-the-Box and vaulted the splintered barrier to confirm his kill.

A wicked red plume burst from Dietz's leg and flew away from the window while the dirty cop was still in mid-air. Pain wracked his nervous system and ruined whatever acrobatic foolery had previously occupied his mind. He crashed clumsily atop Brenna's bullet sponge. Silver streaked within the shadow in a blurred line as Brenna needled the nefarious policeman like a sewing machine.

The two remaining thugs leapt through the ruined window in a desperate bid to escape the room which was fast becoming a mass grave. Brenna, weighed down by four times her mass in dead meat, was in no position to give chase. Danny, no longer in the grips of bloodlust, let the petty crooks flee into the night. When he heard no follow-up shots outside, he realized his father must have made a similar decision from the tree line.

Adrenaline faded from his system like the flare that fizzled on the floor and grew dim. Fatigue from the fight - and the hike before it, and the ride before that - began to set into his muscles. Danny heaved a sigh, lowered his weapon, and shuffled into the front room to help Brenna disinter herself from her macabre dog pile.

The former Marine had endured a hard few days and came out of a heated fight none the worse for wear. *Gotta swap the barrel outta this gun,* he reminded himself as he unthreaded his suppressor. *Lose this one in a dumpster somewhere in Bozeman after an acetone bath.*

His mind already set into motion planning a quick but clean exit from the premises before any authorities arrived. The last thing Danny wanted was for himself or his father to be linked to this mess in any way. "The first thing we need, he announced to Brenna as he slipped behind the customer service counter to help her up, "is a really good alibi."

The last detail Wakefield failed to notice as he ducked down, however, was the shadowy figure that slipped out from underneath the blue Peterbilt truck in the bay behind him.

CHAPTER 25

THE KARAMBIT TORE a savage line across Danny's shoulder blades. Pain ripped a howl from his soul and caused him to stumble to his knees with his eyes closed. His bronze gun fell to the floor and skittered away blindly.

"Squeal, little piggy."

Beneath two bloody bodies, Brenna froze at the sound of her rapist's voice.

"Jay always said you didn't win a fight by doin' all the hittin' yerself." James glanced at the blade that curved forward beneath his littlest finger and the trace of red along its edge. "You win it by bein' the last man standin' at the end." Gage saw the bodies scattered about and stopped himself short before he stepped in front of the window. He took a cautious step backward toward the door to the maintenance bay.

Danny winced and pushed himself back to his feet. "You'll be James, then."

"Jay was supposed to meet me at the truck if anything happened," the last remaining Gage looked back into the shot-up bay and the bodies which laid in pools of their own blood.

"You can catch up with him in Hell." A dozen or more paces separated Danny from James. The former Marine mustered all of his hate and focused it like a laser designator at the lowlife in front of him. *Drug mule,* a dark voice in the back of his mind called. Wakefield pulled the Kabar from his hip. *Murderer.* Slowly, step by step, he found the strength to keep pushing himself forward. *Rapist.* "I'll arrange the meeting."

Danny launched himself the last few yards. He slammed into James like a dirtbag seeking missile armed with murderous intent. The *karambit* slashed toward him in a deadly right hook, which he blocked with his left arm and answered with a momentum-powered thrust from his own blade.

James slipped sideways and avoided being skewered. His weapon hand shot upward and drew a red line across Danny's left forearm. Wakefield disengaged and shook the fire out of his wound.

First rule of knife fighting, Danny reminded himself. *You are going to get cut.*

Gage's eyes flashed in the bay's low light. The shadows and highlights on his face twisted into a murderous smile. For a moment, the visage of Guy Fawkes' humorless grin flashed in Danny's mind. A new surge of anger fed his fury.

Wakefield lunged once more - this time for a nearby tool chest. He scooped up a four-way tire iron and threw the big steel cross at his foe. James ducked the incoming missile and was still off balance when Danny, less than a step behind the steel distraction, tackled him and drove him backward into a nearby car.

The impact from both men dented the car's door and punched a spiderweb into the corresponding window. The former Marine brought the butt of his heavy weapon's grip down onto Gage's head hard. He held his foe in a bear hug and hammered James in the skull again for good measure, then drew the knife to his ribs and stabbed forward.

Either blind luck or uncanny skill caused James to fall forward at the last second. The Kabar's blade *screeched* across metal. A low slash from the *karambit* drew more of Danny's blood - this time, from his left thigh. Only a last-second shift of his leg saved Wakefield from having his femoral artery opened. Gage stumbled, but came back up fast enough and far enough away that Danny never got a chance for a follow-up attack.

During times of terminal stress, the normal human mind inevitably became an utterly useless jumble of random impulses. But under those same conditions, a trained mind always reverted to its basic training. As he grew more tired with each breath spent and every drop of blood which trickled beneath his feet, all higher reasoning disappeared from Danny's consciousness. The nimble fighter in front of him became a formless target... a man-shaped punching bag whose only feature was the steel claw which jutted from its hand.

Special Agent Daniel Wakefield of the United States Secret Service disappeared from existence. He was finally and truly on his metaphysical vacation. In his place stood Private Wakefield, United States Marine. And Private Wakefield only knew one thing. Attack.

What makes the grass grow? the invisible drill sergeant yelled from everywhere around him as Private Wakefield rushed the anatomical target in blind fury.

Blood! Blood! Blood! The curved talon swung toward the eighteen-year-old Marine. In a move that would have made Chesty Puller proud, Wakefield used his left hand to guid the *karambit* into his own left thigh. He buried the blade deep into his own thick muscle, then held it there with pure grit and unbreakable will.

Why is the sky blue? the unseen instructor demanded. Private Wakefield held his Kabar high above his head and reversed his grip so the massive blade became a giant ice pick aimed at his green canvas nemesis.

Because God loves the Corps! The heavy combat knife plunged into its target from above again and again. Each time Private Wakefield buried the blade up to the hilt, a little more sand poured onto the ground.

Pain is weakness leaving the body.

So much weakness left Wakefield's left leg that the limb collapsed. The Marine fell to his side. His target fell away from him. They both hit the ground at the same time. Daniel aged years in a microsecond. And the canvas sandbag became a guy with dirty blond hair who leaked vital fluid as he crawled across the cold concrete.

Danny wanted to finish his foe. He wanted to kill the evil bastard before he could slink away. But his body wanted to lay there on the ground. His right hand fought to hold his knife, but it was getting tired. His left hand started to pull him toward his enemy, but then slipped on a trail of his own blood and dropped him and desperately tried to clamp down on a gushing wound in his leg.

James Gage coughed and dragged himself closer to the big blue truck. Closer to escape. The open road was the criminal's avenue to freedom. And Wakefield knew in his heart that if Gage made it to the street again then he would never be caught.

A canon sounded in the cavernous workshop. and halted Gage in his gruesome tracks. Thunder echoed against steel and concrete sang. The ringing in Danny's ears did nothing to muffle the second shot, which blew a significant portion of James Gage's head away from the rest of his skull and splashed all manner of viscera in a rooster tail along the ground.

Danny blinked and saw Brenna standing a few paces away, backlit by some angelic light, and pointing his .45 at Gage's body as if she dared it to move again.

CHAPTER 26

"SANDERS COUNTY FIRE crews are battling a huge blaze at an industrial building this morning." Danny listened to the radio from the passenger seat of his own Jeep. "News on Two's very own Marcia Hunt brings you the latest live from the scene now."

The as-yet-risen sun burned a yellow line across the eastern horizon. The undersides of clouds glowed in a soft salmon orange. Their shadowy tops were mounds of periwinkle against a navy-blue sky. To the west, snowcapped mountaintops shone in bright contrast with their still unlit faces and the dark forests and fields beneath them.

"Thank you, Greg. I'm standing here with Sanders County Fire Marshall Ron Bolton. Marshall Bolton, please tell us what happened here and what's going on behind us."

"Well, it looks like a gas tank at the back of this mechanic's shop ignited. Probably someone careless with a cigarette on their smoke break. That's really all it takes. Anyway, that initial fire seems to have spread to nearby cars parked in the lot and other chemicals stored here and there around the grounds. Places like this are loaded with cleaners, paints, solvents, lubricants... all kinds of combustible materials. By the time our crews got here, the place was fully engulfed. We've got the fire contained, but there's really nothing we can do right now but let it burn itself out."

Danny switched the radio off and took another pull from the sports drink he had nursed for the last hour. A length of intravenous tubing replenished his lost blood from a bag hung inconspicuously from the back of his headrest. Another tube plugged into his arm provided his depleted body with even more fluids.

"I can't believe they actually bought it," Danny shook his head. "I mean, it doesn't even sound like they're gonna investigate."

"By the time they can safely move around that joint, Son, there won't be anything left to find. Fire that hot won't leave anything but a black scar on the pavement. And that's if the concrete doesn't shatter. It gets hot enough, that slab'll pop like corn."

In the aftermath of the previous night's firefight, David Wakefield treated his son's wounds, then set to staging an industrial accident of sufficient scale and plausibility to remove any trace of what had truly happened or inspire any thoughts of foul play. It was the most efficient way the former cop knew to cover everyone's tracks and eliminate all forensic evidence from such a complicated crime scene.

"What I can't believe," David continued in a tone that told his son that the conversation had become a lecture, "is that with all that crap in your Go Bag, you don't keep a pint or two of blood and a banana bag." The elder Wakefield clicked his tongue against his teeth in a *tsk-tsk-tsk* as he drove further south along the interstate. "I mean, all the bullets in the world won't help you if you've got an arterial bleeder."

"Thanks again, Dad. And not just for stitching me up."

"It's just a patch job. It'll hold for now, but we'll swing by an urgent care clinic in Bozeman and have them do you up right."

"Wild animal attack," Danny smiled. "I *have* been hunting mountain lions lately."

"Fair enough. Just be sure to roll down your sleeve and give 'em your other arm if they want to stick you. Fresh track marks raise questions."

"Like, 'where did I get my interventional care?'"

"Like, 'how long have you been shooting up?' You *are* a dirty fed, Son. And everyone knows feds are all either doing dope or sniffing blow."

Under better circumstances, the jocular ribbing would have brought a laugh. But the last few hours left Danny in a humorless mood. He fought the urge to breech the subject for a hundred miles, but the younger Wakefield could no longer hold his tongue.

"Why'd you let her go, Dad?"

David sniffed. "Stopping her wasn't my priority, Son. Taking care of you was. And still is."

"Yeah, but -"

"Son," David stopped the ensuing argument before it could start, "you lost a lot of blood. You were pretty out of it back there while I was patchin' you up and loading up our gear an' horses. Your lady friend did a bang-up job helpin' me clear the place, by the way."

"I'm not sure she's my friend," Danny grumbled.

"Are you sure she's your enemy?"

"I'm not sure I wanna think about it."

"Fair enough, Son. Now, there's a time to go all out and there's a time to cover your ass. Like I said: you're not a cop, so you don't understand. But it's all a game, Son. On good days," he held up his hand as if it was part of an imaginary scale, "you win. Some days," he flipped the scale, "they win. The only way to play is to do your best, do what you think is right, and learn to live with the consequences."

Danny drummed his sport drink bottle with his fingertips and thought about the lesson his father was trying to impart. A memory crept to the forefront of his mind. "Maybe that's what Hemingway meant," he offered aloud. The elder Wakefield's confused brow begged for a deeper explanation. "It's something Ernest Hemingway said. They taught it to us back in the Corps. 'There is no hunting like the hunting of man, and those who have hunted armed men long enough and liked it never care for anything else.'"

"Nice."

"That's the sport. Get it? Hunting bad guys. It's like you said, Dad. We can't take it personally. It's just a game."

"True," David slowly agreed, "but it's one you have to play to win."

After they spent half of Christmas Eve at an urgent care clinic to properly patch the wounds caused by Montana's most enigmatic mountain lion, the Wakefield men returned to David's ranch house and did their best to redeem what was left of the holiday. Miss Kitty brought her daughter, the songbird Stacy, and her sweet grandchild over for a bountiful dinner filled with cheer and what might have been a little too much curiosity on Stacy's part about the nature and extent of Danny's wounds. Stockings were exchanged. Snacks were enjoyed. Beverages were consumed. And at the end of the evening, Daniel retreated to his bedroom and began the process of unpacking everything and repacking whatever he decided to take back with him on the long drive back to Washington.

Hastily tucked into a duffle bag, Danny found the .357 Magnum revolver he had lent to Brenna just a few days before. He opened the White Rhino's cylinder out of well-established habit and, with his mind a million miles away, hit the plunger to clear the drum of any casings. Brenna had not fired the gun since she practiced with it here at the house under the name Anita - a name that was friendly enough at the time, but in Danny's mind would just never seem right again.

Whereas a half dozen brass cartridges were expected to fall into his outstretched hand, Danny's palm was instead filled with scraps of paper. He looked again more carefully. Six small pieces of paper, one from each port in the cylinder, sat in small rolls about a third of an inch in diameter.

Special Agent Wakefield's curiosity piqued. He placed the gun and five of the mysterious scraps atop his dresser. The last piece, however, he unrolled cautiously. Danny had learned the hard way that Brenna Jacobs was equally tricky and dangerous. There was no telling what a woman like that might do - either for fun, profit, or revenge - if she was motivated. Or bored.

The unfurled paper was a note, simple and harmless enough. It featured an address, a date, and a dollar amount. Curiously, Danny examined the other scraps of paper. Each of them featured an address or what he recognized to be geographical coordinates. Each of them sported a date within the last fourteen months. And the dollar amounts scribbled on each of the notes were simple two- or three-digit figures followed by the letter *M*. For millions.

Danny quickly shuffled through the scraps again for one address in particular. *There,* he nodded. *This one's right here in Montana. And the date is just a couple of months ago.* The wheels of Special Agent Wakefield's mind turned in consideration of the myriad possibilities and implications of what this information, so discreetly passed to him, might mean.

*   *   *

Danny strode up the paved steps to an opulent house which was large enough to serve as a luxury hotel. Behind him, a plain gray Chevy Impala - temporarily commandeered from the nearest federal government office's fleet - idled so the heater could maintain a comfortable cabin temperature. Ahead of him, oversized doors with ornate scrollwork carved into their faces and floor-length stained-glass windows on either side screamed, *Go away, peasants!*

The doorbell button summoned a chorus which pealed and rang softly inside the mansion. A moment later, the portal opened slowly to a middle-aged man in a silk robe and pajamas which Danny strongly suspected cost more than the suit he dug out of his travel bags. "May I help you?" the man inquired with ill humor.

"Good morning, sir. I'm Special Agent Wakefield," Danny held his badge out for inspection.

"It's Christmas morning, Agent Wakefield," the man grumbled. "And I'm a United States Senator."

"And I'm the Secret Service," Wakefield pushed his way through the door. "I'm sure this'll only take a minute. Nice place you've got here."

"Thank you."

"With respect to your time, Senator Bridges, I'll cut right to it." He swapped his badge for his phone and the picture of the hitwoman he took days ago at the Ninepines Lodge. "Do you recognize this woman, sir?"

"I do not."

"Do you think anyone else here might? Your wife? Kids, maybe?"

"They most certainly would not," Senator Bridges protested. "What is this about, Agent Wakefield?"

"You're lying," Danny sniffed. "I mean, it must be second nature to you by now, being a sitting congressman and all. You see, the only way you could possibly know that nobody else here knows who that woman is if *you* are the one who knows, but you've also gone to great lengths to keep her secret." Wakefield leaned in closely. "So, what is she to you? Your secret daughter?"

"My daughter is a sophomore at Carroll. And she went with some friends to Cancun for the break."

"Mistress?"

"How dare you?"

"George," a woman's voice called from what Danny assumed was the luxury home's parlor, "who is it?"

"Nobody, Grace," the man called back to his unseen wife. "Just someone who is lost." When his eyes returned to Danny, they were as cold and hard as steel. "Now, listen to me, Agent Wakefield. I sit on a number of committees, any of which can make your career evaporate."

"You know, I made a few calls on the drive here," Danny admitted softly. "It seems that your campaign took in a lot more money than it spent on advertising last year."

"How would you -" the man started. "Right. Treasury Department. Well, then, you are probably also aware of the fact that we stopped spending money on the campaign after my opponent died of a heart attack."

"Indeed I am, Senator Bridges. And that particular detail makes things even interesting to me."

"What's so suspicious about not spending money? Some people would call that 'fiscal responsibility.'"

"Oh, I barely care about the money part," Danny corrected lightly. "But the heart attack part. That's just *fascinating*. Because you see, sir, the woman in the photo - the person who gave me your home address - is an international assassin who knows a thousand ways to disguise a murder." Senator Bridges stood silently at the soft implication, so Wakefield hardened his tone a bit. "You know, like, by using certain drugs to fake cardiac arrest in her target."

Senator Bridges froze. "How dare you -"

"And one of my associates hacked into your late opponent's doctor's records, Senator."

"- on Christmas morning, of all -"

"It seems the late Mr. Jeffries had no prior history of heart disease."

"You can't seriously think -"

"Senator Bridges," Wakefield held up a finger in warning, "we can do this the easy way, or the hard way. The easy way, you come quietly with me now, you answer some uncomfortable questions, and maybe you still get to enjoy Christmas dinner with your wife."

"Get out of my -"

"The hard way," Danny continued unfettered, "is that I pull a warrant out of this pocket," he pointed to his winter dress coat, "handcuffs off of this belt, and after I none-too-gingerly drag your ass away, I spend the next few days here with a forensic team and a news crew. We tear this lovely home to pieces looking for evidence of anything wrong you've ever done in your life. There're more than forty-thousand federal laws on the books, Senator. Statistically speaking, you and your wife are probably felons *by accident*. You will spend the holidays in jail answering for every crime you've accidentally committed, anything you did on purpose and thought you got away with, and anything else we can make look bad for you. You might not lose your seat immediately, but the blood in the water will make your re-election bid in two years a feeding frenzy."

Danny politely helped Senator Bridges into the sedan's back seat, then made his way around the vehicle to the driver's door. He paused for a moment at the curb, reached into his jacket pocket, and withdrew a small piece of paper. The Secret Service agent unfurled the note and read the next clue left for him by his enigmatic dalliance.

It was all he had left from the woman with whom he'd unintentionally shared his vacation. All searches for her passport, any ID they could find in any country anywhere on the globe that cooperated with an information request, even a search through un-compartmentalized classified networks... not one single investigative tool at his disposal yielded any answers about his mysterious companion

The woman was anyone and nobody. She could be anywhere, yet was unfindable. The only thing Special Agent Wakefield had to work with was a handful of cryptic clues which could lead to anything - or nothing at all.

The game is on. Danny looked down at the scrap of paper again and smiled. *So tell me, Brenna Jacobs: What other treasure have you given me?*

EPILOGUE

"EXCUSE ME, SIR," the pasty-faced technician squeaked, "but there's something you should see.

Michael Coffield was a meek and mild-mannered employee whose many years at the NSA went as unnoticed by his colleagues and supervisors as the Agency's own activities went by the general public. When his unsung talents landed him a previously unheard of position providing unspecified support directly to the Secretary of Homeland Security, nobody back on the East Coast knew he left - or where he went. Or cared.

"What is it?" Secretary Lehman gruffly demanded.

"Unusual activity on the network over the holiday," Coffield explained. "Inquiries made into an asset the Agency uses from time to time." With a click, the mousey man called up a picture of a beautiful black-haired woman. "Brenna Jacobs."

"What kind of inquiries?"

"She inexplicably appeared on Homeland Security's radar about a week ago." Michael consulted his notes. "Special Agent Wakefield - the investigator from the Constitutional Killer case all over the news this year - was allegedly on leave when he linked up with her by means unknown and for reasons which remain unclear."

"Yes," the DHS overlord hummed. "He was one of Noah Wiley's guys back in Analysis. Wasn't he?"

"He still is, sir."

Secretary Lehman sounded a *harumf*. "I thought Wiley said he was getting out," he mused aloud. "You said 'allegedly on leave.' What was Wakefield really doing?"

"We're not sure at this time, sir."

"Does it link back to us?"

"Wakefield's been active over the holiday break, sir. After Thanksgiving, the guy basically crawled under a rock. Now it's New Year's Eve and he's bouncing around like a squirrel on meth."

"Does it link back to *us*?"

Coffield swallowed hard. "That list of names you gave me, sir. The Circle, you called them. Some of Wakefield's browser activity on the government networks - classified and unclassified alike - starts to approach some of The Circle's interests. And Jacobs has a history doing odd jobs for The Circle from time to time."

"The Circle's interests are broad and complex," "Is Wakefield becoming a problem?"

"Not quite yet, sir. But he could be in the future."

"Then we'll deal with it in the future."

"But isn't weeding out potential threats what we're here to do?"

"You're doing a good job, Coffield," the Secretary assured him. "This is important work." Lehman fanned the pen in his hand through the air. "Keep an eye on Special Agent Wakefield. Let me know if any of this - or anything else - compromises this program or The Circle."

"Of course, sir."

"I'm headed back to Washington. I'll see you next month, Coffield. Unless something comes up."

"Yes, sir."

When Garrett Lehman walked out of the unnamed industrial building filled with monitors and hidden in the middle of nowhere, the structure's population was halved. Other than his lackey, Coffield, Secretary Lehman was the only living person with access to the nondescript building. Even the people who built the corrugated steel building were half a world away - and unlikely to ever return to the States alive.

Lehman slid into back of the black Mercedez the taxpayers afforded his position. Behind the wheel, a somber looking man half Garrett's age kept the engine running and soft classical music in the climate-controlled air. "Home, Charles," the Secretary ordered his driver. Born mute, the chauffeur nodded slowly and started the car gently down the gravel driveway which led to a road… which led to a road… which would eventually lead to civilization.

Garrett Lehman's mind was not on the winter drive, or the holiday. He spared no unnecessary thought for his estranged wife, an aging heiress who was on vacation in Italy with her latest beau. His assistant allegedly sent his children - scattered across the map as they were - Christmas cards with Garrett's name convincingly signed on them. Neither did he really have time to spare for some rogue agent who randomly flitted about in the wind.

No. Garrett Ambercrombie Lehman had history on his mind. Some of that history was written. Some of it all-but-forgotten. Some of it was kept secret. But the facet of history which demanded the newly minted Secretary of Homeland Security's attention was the part which had not yet happened.

The full weight of history was set into forward motion. Its course was guided by players whose power was transcendent: The Circle. They were a collection of titans among mere ants.

And if some lesser being - some mere plebeian - thought for a moment that he could inconvenience them, there was no force in Heaven or Earth which could save his insignificant existence.

MOST DANGEROUS GAME

Recommended Playlist

I listen to music while I write certain scenes in order to keep focused on that moment's particular mood. I also usually listen to music while I read for the same reason. I hope the songs that helped this story come together for me as a writer breathe life into it for you, my readers.

"Take Out the Gunman" - Chevelle. *La Gárgola.*
"Gone Away" - Five Finger Death Punch. *A Decade of Destruction.*
"Running Up That Hill" - Track and Field. *Running Up That Hill - Single.*
"Cowboy" - Kid Rock. *Devil Without a Cause.*
"Emotionless" - Red Sun Rising. *Polyester Zeal.*
"Hurts Like Hell (feat. Fleurie)" - Tommee Profitt, Fleurie. *Cinematic Songs - Vol. 1.*
"Everybody Wants to Rule the World" - Lorde. *The Hunger Games: Catching Fire (Original Motion Picture Soundtrack).*
"Click Click Boom" - Saliva. *Every Six Seconds.*
"Rx (Medicate)" - Theory of a Deadman. *Wake up Call.*
"Person of Interest" - Immediate Music. *Trailer Hits.*
"Refuse to Dance" - Celine Dion. *The Colour of My Love.*
"State of My Head" - Shinedown. *Threat to Survival.*
"In the Air Tonight" - The Protomen. *The Cover Up (Original Motion Picture Soundtrack).*
"God's Gonna Cut You Down" - Johnny Cash. *American V: A Hundred Highways.*
"Lockdown" - Steve Jablonsky. *Transformers: Age of Extinction (Original Motion Picture Soundtrack).*
"Chevaliers de Sangrael" - Hans Zimmer. *The DaVinci Code (Original Motion Picture Soundtrack).*

- DEJS

ABOUT THE AUTHOR

DARYL E.J. SIMMONS is a distinguished former naval intelligence analyst and decorated veteran whose career includes multiple combat deployments embedded with Special Operations elements. During his career in public service, Mr. Simmons served as the policy advisor to American and Allied leaders on matters of global security, counterterrorism, counternarcotics, counter piracy, and counter-human trafficking. Mr. Simmons has hunted terrorists and drug traffickers on five continents. He is an esteemed expert on international relations and critical strategic problem sets.

Mr. Simmons graduated with honors from the University of Tulsa. He moonlights as a consultant specializing in policy development, asymmetric threat analysis, and fielding unconventional solutions to complex problems in both the government and business sectors.

When he is not writing, Mr. Simmons hosts his podcast, *The Daily Dose of Daryl*. He is an avid public speaker and vocal advocate for veteran causes.

And now an excerpt from "After the West," an all new sci-fi western by Daryl E.J. Simmons!

And here's an excerpt from "After the West," an original sci-fi western adventure also written by Daryl E.J. Simmons. Look for it now!

"Billie English?" a passing patron looked upon her in amazement. "You're Billie English?" Noah chuckled as his companion cursed under her breath. "Billie English!" the drunken behemoth rose from one of the tables toward the middle of the room. "You killed my cousin in Abilene!"

Noah looked at her in disbelief. "You shot a guy in Abilene?"

"No," Billie sized up the angry dude - who was a real bear of a man - and shrugged. "But I did hang a few. Tossed one off a bridge, too. Oh, and I ran over some with a -"

The man-bear pushed past his companions and stomped across the floor. "I'ma get you fer what you did to Gus!"

"Gus?" Billie could not place the name. "Gus... Gus Turner?" she guessed.

The giant answered her question with a haymaker punch so wide that Noah had to duck down onto the bar in order to avoid being hit by the thrower's paw accidentally as it flew along the way toward its real target. Billie jerked her head backwards to slip the wild punch, then bounced back forward and clocked her oversized assailant over the head with her mostly-full whiskey bottle. The angry redneck giant staggered, then caught her across the midsection with a delirious - but powerful - backhanded blow.

Billie flew backwards into another patron, who spilled his drink as he was crushed against the bar. He rebounded and threw the woman back into the fray with a brawler more than three times her size. She squared off against the big brute and raised her hands to defend herself.

"Gus Morris?" she tried again. The big man charged her again with his fist cocked back, but when his punch flew, Billie slipped to the outside and let the man's momentum carry him into the guy who just threw her back into the fight. A fist the size of a small melon smashed into the seated dude's face and knocked him out cold.

The unconscious guy's buddies jumped up with a yell and piled onto the violent giant. A flurry of fists and feet overwhelmed the bigger man, until he reached out blindly, grabbed the dude on his right, and used that guy like a meat hammer to clobber his own drinking companions.

Billie used the distraction and the distance to rush at the big guy from behind. She dove low and snapped a vicious kick into the back of his knee. The joint buckled. The dazed man staggered uncertainly. Billie cradled the compromised joint against her shoulder and launched herself upward, toppling the giant with a crash. She hugged the guy's leg - which was, itself, almost as massive as she was - close to her chest and drove her tough leather boot hard into his vulnerable nether region.

"Gus Washington?" She kicked again. "Gus Jenkins?" Another kick brought tears to the man's eyes. "Gus Filmore?" Billie scrambled the guy's eggs with yet another kick. The giant threw up all over Roxy's floor. Most of the men in the saloon winced in sympathy. Several of them cradled their own frontside, clenched their knees together, and hissed in horror.

Billie tossed the weeping whale's leg away and regarded the rest of the room. "Who else wants some?" she dared.

"Day-um." Noah wiped a tear from the corner of his eye, then finished his whiskey. "I'm thinking maybe you really might *be* Billie English."

Breathing hard, the bounty huntress signaled for a replacement whiskey bottle. "Sorry for the ruckus, Roxy." Her hard eyes darted toward Noah. "Sheriff said someone here could look at my bike? I'm leavin' in the morning."

"See my baby brother about that." Roxy pointed to a pint-sized patron in grease-stained coveralls whose legs dangled from one of the stools at the bar's far end.

"Thanks."

Made in the USA
Coppell, TX
21 February 2026

71936934R10184